Happily and Madly

Happily and Madly

ALEXIS BASS

A TOM DOHERTY ASSOCIATES BOOK NEW YORK

This is a work of fiction. All of the characters, organizations, and events portrayed in this novel are either products of the author's imagination or are used fictitiously.

HAPPILY AND MADLY

Copyright © 2019 by Alexis Bass

A Tor Teen Book
Published by Tom Doherty Associates
175 Fifth Avenue
New York, NY 10010

www.tor-forge.com

Tor® is a registered trademark of Macmillan Publishing Group, LLC.

The Library of Congress Cataloging-in-Publication Data is available upon request.

ISBN 978-1-250-19591-3 (hardcover)
ISBN 978-1-250-19592-0 (ebook)

Our books may be purchased in bulk for promotional, educational, or business use. Please contact your local bookseller or the Macmillan Corporate and Premium Sales Department at 1-800-221-7945, extension 5442, or by email at MacmillanSpecialMarkets@macmillan.com.

First Edition: May 2019

Printed in the United States of America

0 9 8 7 6 5 4 3 2 1

To Lea, for naming the poison

Happily and Madly

Chapter 1

The New Brown Family is portrait perfect. They are each seamless in their own way. They look alike even though they are patchwork pieces of different families, strung together not by DNA but by true love.

George is the father. He is tall and broad-shouldered, carrying some weight in his stomach the way men his age are inclined to do. His hair is rich in color, speckled with gray, but still there, full and thick enough for him to run his fingers through, and according to him, that is what matters. Trisha is the mother. A thirty-six-year-old who looks exactly her age, despite the new-mom short-bob haircut, with blond hair and grown-out roots, and large breasts, which she always covers, but are still the second thing you notice about her, after her kind smile. Chelsea is the oldest daughter. She just turned eighteen. She looks like Trisha except smaller, with long, luscious hair and tan skin and the glowing radiance of being a daughter by choice instead of by circumstance. Phoebe is the baby, a perfect pink package that gurgles and coos. She is a bundle of spit-up and potential. The most basic definition of *love child.*

The four of them stare back at me smiling as they stand in the airport terminal holding a handwritten sign, something probably done last night over a table covered in Magic Markers and glitter and glue, while eating cookies and sipping on lemonade.

"Welcome, Maris!"

I don't look like them. I do not have a smile for every occasion. I do not glow. I am a daughter entirely by circumstance. Baggage from George's first marriage. Nothing about me is beautiful or precious, and my shadow is the first thing you would notice.

It is only my third time seeing the New Brown Family in the two years since they have been in existence, but I hug each of them, tell them, "I've missed you, too." I only pretend to hug George. They all hug me back, except Phoebe, who, at only ten months old, maybe isn't old enough to entirely grasp the concept of an embrace. She stares at me with eyes too big for her face and lips pursed in a grin—*familiar* lips on a *familiar* grin. We have the same mouth, courtesy of George. I note familiarity in her eyes, too. And her chin. When she laughs, I'm relieved that the sound is altogether alien. She and I will never know the same kind of joy.

"We're so happy you're spending the summer with us at Cross Cove!"—they all say this to me, but in different ways.

They are lying.

The New Brown Family would like to be the kind of family

that's effortlessly welcoming. A family that can extend itself to sustain the debris of George's past. But that is the one thing they are not.

"Me, too," I say back. I would also like to be effortlessly welcoming. I would like to be able to mold and fit; for my absence to be a real vacancy in their lives; for our reunions to feel like a relief. The kind of daughter that meant it when she said, "Congratulations," to a tuxedo-clad George with birdseed in his hair after he exchanged vows with Trisha last year. A girl who had happy tears in her eyes the first time she held her brand-new baby half sister in her arms instead of tears of fear. Someone who felt lucky to have been gifted a stepsister three months older than she is, with whom she may have a lot in common, other than a shared father now that the adoption has been official, making us all the Browns.

We walk together, staggered in a row on our way to baggage claim, and I give them a smile that I wish were genuine.

"This summer is going to be different," George told me on the phone before I came.

And it is sure to be. But not in the way he thinks.

Chapter 2

This summer is designed to give my mother a break, though neither George nor my mother is saying that. They say: *What a great opportunity to reconnect with your father.* And: *It'll do you good to get out of the desert and feel that New England ocean breeze.*

They are right in some ways. My relationship with George could use some resuscitation. And I did need to get out of Phoenix, where I was getting boxed in by the sun and the heat and by the general monotony of having lived in the same place for my entire life.

"So what's it like there?" my mother asks over the phone as I unpack. I've been gone a whole ten hours, and her voice already sounds considerably lighter.

She doesn't really want to know about Cross Cove, how it's both charming and vast, exquisite and picturesque; a few hours from the closest city, but still with that feeling of being far removed. About the sizable beach house right on the water George has rented. The kind of money he never spent on us. The kind of money we didn't know he was up for spending.

I glance around my summer bedroom, full of white furniture, a bright blue comforter on the bed, seashell and lighthouse décor on the walls and on the dresser. A big picture window that probably will light up the whole room when the sun rises.

"It's nice," I say and leave it at that. Me coming out here was her idea, which says volumes since even though it's been around two years since she found out that George had been cheating on her, and that not only was he leaving her to marry the woman he'd been seeing, he was also expecting a child with that woman, she still cries about it sometimes and she never says their names. For a long time, she could barely get out of bed. George left both of us for the New Browns, but he is still legally obligated to me.

"And everything's okay? With George and . . . everyone?" I think it really might be physically impossible for her to say their names.

"Yup." I zip up my suitcase now that it's completely unpacked and shove it under the bed. "Everything will be fine, Mom. I'll make the best of it."

"And you're not talking to Trevor, right?"

"No, of course not."

"I'm serious, Maris. He's not good for you. He's not someone you need in your life."

I've told her the truth about not speaking to him, but I don't blame her for not believing me.

Besides, it's easiest for her to blame everything that's happened on my ex-boyfriend Trevor, who is older and consistently smells like weed and always drove too fast down our residential street, because he never did care if my mother liked him or not. Trevor doesn't hide that he knows how good-looking he is, and he wears his ego on his sleeve. When I didn't come home at night, I was usually with him. When I skipped classes, I was usually with him. He's the one I was with when I got caught vandalizing the new spring training stadium on a dare that sounded like the exact right amount of risky at the time it was proposed. He was absent from the hospital the night he wrecked his car, and I had to be rushed to the emergency room for what turned out to be two broken ribs. And it was his party favors that got me arrested that second time.

My only defense is that I tried hard to keep all the fun we had a secret and did everything behind my mother's back. It wasn't hard for a while, when she started taking the night shifts at the hotel because she was too sad after George left to face the bustle of the day.

Sometimes my mother blames George, too, insinuating that I only started getting into trouble and hanging out with Trevor and *his crowd* after he left. But that was the crowd I chose, the ones who could keep up, the ones who weren't going to tell me no. And Trevor was the one I chose, with his easy life and his fearless attitude. So now she's put nearly three thousand miles between Trevor and me and placed me back with George. Her cure-all.

George blames Trevor, but he blames my mother more. I can see it in the way he looks at her. He yelled at her in the hospital that day after the car accident, "Where were you when she started going off the rails?" and my mother screamed, "Where were *you*?"

They both left me for a while, but in different ways.

On the phone, I tell my mother everything she wants to hear, needs to hear; that I'm done with Trevor. That I'm content being here with the New Brown Family, even George. That I've had enough with adrenaline highs and risky ventures. Fast cars and fast boys. Dares and challenges and never backing down.

"Good," she says, pausing to sigh, probably out of relief. *"Good."*

"You don't have to worry," I tell her before we say goodbye.

When I hang up with my mother, Chelsea knocks on the door connecting my bedroom to the bathroom that adjoins our rooms, and I wonder if she's been listening. She doesn't wait for me to say, "Come in," before she enters.

"The fireworks will be starting soon." Her smile fades when she sees that I am not smiling back. I don't know if she is afraid of me and will avoid me the best she can this summer, or if we are going to continue being uncomfortably polite to each other, like we usually are. "You have to see them. I hear the fireworks are magic here; they light up the entire sky, the entire cove."

"That's okay," I say at first. I'm still used to retreating around them. "I mean, yeah, I'll come." Because this is a new summer in a new place, with a new family, too, sure, but it is still mine, and why would I ever want to miss a fireworks show that's just been described as *magical*?

A bright smile invades her whole face. She waits for me to find my sandals, and we walk out together.

I follow her down the stairs, all the way to the back of the house, and out the kitchen door. We walk through a screened porch where Trisha is sitting, rocking Phoebe and feeding her a bottle, with George seated next to her, his arm acting as her headrest. We go down a short flight of stairs, landing in sand dotted with beach grass. I can hear the sound of the ocean in the distance, and we continue down the path until the beach grass disappears and there's a beach stretching in front of us, leading to a low tide and the bay. Chelsea flounces toward the water like it's effortless, but I find that the sand is heavy and hard to walk through. I try to remember the last time I was on a beach, walking on sand. I was fourteen, and my mother and I had accompanied George on a business trip to Florida. He worked the entire time. He never came to the beach with us. He never sat like this, content in the quiet with my mom, the way he's sitting with Trisha and Phoebe.

Chelsea and I get closer to the water, and the sand turns hard and wet and easier to walk on.

Chelsea's out of breath. "This is Cross Cove," she says, motioning to the horseshoe-shaped shore surrounding us. The cove is uneven. On our side, the houses are low, right on the beach, but as it curves, a cliff starts, growing taller and steeper as it inches around the cove. The houses get larger and larger and more and more removed from their beaches below. They are etched in the cliff, their open windows like hundreds of lanterns.

"You've been here before?" I ask.

"No, but I've always wanted to come here. Ever since I heard about it, I've dreamed of spending a summer here. Mom and Dad wanted to go somewhere tropical, like the Bahamas or Hawaii. But I convinced them." She points straight ahead. "That's the Duval summer estate." I let my gaze follow her direction, though all I can really make out are a few white lights. "That's where my boyfriend lives over the summer. His name is Edison." She gives me this lush, giddy smile.

And the truth comes out—the real reason she chose this spot for our summer vacation. I can see her begging George, probably even saying, "Please, Daddy," in a way that never would've worked on him if I'd said it. The girls of the New Brown Family have him wrapped around their fingers, where my mother and I were stuck butting heads with him.

"Congratulations," I say in response to both her wealthy boyfriend and that she managed to convince George to spend the two months of his collected vacation out here.

Chelsea laughs, which I hadn't expected. "I am so lucky," she says—no hesitation in her voice. In a way, I like that she owns this—she has a boyfriend with a large cliff-side summer mansion, and she is absolutely not ashamed that this is part of what she likes about him, enough that he was one of the main reasons she talked her family into coming out here, when they could have gone anywhere. "He'll be here in a few days, when he gets back from London."

I remember vaguely hearing about Chelsea's boyfriend attending some prestigious international university when I'd visited the New Browns in December, four months after Phoebe was born. I'm surprised they've lasted this long, given his distance. Trevor was all about the here and now and would've forgotten about me in a week if there was an ocean between us. He's probably already started to forget, already started replacing me with summertime girls who find his aloofness a refreshing quality.

She points to the curve in the cove. "The Covingtons live there. They have the deepest beach, so they do the fireworks show every night." She blushes, like she gets that I'm wondering how she knows about this. "It's not a secret," she says with a shrug.

Generations of families have summered here, she claims. She regales me with the tale of Edison's family, a rags-to-riches story, in which the eldest Duval cashed in all his chips to start his business in the '60s, and how it grew and doubled, then tripled, then quadrupled. She reminds me that she grew up poor: no winter coats, too-small boots, canned beans for breakfast, lunch, dinner, before George, until George. Her father and mother were high school sweethearts, but he died in a car accident shortly after she was born. George is the only father she's known, she says.

"I want to spend every summer here," she says, her eyes alight in a way that makes me jealous. This place—the dream of this place and the idea of it—is what feeds her and fuels her. This is what makes her feel alive; this is all it takes. It seems such a simple and shallow thing to cherish, but at the same time, I can't fault her for wanting the things she has always believed to be out of her reach.

"Sounds nice," I tell her.

There's a loud popping noise that I can feel in the base of my stomach, and the sky ignites in a shower of red and blue and green lights.

"Isn't it beautiful?" Chelsea asks. Her head's tilted back and the colors from the fireworks streak across her face. She looks *alive,* relaxed, happy—every part of her; free.

"Yes," I admit, staring up at the sky.

There's something unnerving and exhilarating about being here, surrounded by the beaches and that cliff with windows looking down on us, the bay like a moat between us, the waves ridged and high in the distance.

"I think it will be a good summer," Chelsea says.

I nod. I'm thinking, *It has to be.*

Chapter 3

The walls are thin in the New Brown Family's summer rental, even for as big as it is. That night, I hear very clearly all four times Phoebe screams bloody murder from her crib and all the giggling murmurs from George and Trisha, full of wine and feeling very much like they're on vacation. He never acted this giddy with my mom.

I can hear Chelsea, too, on the phone with her boyfriend as she lies in bed.

"Eddy, don't tell me you actually like oysters?"

"What—how did you guess that salmon was my favorite?"

"Remember that night—yes, yes—right, right. And the water was so cold!"

It all makes me feel so lonely and so bored—a twitch that starts in the tips of my fingers and travels through my veins—that I send Trevor a message, like a bad habit. *Hey there.*

As expected, he writes back. *Come over.*

I turn off my phone instead of explaining to him yet again that I'm not there. By far the best thing about Trevor is that he's good at living in bliss, no matter what's in front of him, no matter what happens to him. Some would call it the most severe case of denial, but it's not. It's a gift. Trevor can build a whole world and let in only what he wants—only good things. Only exciting things. He can keep out the bad and the boring. In Trevor's world, there is no word for *consequences.* He drinks like he doesn't care about blacking out, runs like he's got the lung capacity of a whale, kisses like he's in unbridled love, and wakes up every day like he's got a clean slate.

This makes him a bad person, according to my parents—according to a lot of people, actually. But it was what I liked most about him. It was what I envied most about him, too.

I admit Trevor was a horrible boyfriend. Forgetful. Unfaithful. Unreliable. But he was also the perfect escape. He knew the secret to really truly not caring, and that is why I chose him. Being with him was to effortlessly live moment by moment—to let each second explode and then slip away entirely. And that's all I ever wanted; that's how I wanted my life to be all the time. Not many people understood that, but Trevor did. So unsurprisingly, it couldn't last. And we were ultimately pulled apart not by Trevor's unfaithfulness or his aloofness. What truly ended things with us was Trevor's desire to blur the lines of reality, to take it too far. I always knew about the cocaine he liked, and that he probably liked me even more because I didn't make him share. He'd send the adrenaline right into his system instead of working for it, and when we were busted for running a red light in a car Trevor's aunt had finally reported as stolen and they made us get out of the car on the side of the road, they of course found the small almost-empty baggy in his pocket and the nearly full untouched baggy he'd decided to keep in my purse. I didn't know it was there, or I would have hidden it better or distracted the police officer and tossed it. That is not the kind of trouble I wanted to waste my time with—waste my life with. No one believes you when you say that it's not yours, that you're not interested in it, because that's exactly what someone found with an illegal substance in their purse would say.

Some things aren't worth the trouble. I get it now. Trevor turned out to be one of those things that doesn't last and shouldn't.

I guess I should be glad for him, despite the expired fun. He is the reason I'm here and not in Phoenix. Without all this "concern" I've generated over the past few years, with his help, the New Browns would probably be here on their own, the way they are accustomed to vacationing. Everything for a reason. That's what I was told by the only person who ever gave me advice worth listening to, the only person who ever spoke about life and death in a way I could understand.

I met her the last time I was on vacation with George, without my mother. I was twelve. We must not have been more than three hours from Cross Cove, but we might as well have been on another planet. We stayed at one of those extended-stay, pay-by-the-week motels, and not the nice kind that serve breakfast and have a recreation room. We were there for almost a week before my mother came, and when she saw where we were staying, the mold on the carpet, the smoke stains on the walls, the rust in the shower, they had a huge fight. If George was there for work, why didn't the company pay for a nicer hotel? Why weren't they paying at all? We moved to a better place down the street just a few hours after she arrived, even though George was cranky about spending the extra money.

I was actually sad to go; I'd liked being there, even if George did leave me alone a fair amount of time. George sucked up to me, since he was gone constantly, giving me handfuls of change for the vending machine at the bottom of the stairs before he left each day. I could watch as much TV as I wanted and eat as much candy as I wanted, and all I had to do was not leave the premises and promise not to go swimming in the questionably colored pool or talk to anyone. I followed all of these rules, except one.

The woman staying next to us had long silver-and-red hair and dark eye makeup and deep wrinkles. She burned incense, and the smell of fire and dying flowers came wafting out of her room whenever she opened the door. She didn't sleep in her room. She arrived every day midmorning and left a few hours after it got dark. People came to visit her throughout the day. All kinds of people. Some of them left, squeezing her hands and kissing her cheeks, telling her, "Thank you, thank you, thank you." Others cried, shook their heads, said, "I can't believe it, I can't believe it," and she would be the one to kiss their cheeks, take their hands.

She noticed me one day, sitting on the hot cement, eating Skittles, letting my feet dangle through the railing, staring down at the green, murky pool I wasn't allowed to swim in.

"What's your story?" she'd asked me.

No other adult had ever asked me that, an all-encompassing question about my life. No one had ever called it a story, like it was an adventure.

"I don't know," I answered honestly. Then I thought of many things to say. I told her I was there with my dad, all the way from Phoenix. I told her about the time I won the spelling bee in third grade and that I would be playing soccer next season for a team called the Sun Angels.

She nodded. There was something friendly about her even if she didn't really smile.

"What's your story?" I asked her, being polite, but also genuinely curious.

She laughed; it was this raspy sound.

"My story doesn't matter," she said. "I tell the stories."

"What do you mean?"

She was a fortune-teller, she said. She could intuit the future, see the paths people would take in life. They paid her and asked her questions, and she told them about the journey their lives would be.

"How do you know?"

She shrugged. "I know." She said it like it was a fact, so simple and true it required no explanation.

That was good enough for me. I could hardly sleep thinking about it. The next day, after George left, I waited until I was sure the fortune-teller was alone in her room, and I presented all of the change I had been given for candy to her, asking how much of my future she could tell me.

"It's better not to know, believe me," she said. But she was counting the coins, making small piles on the end table.

"But every day you have so many customers."

"Those people are desperate."

"But . . . I want to know, too." I wondered if I was just like them: desperate. But I also didn't care and wondered how to convince her that I was desperate enough that she needed to tell me my future.

"What do you want to know?" she said, lighting a long skinny cigarette.

This astounded me, the specificity of what I was supposed to want to know about my own life, which felt like it had barely started.

"What do the others ask?"

"Many things. About job promotions. Cheating spouses. Love. Death. You name it."

"What do they ask you about death?"

"When they will die, how they will die; when people they are close with will die; when people they hate will die."

"And what about love?"

"Oh, everyone asks the same thing about love."

"What?"

She gave me this flat expression, like I should know, even me, and the thing is, I think I did know. "They ask if they'll fall in love; if there is someone out there who will love them."

"That's what I want to know."

"Are you sure?" Her lips were curving up as close to a smile as she ever got, so I allowed myself to smile, too, as I watched her scoop up the change and put it in the maroon bag next to her bed. I didn't care if asking about love made me predictable or ordinary—in that moment she was about to tell me about falling in love; she would confirm it was coming for me. Just like the movies, all those stories I'd heard. I was delighted.

I nodded, already feeling my face get hot.

"It's going to happen to you," she said. My stomach started to flutter. "You will fall happily and madly in love."

"With who?"

"Let some things be a surprise. Trust me. You'll meet who you're supposed to meet. They'll take you by surprise, and you will be a surprise to them, too. You'll do anything for this person. And they will do anything for you. You'll know, *this is it*, because it will feel so intense that you'll wonder how you ever lived before this person. You will do whatever it takes to be with them."

This sounded so enchanting. A love so great it would make me happy and mad. And I wouldn't be alone. There would be two of us in the adventure together. I couldn't wait.

A couple of nights later, my mother arrived, and she and George fought. I went outside to get away from it. The fortune-teller came out of her room and stood beside me.

"Those are your parents yelling? They are very loud. Don't they know we can all hear them?" I liked that she didn't dance around topics; she was straight and honest with me. She smelled like stale cigarette smoke and too much liquor, but I didn't care. I was glad she was there.

"They always fight."

"I'm sorry," she said. "Love is the best and worst thing that ever happens to a person. Sometimes the worst wins. You'll get to leave them one day at least."

This made me sad, and I started tearing up. I didn't want to leave them. I wanted us to all be together; why was it so hard for them to be together?

"One day, that won't make you cry," she said. "You'll be okay with leaving them. You'll be ready."

"I guess."

"It's true," she said.

"How do you know when people are going to die?" I asked her, something I wanted to know ever since I'd listened in on a few of her sessions the day before. She told one woman her father's cancer was going to go away. She told another she needed to get her liver checked before it was too late.

"I just do," she said.

"You know when I'm going to die?"

She looked down at the pool and didn't say anything for a while.

"I don't know when anyone is going to die," she said. "But it's something we all do."

This confused me. "You lie to all those people?"

She took her time answering me. "Most people only want to be told what they already know. And for the privilege of my services, people make appointments. I have time to look them up. Some people show so much of themselves on the internet. And I've lived in this town a long time; I sometimes have a mutual acquaintance with a client that can tell me what I need to know so I'll know what I need to say. Arrests are public record. Deaths are always documented. And I have a friend working at the hospital who will send me medical records if I offer the right price. And everyone has a price, never forget that."

"It sounds sneaky." This broke my heart because if she lied to those people about dying, maybe she also lied to me about falling in love—happily and madly, the way I'd always dreamed.

"Everyone hears what they want to hear, no matter what I say." She flicked ash from her cigarette and watched the white flakes drift to the cement. "It's not all bullshit. People live in two worlds, one where they convince themselves to feel how they think they're supposed to feel and one where they are honest about their feelings." She turned to me like she wanted to make sure I was listening. "Every person we come into contact with plays a role in our future, if we let them, and I am no different—just someone else they've elected to alter their path. Coincidences are fate made obvious, but no one ever takes the time to notice. Everything for a reason, everything for a reason."

I heard every word she said; she knew the power she had and she didn't care. "I don't think anyone wants you to tell them they're about to die unless they really are."

"We are all going to die someday. It could be tomorrow. It could be in ten years. It could be in fifty years." She studied me and I wondered what she saw, looking at me the careful way she was. "You probably won't even make it to your eighteenth birthday."

"But you don't know for sure," I said. My chest felt heavy, and I felt so tired all of a sudden. "You can never know."

She put her hand on my shoulder. "That's right," she said. "You should remember that, too. Life is short. And it can be very deceiving. Never forget."

She stayed next to me leaning against the railing, until my parents made me come inside to pack my things. Even though she could tell I was mad at her, I liked that she didn't leave me to sit there alone.

When we left that night, her door was shut, and she was probably already gone. I didn't get to say goodbye. I never got to say thank you.

I think about what she said all the time. So maybe she was a con artist, but as the years go by, more and more of what she said to me makes sense, about the lies she tells, how little they matter in the grand scheme of things. Because we are all going to die—that much is true.

And as I lie in bed, the house finally getting quiet, my room darker than I'm used to with no streetlight right outside my bedroom window and no sound of cars or neighbors slamming their doors, not even crickets, I think how lucky I am to be out of Phoenix for the summer. That getting in trouble with Trevor had really gotten me in over my head. That not being happily and madly in love with him was a blessing and a warning. I came out here knowing that I wasn't going to let George or the New Browns stop me from turning this into the best summer of my life, and I'm not going to give up now, even when loneliness strikes me so hard that my chest feels hollow and my legs start to itch. Because you never know.

Chapter 4

I spend the next morning lying in bed listening to the New Brown Family move through the house, gathering in the kitchen, chatting about where they want to take the boat today and what strange and lovely dreams they had last night. They're so at ease. They have a groove, like they've spent a million mornings together, like they belong together. Deep down I know: they do.

"Should I wake Maris?" Chelsea asks.

"Better let her sleep," George replies.

I come down a while later and intrude. Chelsea offers me coffee—*You drink coffee, don't you?* Trisha is making eggs—*How do you take yours?* George is silent because George doesn't know the answers either.

Phoebe reaches for me from her high chair as I pass by with my coffee. She smiles at me, mouth open, and looks me right in the face, like she understands that there's no reason to be afraid. She grasps for me with one chubby baby arm, wiggling all her fingers. I tentatively hold my hand out to her, and she grabs my pointer finger and squeezes it with all the force of her tiny hand. She's stronger than she looks, and she smiles like she knows it. I smile back at her as she makes an indecipherable noise, half giggle, half exclamation. The need to bond with her is alarmingly urgent—I want to pick her up and hug her; I want to feel her grasping hands pinch into my skin. The New Brown Family is smiling, too, but their stares are unwavering. They are *watching*. They are cautious. It doesn't matter that Phoebe is my half sister, too; I am still not to be trusted.

"We're taking the boat out today," George says.

"You'll come, won't you?" Chelsea asks, the hopefulness already slipping from her face as she waits for my answer. She is used to the Maris at her mom and George's wedding, who left right after they cut the cake to catch the red-eye back to Phoenix, and the Maris who spent Christmas Eve hiding out in the New Brown Family guest room, talking to her boyfriend on the phone with the door locked.

"Of course," I say with a smile. "Sounds like fun."

Forty minutes later, I find myself riding out of the cove on the New Brown Family's summer rental boat named *Vienna*.

The ocean is beautiful, blue and transparent. It glistens against the sun. It's inviting even. I like it all the more as we're soaring above it, bumping over the waves, getting sprayed with their mist. George drives us in line with a herd of other boats also leaving their homes in the bay.

Our destination is a place called Honeycomb Island, a mass of white sand with a forest center. George announces that it's rife with hiking trails, though by the time we anchor the boat and unload all of our stuff, mostly all Phoebe's things, and find a spot on the beach and have lunch next to all the other families scattered across the sand, it's clear none of the New Browns are ambitious enough to go for a hike.

Two hours of sunning myself while Chelsea and George stand in the water tossing a Frisbee, and Trisha and Phoebe splash in the tide and cheer them on, is about all I can take of the sight of George and the new loves of his life. We—his former family—were never *this* happy. He was never *this* thrilled to be with us. We weren't the ones he wanted to be with, and we could feel it deep in our hearts.

"I'm going to go exploring," I declare, sliding on my flip-flops and slipping my gray sundress on over my swimming suit.

"Okay—" Trisha looks up at me, unable to move from where she's kneeling in the sand because if she lets go of Phoebe, Phoebe will charge into the ocean. "I guess that's okay."

"You want me to go with you?" George calls. He glances at Chelsea. "We could all go." But Chelsea's smile is reluctant.

"Come play with us!" Chelsea shouts. "This game isn't as lame as I thought it'd be." George replies to this by splashing Chelsea. She shrieks with laughter and Trisha laughs, too, like she thinks this is the funniest thing she's ever seen. Even Phoebe, who is supposed to at least half be on my side, is clapping.

The New Browns want to stay here, in the same spot, when there is a whole island to explore. They don't care that we have no surprises coming for us on this beach, that this is *it* for the afternoon, for the day, maybe for their entire damn summer.

"No, it's okay," I say. "I'll be right back."

"Be careful!" Tricia says.

"Don't go too far!" George says instead of "Don't ruin the summer for us."

I whirl around to give them one last wave, but another session of the New Brown Family bonding has begun and they're not even watching me as I move off the sand, into the beach grass, before disappearing into a forest of tall skinny trees with thick branches crisscrossing.

What's the saying? If a tree falls in a forest and no one is around to hear it, does it make a sound? And so: If I'm not missed, was I ever really here?

Chapter 5

The farther into the island I get, the larger the rocks are, the thicker the trees are, the broader their trunks; the older trees are lying down, and there is moss on the hard-dirt ground, and soon, above me, there's a canopy of leaves, a tangle of snaking branches, and my feet are gliding over wet earth. There are a few signs announcing trailheads. I ignore them.

I keep wandering my own unbeaten path until I can't hear anything, no conversations in the distance, except the faint sound of the ocean barreling into the shore.

There's a break in the quiet, a twig snapping. Then another. And another. And I know I am not alone anymore.

I step behind a tree, my eyes scanning the area in front of me for signs of movement. I didn't consider wild animals when I decided to roam off on my own. I also didn't consider that someone else might be out here, off the path.

He's hard to spot at first, popping in and out of view, sprinting quickly through the greenery—or trying to. He's limping, but still moving fast. He's tall and dressed all in black, covered in dirt. There is mud streaked across his face, but I think he looks about my age. As he gets closer, I can hear his rapid breathing louder than the sound of his feet pounding into the ground, his leg dragging. He falls against a tree, either trying for a rest or because he can't make it any farther on his bad leg. That's when he sees me. His eyes widen. For a second, we stand there staring at each other from across the expanse of wilderness.

I wait, gauging whether my presence is a good or a bad thing to him.

Maybe I should run. *What is he running from?* But he's already seen me. And he doesn't seem dangerous. He looks hurt and terrified.

"Do you need help?" I call.

He opens his mouth like he's about to say something, but he's still breathing too hard to speak. There's something in his face—an expression of despair—that makes me start toward him. He shakes his head, but I keep walking. For a second, when he sees I'm not going to turn away despite his insistence, I see the crack in his fear, and relief passes over his face, like he is letting in the smallest dose of hope, and I know helping him is the right thing to do.

But then I hear the other noises: a whole chorus of stampeding feet. The boy glances quickly over his shoulder. His eyes scan the trees, like they are searching for somewhere else to go, somewhere else to hide. I can see silhouettes in the distance, darting between the trees, coming toward us. Three, four, maybe five people—all guys, judging by the sound of their yelling, though I can't make out what they're saying.

I'm still standing in front of the boy, listening to the voices getting closer, watching him grow tense as he hears them, too. Maybe right now I should be tearing out of here and hiding, getting far, far away from the middle of the island.

He speaks. "Will you help me get behind that rock?" His voice is hoarse and struggling. He nods at a moss-covered boulder coming off a small creek about three yards away. "Please," he says when I glance behind me. If I ran, where would I go? And the boy is desperate. Now that I'm close enough to him, I can see that there is not only mud on his face, there is also blood.

"Yes," I say, because my heart is racing and I'm afraid in that compulsive-glorious way I'm accustomed to.

Without hesitation and without warning, he throws his arm around my shoulders. "Go, go!" he whispers as we slide over the slick wet ground of moss and leaves and mud and pebbles.

He's heavy, and his left foot drags. I can feel his heart beating quickly, and soon my heart rate matches, and I'm out of breath, too. We fall when we get to the rock. He scrambles to press his back against the cold stone, drawing his legs up in front of his chest so every part of him is as close to the rock as possible. I follow suit, getting in the same position, and he reaches out, pulling me in so I'm right up next to him.

"Shh," he says.

This time, I feel it all over. Vivid and enraged fear. The kind of fear that starts in my toes and makes my heart beat quickly and turns me into someone with no limits by the time it reaches my brain.

The footsteps are louder now, the voices clearer. These are not boys. They are men.

"Finn!" they shout. "*Finn*, we know you're out there!"

I glance at him, and as if he knows I'm about to ask if he is Finn, he puts a finger to his lips, signaling me to stay silent.

"Maybe we can still work something out." Their voices are scattered.

"That's all we wanted, man. To make a deal."

"It doesn't end this way, and you know it."

They laugh, but there is anger, frustration, and wickedness in their low chuckles.

The boy—Finn—is trembling. He brings a shaky hand to his lips again. He does not seem to trust me, even though I haven't made a sound. Even though I helped him.

The voices are spreading out and getting closer. They aren't shouting to Finn anymore; now they speak to each other.

"He could barely walk; he's here somewhere." This, to the left of us.

"How's your neck, Archaletta?" This, to the right.

"How the hell do you think it is?" The voice that says this is weak and nearby. "I can't believe that motherfucker stabbed me."

"Maybe he made it to the shore, after all."

"He wouldn't risk being seen."

The voices are closing in on us. They are going to find us. The boy knows it, too. He hugs himself tighter, looking to the sky like he is begging for mercy, pinching his eyes shut, then letting them fly open, like he is too afraid to be in the dark.

Even though I am scared, even though we are surrounded, I am not petrified by fear. I never am—not for long anyway. My adrenaline gets going, and my brain starts working, analyzing the situation, and then all of a sudden, I see the way out so clearly. For the handful of things I got caught doing, there was an armful of things no one ever found out about. And I have an idea now that might save us. Maybe they will only want the boy. There is a chance I could be collateral damage. In my experience, there are almost always casualties of some sort. But taking the risk—it's better than squatting here waiting for them to find us.

I feel around in front of me for a stick or something sharp and find a small jagged rock with a rough edge. It will work. Beside me, Finn is shaking his head—he doesn't know what I'm up to, and he doesn't like it. I ignore him. I drag the pointed edge of the rock across the side of my wrist. The skin breaks, and blood oozes out of my arm and drips down my hand, but I'm a pro at stifling pain, keeping it quiet.

Finn's mouth hangs open. I hear him whisper, "Don't!" as I dart out from behind the rock. My shoes slide over the slick ground, but I'm careful. I am confident none of the surrounding men hear me. And they will not see me until . . . now, when I am crouched in position by the side of the creek, pretending to clean my wound.

"Hey, what's that—there?" A man a few feet directly in front of me wearing a red hat points. The others gather quickly, and I scramble up as though I'm startled to see them.

There are three of them. They all look as though they're in their midtwenties, maybe. They have gruff faces and stern eyes. Like Finn, they are dirt-covered, blood-covered. One of them is badly injured. His shirt is off and tied blood-soaked around his shoulder and neck in a makeshift bandage.

I act like I'm surprised and frightened by their presence. Really, I am roused by it. I can feel my blood pumping furiously through my body. It's like that time I was fourteen and floating down the river, and I jumped off my tube with the older kids, the ones who drove us there. I climbed the hot rocks and stood on the ledge, about to jump off the twenty-foot cliff as all those eyes from the water down below stared up at me, and I had no idea if the water was deep enough or if anyone had ever been hurt before. But the older kids were doing it, and I desperately wanted to feel what it was like to drop through the air, even if I was so afraid of the landing. And when I pushed off and felt the wind in my hair, I knew that it'd been worth it.

The one in the red hat puts his hands out in front of him, motioning for me to calm down, as though he's anticipating that I'm going to scream. Now that I see how skittish he is, my fear starts to disappear and is replaced with confidence that I'll be able to tell them whatever I want, and they'll believe me.

"What are you doing all the way out here by yourself?" His voice is fake and pushy and degrading, like he's scolding a puppy. His face registers irritation as soon as he hears himself. I recoil accordingly.

"Jesus," the one with the apparent stab wound mutters—*Archaletta*, that's what they called him before. He has crystal-clear blue eyes, made drastic against his dark hair.

"Do you need help?" the one in the red hat says, using his real voice this time, annoyed, but genuine. He nods at my hand, dripping with blood.

I respond by looking pointedly at them and all their obvious wounds.

The one in the red hat nods, still irritated. "Don't you worry about us, we're fine."

"Just a minor accident," the shortest one says.

Archaletta mutters, "Yeah, right," as he adjusts his makeshift bandage.

"I got lost," I say, keeping my voice tentative. "And I fell." I hold my wound close to my body. "I was trying to rinse the dirt out." They all look to the creek I'm standing by.

The shortest of the group shakes his head. "Damn, sweetheart, you gotta be careful."

"Listen, through those trees, straight ahead this way." The one in the red hat motions to the right, the direction I came from when I left the New Browns. "That's the fastest way to the shore. Someone can help you there."

I nod, clutching my wrist. "Okay, thanks." But I am slow as I move across the creek, eyeing them warily. Really, I'm waiting. If they are really serious about finding Finn, I'm sure they are dying to ask me what I've seen, *who* I've seen, being the only other person out here.

"Hey." It's Archaletta that breaks. "You didn't happen to see another guy—brown hair, messy like us, younger, tall . . . you didn't see him come through here, did you?"

"We're looking for our buddy," adds the shortest.

The one in the red hat shakes his head and puts his hands on his hips, looking away. I think he must know it was a bad idea to ask me. I bite my lower lip and wait a second so it seems like I'm taking great care in my decision to answer. I tell them, "I hid from him." I look to the ground, as though I'm ashamed. "He was . . . limping or something."

"Yeah," the short one says. "We veered off trail, it's pretty rough and—"

I'm still playing scared with my eyes locked on the ground, so I can't see who's cut him off, though my guess would be the one in the red hat. I glance up when I hear footsteps, indicating one of them is moving toward me.

"Did you see which way he went?" Archaletta says, eyes sincere, and he takes another step closer. He's close enough to touch me, and he does it. I tense, but he still puts his hand on my shoulder, lifting my hair back, exposing the dirt smeared there from helping Finn.

I wince a little, not too overdramatic, though I can see the one in the red hat cursing at the sky under his breath for the way Archaletta is interacting with me. An injury is the best guise—something I learned was a good antidote for getting out of trouble. The time I was caught trying to steal the test key off my teacher's computer? A few tears and a bruise across the collarbone made them forget they might've seen me pull a flash drive from the laptop. This is the rule: make them think you are fragile; even better if they feel sorry for you. It's an exposed weakness to hide an inner strength. It's why I knew I had to cut myself before I could talk to them. It's what's making Archaletta so brazen now, in the way he's speaking to me, touching me.

Again, I take my time before nodding. I point in the direction they already seemed to be going anyway. Past the rock and away from Finn hiding behind it. Their eyes are scanning the trees; they're telling one another, "He probably thought he'd be secure by the waterfall," and "Maybe there's an outlet we don't know about."

"Thank you," Archaletta says, nodding at me.

They are quick to be on their way, but the one in the red hat stops.

"Why didn't you try to hide from us?" he asks.

"There were too many of you," I say. I shift my arm to remind him of the reason I was out in the open in the first place. It's a good excuse.

Archaletta and the shorter one appear to be satisfied immediately with this answer, not really giving me another glance. But the one in the red hat furrows his brow and opens his mouth slightly, like maybe he has more questions. I shudder and clutch my arm. It works. He does not like that I am easily spooked. He can sense that I am unpredictable even if he doesn't trust that my fear is real.

I start moving as soon as they do. They head straight; I go to the right. They move quickly, and so do I. When I can no longer hear them or see them, I slow down. I turn around to go back for Finn. Because if it were me, I'd want someone to come back for me. I'm still in escape mode, adrenaline pumping. I don't know if we have much time before they come back this way to look for him.

"Over here." This voice is too hoarse and rough to be from one of the men, but it still startles me. Finn is a few feet away, leaning against a tree, no longer by the rock. He is motioning with filthy hands for me to come over.

I rush over to him, my blood still surging, my hands completely steady, and help his arm around my neck. "That way," he says, and I stop. He's pointing in the same direction that I told Archaletta and the others to go to look for him.

"It's okay," he says in my ear. "There *is* an outlet they don't know about."

Chapter 6

We move through the trees, hobbling over the wet dirt. I try to listen for the sound of the ocean getting closer, but I can't hear anything above our ragged breathing and the sound of my heart beating in my ears. All I can smell is salt and steel and soil. We are fleeing through the enshrouded part of an island, but I could be careening out the back door of a party about to be broken up by the police, or climbing out of my bedroom window in the middle of the night—the feeling is the same. Like I'm escaping so much more than the people who might stop me, like I am setting myself free.

"Not much farther," Finn promises.

Soon, he directs us through a curtain of vines and bushy plants, and we practically fall into a small pool of water. We are up to our hips in ocean water, surrounded on one side by a rocky wall with water sliding down it, but not with enough force to make a real waterfall. On the other side is thick vegetation. Short and stalky trees and overgrown brush. There is a black, pointy speedboat anchored in the water, half-covered by the overgrown shrubbery and vines.

I think I hear Finn say, "We made it."

He lets go of me to fling himself farther into the water, bobbing under and emerging through a cloud of dirt and blood. I wash myself off, too, cleaning away the remaining blood on my wrist and letting the water rinse away the traces of mud Finn left stamped across my arm and around my neck.

"Holy shit," I say, bending forward to catch my breath, letting the relief flood over me, those tingles of excitement hitting me like needle pricks all over my skin.

Finn smiles at me. For the first time, a real smile, and I get it— danger, escape, it's best when it's shared with someone else. *Partner in crime* is a saying for a reason. And sometimes, even if you are still scared, when your mind knows you've won, your mouth automatically responds.

"What was that all about?" I ask. "Who were those guys?"

Finn glances at me over his shoulder as he grabs the rope bobbing in the water and attempts to tug the boat loose from the branches. On his first try, he topples over, like he can't quite stay balanced on one foot to use enough strength to move the boat. He's a little more successful the next time he pulls on the rope, and even more successful the third time, when I help him. The boat glides toward us, coming out from under all the debris.

He pulls himself up on the edge. Without proper use of his left foot, he ungracefully falls in. He pops up quickly.

I wade out to the boat, where the water comes up almost to my shoulders, get a grip on the edge, and throw myself in, too.

"Come on," I say. I nod toward the steering wheel, keys missing from the ignition.

"Oh," he says after a moment, when he realizes I'm waiting for an answer. "I can't go anywhere yet. They might circle the island before they take off. I'm going to wait them out. When I'm sure they're gone, then I'll leave."

This is, as it seems, the worst plan I have ever heard.

"But what if they find you while you're 'waiting it out'?"

"They won't." He peels off his wet shirt and grabs a water bottle from a cooler on the boat. He tosses a bottle to me, then takes one for himself. I can't help but stare as he leans against the edge, tilting his head, drinking as fast as he can, as the sun makes the water droplets clinging to his skin shimmer. There are cuts on his side, a few bruises on his shoulders and by his neck, and his foot is swollen and bleeding below the ankle. There is a dark bruise under his eye, covering most of his left cheek, shading the side of his nose. The image I get is one of Finn being held down by his neck and shoulders, getting punched in the face. I still notice that he is beautiful.

Finn finishes off his water and lets the empty bottle fall to the floor as he grabs another. He looks up, asking if I want more, but I've been too busy staring and have barely taken a sip, so I shake my head.

"But how can you be sure?" I say. He slowly looks me over. I wonder if he's questioning why tricking people came so easily to me and if he can sense that what happened gave me a kind of rush; if he looks at me and sees a junkie, grateful for this hit of adrenaline, drawn to this kind of danger, and high off the escape.

"Because they don't know the island," he finally says. "They won't know where to search—they definitely won't know to look here. This is the kind of place you have to know to look for."

The characteristics of a perfect hiding spot, I think—I'll give him that. My perfect hiding spot back home was the front seat of my dad's car when it was parked in the garage. The only place in the house where I couldn't hear them yelling at each other. And when I went missing, when I was in trouble, my parents always called my phone, sent a million texts; never truly tried looking for me. They gave up after not finding me in my room. They would never suspect I was so close.

"How will you know when they're gone?"

He shrugs. I can see a little bit of hope slip from his expression. Good. He's starting to understand.

"This is a terrible idea, even with the perfect hiding spot," I say to make sure he knows. There was something determined about those men, and they were angry.

He raises his eyebrows. "What would you have me do, then?" There's an edge in his voice.

"We leave now"—I'm talking a million miles a minute—"going as fast as we can—how fast can this thing go?"

He smiles again, his eyes on me like he's watching me, like he's looking for something, but they still seem sad. Like he wishes it could be that simple.

"I'm surprised you aren't listening to me, after I saved you out there."

"You're right, you're right—you saved my life. Thank you, by the way. But I'll have to take it from here. And I'm going to wait it out."

He gets up and opens a compartment below a seat on the

inside edge of the boat. He pulls out a first aid kit. I watch as he rummages through its contents until he finds the sanitizer and a bandage. He holds it out to me. "That'll get infected." He motions to my wrist.

I hesitate, because I still think he is making a mistake staying here like a sitting duck, but he's right about my cut, so I take it from him.

"The least you can do, I guess, since I saved your life."

It's not really that he's being nice; it's to nudge me on my way. Clean yourself up, and then scram.

"You really thought they were going to kill you?" I dab my cut with the sanitizer, pressing hard against my skin with the bandage to quell the stinging.

"What—no." He shakes his head. "No, they weren't going to kill me. Of course not."

"You just said I saved your life."

"It's an expression. You rescued me, sure. I needed badly to get away from them, and you made that possible. That's why I said that."

I don't believe him.

"What did they want?" I ask.

He ignores me, sifting through the first aid kit again, then devoting all his concentration to shaking out the instant cold pack before he sits down and begins fashioning it to his ankle using a compression bandage.

"You'll want to elevate that to keep it from swelling," I say.

"You're sort of . . . bossy, you know." But he's smiling again, a barely there upward tug of his lips.

"And yet you refuse to listen to me, to take any of my advice, even after I saved your life."

He stares at me for a moment but does not elevate his ankle. "Again, the only thing I was in danger of is a concussion. They would not have killed me."

I nod. Sure—except: "But you stabbed one of them."

He leans back against the seat and this time doesn't look directly at me. "It was self-defense. I didn't mean to. I wasn't trying to hurt him. We were in a fight—they outnumbered me. I did what I had to do to get away."

He doesn't know it's always best to stick to one excuse. And also that the best way to get someone to believe you is to make eye contact.

When he looks at me, it's only to make sure he's convinced me, his expression asking, *Okay? Is that good enough?*

"Why were you in a fight?"

"What's with the interrogation?" He throws his hands up, but his smile counters his annoyance.

I watch him, trying to gauge how truly irritated with me he really is. "Just making sure I saved the right side." I wait for another slight, can't-help-it smile, and he does not disappoint.

"Money—I owe them money," he says. "Isn't that why everyone fights?"

"I've always thought physical violence was a stupid way to get money from someone."

"Right." It's all he says.

"But now maybe you'll pay what you owe them."

"Maybe."

"How much money do you owe them?"

"It was just a poker game."

"How much?" I ask again.

"A lot." His face scrunches like he's concentrating. Likely he's trying to pick an answer out of the sky but wants to appear serious about this topic.

"Do you need help coming up with it?"

"Are you offering me money?" He laughs, shakes his head. "It's fine, I don't know—I can ask my parents to help or dip into my savings or something." Too many answers. "What?"

I am staring at him with a look of indignant surprise. They were going to beat the shit out of him, kill him probably, and he chose to meet them here in the deserted part of the island, carefully hiding his boat like he knew he would need to stay hidden, just for money that he can simply borrow from his parents or get from a savings account? Something does not make sense. Also, he is a terrible liar.

"You are a terrible liar."

"I'm not sure why this is any of your business." He breaks open another cold pack and lays the large clump over his eye.

"I was only trying to help." Now would be a good time to storm off; he's lying to me and treating me like I'm getting in his way, and whatever is chasing him isn't my problem. But—"You're doing that all wrong."

"Is there really a wrong way to hold ice to your face?"

He should be using a smaller cold pack that won't be so overwhelming against the bruising on his face. And that's not the only thing he's doing wrong.

I grab the large cold pack from him and press it against the other side of his ankle, grabbing a towel that's resting on the seat and using it to cradle his foot. It also helps hold the cold pack in place properly, to give his whole ankle the icing it truly needs. I pull his foot up, laughing to myself at how this surprises him, and he grips the seat with both hands to balance himself as I set his foot on the driver's seat so it's nearly elevated. I break apart and shake out another cold pack, this one much smaller, and place it carefully over his cheek. He cringes when I move it closer to the bruising by his nose. Almost instinctively, I press my free hand against his shoulder to calm him. He breathes out slowly, keeping his eyes on mine.

I like that he's letting me do this—that he knows to trust me, even though I'm peppering him with questions and opinions, and he's seen what a brilliant liar I can be and how much better I am at it than he is.

"Take a breath," I say. "It hurts now, but you'll be glad later."

"Are you a doctor or something?" His jaw is still tensed, but he manages a smile.

"I was a clumsy child."

This gets a real laugh out of him, but he doesn't say anything else. He seems like he needs it—the laughter. Even if it's fleeting and shallow. I like that I can give it to him. I brought him to safety, but getting him to laugh somehow seems like a rescue, too.

He takes another deep breath before he looks at me, and when he does, I feel myself breathe out, too. I stare into his eyes, gray and stormy, and realize they are the only part of him that is completely honest. They do not lie, they do not make jokes or excuses, and right now, they are saying thank you. When I first met him, they were desperate; then they were sad. They are the eyes of a person who thought they were going to die.

"I should probably get going." I let go of his shoulder, remembering that I didn't bring my phone and the New Browns have no way of reaching me when they are ready to go.

This is what he wants anyway, to be left alone.

"Do you know how to get back to—"

"I can figure it out," I say. If he wants to be scarce with his information, I'll be limited with mine.

"Okay," he says, attempting to stand as though he plans to see me off like a gentleman. I press down on his shoulder, encouraging him to stay seated.

"Good luck," I tell him, not looking back, *so* careful not to look back at his handsome face, those sad and grateful eyes, that smile full of abandon, as I ease myself over the boat and into the water.

I walk back the way I came. No sign of anyone. Not Archaletta or the guy in the red hat or the short and stocky guy. I pass the creek where I cut my arm, and the rock Finn and I hid behind. There's something there. A small dark object. It's a brick of a phone. Old, too. A flip phone, cheap looking. Probably pay-by-the-minute; untraceable, like he is on the run in all areas of his life. I know it's his phone, not only because we were here behind this rock but because it's speckled in blood.

I open it, power it to life. There's a notification of a text message, and I open it.

What did you see? Hello?

It's the only message on the phone, and it's from an unnamed number. The contacts list is empty, as well as the call log.

It shouldn't surprise me, I guess. But it does. It's been a long time since I've felt this intrigued.

Chapter 7

I was gone for too long. I can see it in the way George's forehead is creased and his eyes won't meet mine. Trisha is quiet; her face carries a forced-pleasant expression. I recognize it. Whenever the principal was left alone with me before the counselor came in to discuss why I'd missed a week of school or why I hadn't turned in homework since the start of the semester, he had this face. This is the look people give me when they are afraid of saying something to make it worse.

We leave Honeycomb Island right away even though there are still hours of daylight left and we'd packed enough food and essentials to stay until dusk. I apologize profusely, but I always do, so George and Trisha are pretending they don't want to talk about it.

"I told you she'd be right back," Chelsea says to them, an unsuccessful attempt to lighten the mood. She doesn't like a single dark cloud hovering near the New Browns. "I told them there was nothing to worry about," she says to me.

"Thank you." It's probably the least I can say if George and Trisha spent the last hour complaining about me not being back yet.

"What happened to your wrist?" George says, more anger than concern in his voice.

I'd removed my dress and wrapped it around the phone to hide it. I took off the bandage on my wrist, too, so there would be no questions about how I got it, and did my best to conceal the cut, which is still red and on the verge of opening again.

"I tripped, and when I tried to catch myself with a boulder, it cut me."

George sighs and goes back to ignoring me.

Chelsea gives me a sympathetic smile, but it is still timid. Phoebe hardly notices me, but when she does, she has a face full of glee. I like that she is not yet old enough to know that her feelings about me should be complicated. Chelsea sits right beside me on the boat ride home, not leaving a seat between us even though there is plenty of room. She doesn't say anything to me, but I think this is her way of being on my side. Like she can see the guilt I feel, or assumes it must be there. The mistake I did make is putting out warning signs too early in the summer—they won't want to trust me to go off on my own again; I'll have to make this up to them somehow.

I receive a fierce text message from my mother: *You need to be more respectful*, which means George called her from Honeycomb Island and told her I'd wandered off and made them all worry.

I knew this was how it was going to be, my behavior in constant question and scrutiny, but now, as George sighs again instead of telling me that I scared the hell out of him by wandering off without my phone, staying gone longer than "I'll be right back," returning with a cut he thinks probably "needs stitches," I feel a twinge of anger.

My mother was the one who had to bail me out when I was arrested for vandalizing the new spring training facilities and when Trevor and I were found with the stolen car and the cocaine. George wasn't looped in until the charges didn't hold up and I was given community service. She was always the one to answer the door when the police brought me home for using a fake ID to get into one of the clubs in Scottsdale, George thousands of miles away not even losing sleep. My mother had to hear the news directly from the counselor and the principal in person that I had too many absences to graduate this year. George heard about this after I'd passed the GED exams. And she was the one who got the call when I was in the emergency room, broken ribs, covered in cuts and bruises. The call George got was informing him that I had been in a car accident but was going to be fine.

Part of me hopes he was a mess while I was gone, wondering if or when or how I would be coming back. I'm afraid he can see it on me, sense it on me, that I wish for holes in his happiness.

Just in case, I tell him, "I'm sorry," one more time.

Chapter 8

Finn's phone rings after dinner, an unfamiliar chiming coming from my beach bag. I rush upstairs to take the call, pretending it's coming from my own phone. As soon as I've got my bedroom door shut tight behind me, I answer it, but keep silent.

There's no sound on the other end. It's a call from an unlisted number.

"Yes?" I finally say when my curiosity becomes too much.

"So it is you." It's Finn's voice, and I feel a touch of satisfaction that he could recognize mine, too.

"Who else were you expecting?"

I hear a grunt that I interpret as the beginnings of a laugh. "Did you find my phone, or did you take it off me?"

Now I laugh, full-on. I'm undeniably happy to be hearing from him. Handsomeness aside, he is the most exciting person I've ever met or could have dreamed of meeting someplace like this, where serenity is the selling point. He has a secret. There's a mystery to him. And were it not for me, no matter what he says about his life not being in danger, he wouldn't even be here to make this call.

"I found it, of course." There's no telling if he believes me.

"Well, I'm going to need it back. Where are you? Staying in the cove, I assume? Can you meet me somewhere tonight to give it back?" He is talking quickly, already back to no-nonsense. "And can you be discreet about how we know each other? The cove is full of people who like to gossip." He clears his throat. "You haven't told anyone about what happened on Honeycomb Island, have you?"

"You think people care what I have to say?" It's a non-answer, and I give it to him that way on purpose.

"Please—" he starts, but he cuts himself off like maybe he knows showing his desperation isn't a good next move.

I've missed this—your move, my move, opponents in a game, who will break first, what lie will be the one that accidentally reveals too much, who will expose their weakness first and have to surrender. The difference is that usually people don't know they're playing. Finn is very aware. It keeps me on my toes, even if currently I am the one holding all the information that's damning to him, and therefore the one winning.

"Where do you want to meet?" I ask.

"There's a lot on the corner of Van Ness and Pine, on the south side of the cove—"

"I know where Pine is." The New Brown beach house is on

Pine. "I can be there at nine." When the fireworks start and every-one will be distracted by them.

"Don't be late."

"I'll be on time. Don't worry, Finn." I hang up before he has a chance to react to my voice saying his name—one last reminder that as secretive as he's been, I still know more about him than he thinks.

Chapter 9

"The fireworks are too beautiful to miss," Chelsea says that night when I announce I'm tired and am going to go to bed. "When else in your whole life are you going to be treated to a private fireworks show every night?" But it's too close to nine for her to really put up a fight without missing the show herself.

Like the first night, Trisha and George gather with Phoebe on the screened porch, and Chelsea rushes to stand in the surf and stare up at the sky with her feet in the ocean.

I escape out the front door, letting the booming from the Covingtons' fireworks disguise the sound of my footsteps and the door shutting. Coming back, I'll have to climb through my second-story window, which would be a challenge except my window is over the garage and there's a trellis on the side of the house, making it easy to get onto the garage roof and through my window.

Using my phone's GPS, I find the property, bare except for a dark two-story house on the corner of Van Ness and Pine, a few blocks from the New Brown Family beach house. It's a big lot with a tall house and a cement platform in front, the beginnings of a driveway. I use the flashlight from my phone to illuminate the darkness. The tall trees encroaching make it darker than normal. There are hardly any streetlights on the cove, so the stars and the fireworks have nothing to compete with. There is no sign of Finn. I look around again. Surely, no one lives here; there's no evidence of people, and it's an unfinished landscape. I shine my light on the house, and as I suspected, there are still stickers on the windows, marking them as newly installed.

The popping of the fireworks starts up again, making me jump. There's a light in the distance. It's Finn holding a lantern. He's more put together now, more so than I expected. Like before, he's wearing dark clothes, but these clothes are nice. Unwrinkled shorts and nice sneakers, a black sweatshirt with the collar of a polo shirt, tucked under, but still visible at his neckline. He looks like someone who might belong here at Cross Cove on vacation. Someone who would get in over his head for something as trivial as a poker game. Someone who would know hiding spots on a vacation island but not know how to properly treat his hurt ankle. His hair is windblown, like he must've arrived here by boat since this is a still night. He seems calmer out here. He's not limping anymore, but there's something else about him, something peaceful, like a real burden has been lifted off his shoulders.

"You're here," he says, joining me on the cement.

I shrug, hiding my surprise over how relaxed he's being about this. The lantern light makes shadows over his face, veiling parts of his expression depending on which way he moves. I can't place how he transformed from the broken person on the island, scared for his life, a somewhat snarky boy on the boat in desperate need of a laugh, to this cool and composed person in front of me now.

I remember the image I had in my head of Finn being held down by the men on the island. I add to the picture, visualizing Finn desperate and reaching for whatever he could find to get them off, discovering a knife in one of their pockets and grabbing it and stabbing at the first piece of flesh he could, then running like hell the moment their hands were off him, not wasting a second of their shock to make his escape. Maybe he is stronger than I think. Maybe he was the one hiding in the brush, waiting for Archaletta, ready with his knife, and it was the other two men who surprised him. There is too much to wonder. And that delights me.

"Did you bring the phone?" he asks.

"What's it worth to you?"

"Really?" He looks away, but his lips are turned up in a smile. "Unfortunately, it's not worth much."

"Yeah, I noticed that." It's old and cheap, but still, it doesn't seem like the kind of phone someone has by accident.

"That's the phone I use when I take the boat out. Don't have to worry about getting it wet."

"But it's valuable enough that you came here to meet me at a construction site to pick it up."

He smiles this bashful smile, because I think he doesn't know what to say. I like making him speechless as much as I like making him laugh, it turns out.

"What really happened to you on the island?" I have something he wants, so it's worth a shot. Maybe, with whatever he's involved in, he is completely guilty. And as someone who is, most of the time, completely guilty, I should be warier of him. But this actually makes me like him more. "Why were they chasing you? What did you do to them?"

He looks to the sky. His shoulders sag as he seems to have skipped over being amused or annoyed and has landed on exhausted. "That's tempting, isn't it?" he says to the stars. "Purge all my secrets to a stranger."

"Hey, better me than a priest."

He laughs, and I realize I'd been waiting for it. I'd been trying for it. I definitely like it too much when he smiles.

"It's exactly what I told you. I lost money during a poker game. I didn't want to pay them. Thought I could get out of it, but, well, as you witnessed, I couldn't. Sorry the truth is so boring."

I reach into my back pocket and retrieve his phone. I hold it out to him. He hesitates, then takes it.

"Thank you," he says.

Why did he hesitate? Because now we'll have no reason to be here together?—which is what I'm thinking. The fireworks crash again, and we both look to the sky. We can see the smoke but not the colorful sparks. I still have time, but not much.

"You're lucky I was the one who found your phone."

We're both still looking at the sky.

I expected him to argue or ignore this, too, but he says, "I know."

"I don't have a lot of time left," I say as another eruption of popping begins.

"That's too bad, because I've got all the time in the world."

That makes me smile and makes me brave enough to say, "I

programmed my number in your phone," instead of letting him discover it on his own as I'd planned. This is a new kind of exhilaration. Putting myself out there to be rejected completely. I've made it personal. I've turned the vulnerability around on myself. My heart goes crazy and my stomach is fluttering, but the rest of me is steady.

"Why?" His voice comes out a little higher than normal. He clears his throat. The idea that I've thrown him off again makes my stomach do somersaults.

Everything about him makes me delirious with curiosity. And I like that he is not quite what I thought, but familiar all the same.

"Because I don't want my summer to be boring," I say.

"Summer is supposed to be boring."

"I need this summer to be better."

"Better than what?"

I smile. "The best. Okay?"

"I . . . can't promise best. I am really a very dull guy."

I laugh at this, and he laughs, too.

The fireworks are getting louder, several bursts together at once. The finale.

"I have to get back," I say, leaving the ball in his court, so to speak. I can't be sure he'll even be using that phone again. He holds out the lantern for me as he follows me down the lot, lighting my way to the road.

"I'm not going to call you," he says. Bold. And disappointing. I pretend like I'm unfazed.

"But I will be here tomorrow night," he adds. "Around eleven."

I pinch my lips together and tighten my cheeks to keep from smiling as large as I want to, giving myself away. "I probably can't make it out until midnight." In a house with a delicately sleeping baby and paper-thin walls, I'll have to make sure everyone is sound asleep before I can attempt a break out.

"I could be here at midnight," he says, trying too hard for a casual tone.

"So okay, then."

He smiles, and I didn't expect him to be so blatant in his response to seeing me again.

"Okay, then," he says as I am walking away.

This is it, I'm thinking—I've only been here a few days, and I've found the mystery that's going to fuel my summer and the boy who's going to make everything worth it.

Chapter 10

All day, I have been waiting for the sky to get dark. Through breakfast, where I tell the New Browns specifics about how I like my eggs, how I take my coffee, so they can start to know these things about me, as though I were really part of their family.

We sit on the beach in lawn chairs that rest unevenly on the sand. I help Trisha fix lunch, peanut butter and honey sandwiches with extra honey, the way she claims George likes them. She is right. George devours both of his in record time. For dinner, we have lasagna, and then we play cards until the fireworks start.

Finally, around 10:30, everyone goes to bed, and when it's time, I charge out into the dark night.

Maybe there is a balance. A good day with the New Browns, a night for myself. But I am not in the mood to contemplate the logic of this for too long.

I'm the first to arrive at the cement slab, and I stare up at the sky. The stars are as dazzling as they were the night before. And it's lighter up there. I can barely see in front of me, but against the night sky, I can see silhouettes of the tops of the trees, the glow of the moon, making everything slightly backlit. It's glorious up there. A shooting star flies across the sky, bright and brilliant, trying to impress me, or rubbing its beauty in my face—either way, my breath flutters and a gasp comes out. I've never seen one before.

"Don't scream." Finn approaches holding a lantern and wearing a backpack.

"Not the best way to announce your arrival." I wait to hear his laugh, but then I look back to the stars. "That was my first shooting star."

He clicks off the lantern and sets it down. He comes over and stands next to me.

"Did you make a wish?"

"Oh no, I forgot!" I downright panic. "Maybe there will be another?"

He laughs at my overreaction. "What would you have wished for?"

"More wishes, of course."

"Where I come from, that's cheating."

"Where are you from anyway?" No one has made Cross Cove their real home. It's a place they go to escape.

"All over."

"Oh, I've been there."

Again, he laughs. Again, the sound goes straight to my pride.

"You're on vacation?" he says, not even waiting for my answer. "Is this your first time here?"

"Yes, and you?" He seems to know his way around the cove; he knew this lot was empty and knew the best hiding spot for his boat on the island.

"I've been coming every summer since I was thirteen," he says. "So what do you think? Other than that it's boring."

"I don't know. It's pretty, I guess. Like living in a postcard."

"That's why people love it."

"Do you love it here?" I ask, shamelessly wanting to know more about what he loves.

"Sure," he says. "Beaches, sun—what's not to like?"

I wish he would turn on the lantern so I could see him better. I've had enough of the stars and am ready to see what his expression is doing as he talks about himself.

"What's your name?" he says. "It's weird that I don't know it."

"Maris," I say. First name only since that's all I know of his.

I hear him shuffling in the dark, watch his shadow scratch the back of his neck. He doesn't say anything.

I've never gotten to know someone organically like this, without having school and reputation to guide me, though I have tried to box him in, figure him out, based on first impressions, because what a first impression it was. You can get to know people slowly and by accident at school, even if you only know their façade. I've known who Trevor was ever since ninth grade. He was a senior. Too handsome and charming for his own good. A known rebel, many suspensions under his belt, a permanent seat in detention. He didn't play sports, but he would sit in the bleachers with his friends, laughing and drinking whatever they had mixed in their Big Gulp cups, garnering more attention and admiration than the football players winning the games—at least from me. So I knew who he was when I started seeing him at parties, chatting with him in the comments of other people's posted photos, pretending to run into him at the burger joint where he worked by the college he was most definitely not attending. And soon he knew me, too.

This makes me think of Chelsea, how she is probably so good at getting to know people who are brand-new to her world and good at welcoming them in; how she's tried with me and I don't know how to try back.

I want Finn to know about me as much as I want to know more about him.

"Turn on the lantern," I say. "Let's go in the house." Not waiting for him, using the flashlight app on my phone to see in front of me, I start walking toward the house.

"What—why?"

He trails after me. I slow my pace when I remember that his ankle could still be sore, and when he catches up with me, he turns on the lantern.

"Because we can."

"I'd bet that it's locked."

"We both know you're bad with bets." I watch him smile as I take the lantern from him and walk around to the side of the house. Lucky for us, and as I assumed since this is still a construction site that probably has subcontractors coming and going, there is a spare key hidden inside the breaker box. I come back and rush up the stairs. I wait until Finn is next to me before I unlock the door and let it swing open.

"Oh, look, it's a house," he says, sarcasm in his voice. I like this side of him, too.

It's unlike any summer beach house I've seen. The New Browns' beach house is bright and charming; this one is exquisite and modern. The outside is deceptive. In the entryway, we're face-to-face with a tall ceiling and an iron spiral staircase. The walls are finished, but the flooring hasn't been installed yet. The staircase leads to a huge circular skylight shaped like a wheel. I walk immediately over to it. Finn doesn't step into the house right away, but soon he's standing next to me, staring straight up at the skylight.

"Whoa," he says quietly.

"Come on." We climb the stairs as fast as we can manage with the limited lighting from my phone and the lantern and the night's sky. We get off at the top story. It's a circular room right below the skylight, with a big window cutout blocked by a blue tarp. He must be thinking the same thing as I am, must be as curious as I am, because when I reach for the top of the tarp on the right side, he reaches for the left side. We yank off the tarp and stand in front of a large window exposing an angle of Cross Cove I haven't seen before. The window faces the downtown area, giving us a view of the glistening water in front of the main docks, the lighthouse in the distance. Of course, *of course*, there is a full moon.

I glance over at Finn, and he is like I am, his face lit up with happiness at this discovery.

"Where are you really from?" I ask.

"Not too far from here. Two hours inland."

It's a broad answer. The closest towns are all two hours inland. "You?" he asks.

"Far from here." But I don't see any reason to play coy like he's doing, so I add, "Phoenix."

He doesn't say anything, not even something predictable like, "Oh, must be hot," or "Wow, you are a long way from home."

"Never heard of it?" I say before the silence stretches on too long. .

This makes him laugh. "Come to think of it, it sounds familiar." He checks carefully to make sure I'm laughing at that—I like that he cares. We take turns, looking at each other, looking at the view, like holding eye contact is too much. A passing breeze moves through the open-air window.

This is nice, but I don't like that he's gone quiet.

"What's in your backpack?"

He grips the strap, like he forgot he was wearing it. "Oh." He seems embarrassed in a way I find adorable, and it makes me even more curious. "It's . . . nothing."

I test the waters and put my hand on the zipper; when he doesn't flinch away, I start to unzip it. When it's nearly all the way open, he swings it off his back and holds it steady for me as I root through it. I pull out a rolled-up brown-and-red plaid blanket.

"I thought if we were outside on the cement . . . we'd need something to sit on." He's still looking down, still being bashful. "I didn't know we'd be breaking and entering." But the floor here is still unfinished, so I spread the blanket out over the plywood.

"What else have you got in here?" I reach in, and again he doesn't stop me. I dig out a bottle, heavy to indicate it's full. I hold it against the light to read the label. Some kind of champagne, though it's not a full-size bottle.

"Oh, um." He shifts from one foot to the other, shrugs twice, like he was bold enough to bring the champagne but not quite bold enough to offer it to me. "Just something I had, you know, lying around." He's smiling a little now that he can see how this pleases me.

"And here I didn't bring anything at all." I tease him and watch him look to his feet again, his smile beaming.

I like that he had some sort of plan for us. He wanted us to sit on a blanket under the stars sipping on champagne. I mean, I guess what else were we going to do, meeting here in the middle of the night—the barrage of possibilities makes me blush on command. I distract myself by opening the bottle.

"I forgot glasses," he says. The cork pops off; I hold it tight in my hand to keep it from flying out the window.

I take the first sip, then pass it to him. I have no idea if this is what is considered "good" champagne, but I like it for the usual reasons, that it's sort of sweet and the bubbles tickle my throat. I like it more because he brought it for us. Taking the bottle from him, I sit on the blanket, facing the window—we'll have a view whether we look up or straight ahead. He eases himself down to join me on the blanket, careful not to put too much weight on his hurt ankle.

"How's your ankle?"

"It's not so bad." He shrugs.

We pass the bottle back and forth one more time. I hold it loosely at the neck because it's cold against my palm. Finn notices and takes it from me, sets it in between us.

"So, hey, what was your losing hand?"

"Excuse me?"

"The poker game. Doesn't everyone remember their losing

hand—especially if they lost big?" I decide to give him the benefit of the doubt about the poker game, even if it sounds like I'm testing him.

"The winning hand was a full house, and that's all that matters."

I know nothing about poker, but still respond with, "That's rough."

"You ever play poker?"

I shake my head, and he smiles in this smug but adorable way, like he knew it and he's onto me. I very much like him being onto me.

"You should teach me."

"Oh, sure, except are you sure you want me to teach you since . . ." He breaks; his face slowly morphs into a smile, like he's on the verge of laughing. I like that he can't keep a straight face around me for too long—I like that I'm the same way right now, anticipating what he's going to say next, deep down already knowing what's funny before he says it. "I'm not very good at it." And now we are both laughing, even as the bruise is still fresh on his face and the stab wound on Archaletta's neck hasn't even had the time to scab. But I don't care. Even more than I like being the one to make him laugh, I like when we are laughing together.

"I like my odds, playing for the first time against you," I say, laughter still in my throat.

"It's not really about winning for me."

"Clearly," I say. "Then what's the point?"

"The game. The bluffing, the strategy, the high stakes."

On the island, he seemed like such an obvious liar—the opposite of smooth and definitely not what I would have called a poker face. Lots of backtracking, too many excuses. Maybe he was just shaken up. Maybe these are things he wants to be but not things he's good at, and he likes the intrigue but doesn't know what to do when it backfires on him.

"Whoa, did you see that?" He reaches out and touches my arm. He points to the skylight.

"I missed another one?" My voice turns shrill, but I don't think he minds; I think he enjoys it, the excitement I have over seeing a shooting star.

We seem to get the idea at the same time. We scoot down so we're lying flat on the blanket and we're gazing at the night sky through the large skylight. In case another one is coming, we aren't going to miss it.

He's closer than before. The fabric of our sweatshirts is touching. If I moved over an inch, my arm would be pressed against his.

"There'll be another one," he says, his voice full of hope, like he's trying to reassure me.

"Who gets the wish?"

He laughs. "If we both see it, we both get it. That's how it works. Anyone who sees it gets to wish on it, whether they're together or not." And as he says that, I feel so, so glad that we are not seeing the same star miles apart.

"What are you going to wish for?" I say.

"If I tell you, it won't come true."

"Those are the rules for birthday wishes."

"Those are the rules for all wishes," he says. "Besides, why would I tell you when your answer is such bullshit? Wishing for more wishes."

"So what would you do with your one boring wish, since you're against cheating the rules of wishing? You'd probably wish for something practical. Like to be better at poker."

It's nice, joking and talking about nothing. I feel lighter with all this laughter, and it seems like he might, too, like we had all this bottled in us as something else, something heavy, and now we're freeing whatever was trapped. Our eyes meet; our smiles match. Screw the sunsets and the fireworks and the sun and beaches. Screw these stars, even. Look at him. *Look at him.* Look at what I can do to his face, and, oh god, I wonder what he's doing to mine. I am probably wearing a smile so big its wattage can be seen from outer space.

"Fine. Let's say we really only get one wish. What would yours be?" I dare to ask, dare to believe I'll get a real response.

"I don't know."

"I don't believe that for a second."

I listen to him inhale, and I think he is about to tell me his one wish. We see it at the same time—the bright burst, the streak across the sky. I reach out for him at the same time that he reaches out for me. And we are gasping and laughing; we can't believe it.

"Did you make a wish?" he says.

I nod. We are closer now, my shoulder against his elbow, my head angled toward him, the same way he's angled toward me. So I know he felt my head bobbing up and down, answering him yes.

"Did you?" I say. He nods, too.

We're both smiling again, laughter sneaking out occasionally. And I know that I am not going to tell him my wish, and he is not going to tell me his. Mine was for more nights like this, with him. He makes me feel every second, like no time has been wasted. To Trevor, living for the moment meant taking that extra shot, snorting that extra line of cocaine, but sometimes it meant the same thing as it did to me, and we ended up breaking into a hotel after hours to use their pool, using my mom's credit card to buy those tickets to the concert we couldn't bear to miss, driving out to Prescott National Forest to camp even though I had school in the morning and he had work. I wonder what it means for Finn. Betting all his money for some exciting game? Trying to get out of the payment, seeing if he could really do it? Taking a chance on a stranger who stumbled onto his secrets, who saved him?

He sits up on his elbows. His eyes slant down to look at me. My cheeks are burning up. Early stage crushing, but this is intense. With Trevor I knew exactly what to expect. He acted exactly how I suspected he would, and that made it easier at least. This. Whatever it is. Is all so new and surprising, and this, *this*, is what's going to make my summer the best it's ever been.

"You'll be here the whole summer?" I ask. He is holding my gaze, and it's equal parts exciting and terrifying, him being this close. I can see the way his bottom lip slightly sticks to his top lip when he opens his mouth to answer and the small shadow his lashes make across his cheeks every time he blinks.

"Yes," he says. "Will you?"

"We rented the house until August." Which is I guess when George's saved and stockpiled and rolled-over vacation time runs out.

He still hasn't looked away from me.

"I can trust you, right?" he says. "You won't say anything about what you saw on the island, not to anyone?"

"I am very good at keeping secrets." I have limited time with him, *always too soon* echoing in my head, pounding now that he's staring back at me looking so sincere. "And I promise I'll keep yours."

When the champagne is gone, we replace the tarp and lock the door to the house. It feels too soon to go and, at the same time, as though we've been allotted limited time together and can't use it all up at once.

I cross my arms to the night's chill, wondering what to do with myself as we walk down to the street.

"We could meet tomorrow," I say—too bold, but I don't care. We're almost out of time.

He gives the usual pause I'm accustomed to before he answers. "I can't."

"What about the next day?" I have given up modesty, dignity, all of it.

He smiles this full-voltage smile at me. Like maybe he's going to throw his self-respect out the window, too, for me. "The next day," he repeats. "You'll see me again, Maris." He looks away, shy, as he continues. "I can promise you."

Oh, I do like him, and he keeps getting better. I like that he's promised me. He trusts me to keep his secret and I can trust him to find me again. He's going to make this summer better—best. He's what I'll have to look forward to every night.

I'm about to say, "Good night, Finn," but what comes out is, "Be careful." He looks surprised, as if no one has said this to him and meant it in his whole life, maybe. He's about to say something back. He takes a step toward me, mouth opening slightly. There's only a foot between us now, and I close it, so I'm right in front of him. I put my hand on his shoulder, and he doesn't back away. I lift up and press my lips to his.

It's not a long kiss, but I feel him kiss me back, his hands lightly on my shoulders before moving down to my waist. I turn around as soon as it's over, hearing his voice say goodbye quietly. He sounds like he's smiling, but I don't want to see his reaction, and I don't want to explain why I did that, in case he decides to ask. I want to be left with nothing but the feel of his lips on mine, his hands on me.

Tonight, I was so happy. I listen to the weight of his steps, getting farther away, and feel the pull of the distance. There's a chance he's lying and this is the last time I'll ever see him. There's always that chance. But for now, stars aligned and gave me this gift. Tonight, they didn't disappoint.

Chapter 11

Once when I was chatting with the fortune-teller while she counted her earnings from the morning and relit the incense, her next client came early and she rushed me into the bathroom and told me not to come out until the client was gone. I stayed in there for several clients though. She forgot about me, I guess, because she didn't realize I was still there until one of her clients opened the door to use the bathroom.

The first client had wanted to know about love. She was already deeply in love, so much that it made her cry, big bursting sobs. She said her love was so innate that when her lover was sad or heartbroken, she could feel the ache in her own chest. She sounded like there was a fist in her throat, like she'd scream if she could.

She wanted the fortune-teller to say that she wouldn't ever lose it, this great love she had finally found, that she had been looking for her whole life. She was afraid that something so good was sure to be taken away from her. The fortune-teller told her that this was the love she'd been waiting for and that because she knew it was precious, she wouldn't let it go easily and that was why she wouldn't lose it ever. The woman was laughing when she left. She sounded happy, but also frenzied—overtaken by relief, lost in this passion she'd found. I was so jealous. I wanted to feel something that wholly, that intensely—I wanted to love someone like that and for someone to love me like that back. I wanted someone to fight for, someone I wouldn't let go easily, no matter what.

The next day, the air is still full of ocean salt, and I'm standing with the New Browns outside a bike rental stand on the main downtown strip, and I think I see Finn standing on the curb next to the mail drop.

But it's not really him.

We are tourists in this land of summer homes, beachfront properties, posh boutiques, gourmet restaurants, boat trips to the island.

Today, that means we ride bikes with matching helmets all in a row on our way to the lighthouse.

"This way," Chelsea calls. We follow her, and she follows the signs.

We reach the lighthouse quicker than I anticipated, and as we stand on the lighthouse deck and stare out over the gray-blue water, I think, now, this second, would be a good time to run into Finn.

A wave crashes against the deck and sprays us lightly with a mist. There's a rush of wind, and the next wave hits us harder. A thousand droplets of water come down on us. Phoebe laughs and claps like this is the greatest thing ever. The next splash is even bigger. Everyone moves away except for me. I close my eyes as the water falls back on me.

I feel a hand on my arm. I open my eyes expecting to see Finn. Chelsea is smiling, shaking her head. "Are you serious?"

There's another splash, and Chelsea tugs on my arm. But I don't move, and neither does she. She squeals as the water rains over us. The water is jarring in its coolness, but being in wet clothes feels good against the sun beating down on us on the ride back.

The afternoon ticks on, and I walk along Main Street with Chelsea, window-shopping, grateful that George has abandoned us to accompany Trisha back to the beach house for Phoebe's nap. Now would be a good time for Finn to appear, too.

These shops are fancy and pricey, but according to Chelsea, people like her boyfriend's family, the Duvals, don't ever have to look at the price tag before they make a purchase. They see something and they can have it. No second thoughts.

And here, I think of Finn—*again*—and the trouble he's in over money.

Chelsea and I play a game. We guess how much things cost. I always guess too low, and Chelsea always guesses too high.

"Is it wrong that I no longer think this is beautiful?" Chelsea says about a metallic sling bag in the imported leathers store when she learns the bag is $790 instead of her guess of $1,500. "This is what my mother means when she tells me to manage my expectations."

She has a sense of humor about herself that is lacking in many other people, this kind of honesty and awareness that isn't at all self-deprecating. For that moment, I'm not thinking about Finn.

We continue to guess prices, and Chelsea goes on and on about her future plans. Studying psychology, graduating in four years, getting her doctorate wherever Edison decides he'd like to work. Spending her summers here, her winters in Switzerland. Paris in spring, *of course, naturally.* All her plans involve Edison and his money.

She is nice enough to ask about my plans for next year but also nice enough to push the conversation forward when I don't have an answer.

We stop for ice cream, spoiling dinner. Chelsea laughs at this crime and orders two scoops for herself.

We get back, and George and Trisha have set up the umbrellas and lawn chairs and are all set for another relaxing evening at the beach. The New Brown Family's idea of vacation involves standing waist deep in the ocean tossing a Frisbee or flipping through recipes on their phones with their feet in the sand, planning what they'd like for dinner.

Their idea of vacation is not mine. It's times like these when I feel like a stranger, only there by default.

I decide to go for a run, burn off the extra energy that's been trapped inside me since we got back from the bike ride, even though it's the time of day when the sun is low and it gets in my eyes. I am still searching for Finn.

Chapter 12

At night, the clouds roll in. The humidity in the air suggests that a storm is imminent. The New Brown Family stays up late playing cards. I tell them I am too tired from my run, and they don't protest. I'm carried to bed by the memory of George sighing his way through Trouble and Chutes and Ladders, and fighting with my mom about the rules of Rummy 500. I listen to the wind pick up, drowning out the sound of the New Brown Family's laughter. I fall asleep imagining a hurricane lifting our house and carrying us away.

But storm be damned because Chelsea is louder than the thunder and gets up before everyone, even Phoebe, and in turn wakes me, as I hear her flouncing around her room, traipsing in and out of our shared bathroom, banging around.

"What are you doing?" I finally ask, standing half-awake in the doorway on my side of the bathroom.

She's in her pajamas with two hangers around her neck, holding dresses, three giant rollers lined up on the top of her head, like the spikes of a stegosaurus.

"Oh, good, you're awake." She rushes toward me. "Edison gets here today! I don't know what I'm going to wear. Do you like the blue one?" She points at the dresses hanging from her neck. Neither of them are blue.

"Chelsea . . . it's four in the morning."

"I'm too excited to sleep! I haven't seen him since August." She starts shaking her head. "I'm sorry, you probably think I've lost it, but it's been so long since I've seen him. We've been together for almost a year, but he left for school three months after I met him, and I just . . . I want to make our reunion special."

"That's barely any time together; how do you know you even still like him?" I am too tired to contemplate if that might've offended her.

"Oh, I *know*," she says, nodding furiously. "We talk every day," she continues, leaning forward to splash water on her face. "But to be in the same room with him *physically*, after all this time, I think I might explode."

"I believe you."

She dabs her face with a towel. "Oh, shoot. Oh no." She flicks her nails. The fresh paint on them has smeared across her fingers and on the towel. "Oh no, oh no. Fuck!" I attribute this minor meltdown to the fact that she's barely slept and is overly anxious. She even stomps her foot.

"It's okay," I say, placing a hand on her shoulder to steady her.

"I can do your nails." Maybe if I fix her nails, she will settle down and let me sleep.

"You will?"

"You have to promise to sit still long enough to let them dry."

Her face melts into a warm smile. "Thank you; you are a life-saver." She has no idea.

We move into her room, stepping over the debris of Hurricane Chelsea, clothes and shoes and hair accessories flung everywhere. Chelsea takes the dresses from around her neck and leans them against her desk. She clears the bed, letting a pile of clothes fall to the floor, and we sit on top of her comforter. I hold her slightly wobbly hand as I apply the light pink polish she's chosen.

"You're shaking," I tell her.

"It's just—he hasn't seen me in so long. I want to look perfect. Because he's perfect, Maris, he's—" She looks away, biting her lip. "He's as good as it gets. And his family—you'll see when you meet them."

Them. The Duvals. There is always awe in her voice and a sparkle in her eyes when she talks about them.

"They will surely be impressed with your nails," I tease, winking as I finish up her right hand. She smiles at me again, and I can see in the way she's starting to calm that she's grateful for someone to share in this excitement, even if I'm the person she's stuck with.

"It's been perfect so far." Her smile falters. "I want us to always be perfect."

"You've said *perfect* like eighty times since you woke me up."

"There's no other word to describe him."

"No one's perfect," I say. Even the flawless New Brown Family has me as the skeleton in their closet.

"You'll see when you meet him."

She's stubborn about this, so I ask, "Well, then, what are you going to wear?"

"*That* is the ultimate question."

She's got a few dresses hanging over her closet door. She explains to me her top choices, but they all carry concerns. The dresses Edison sent her from Paris—too short, all of them. The dress Edison told her once brought out her eyes—but maybe it's too green. The white dress—too innocent. The pink one—too demure.

"How about that one?" I point to the black dress hanging off the back of her desk chair. "You can never go wrong with a little black dress, right?"

Chelsea shakes her head. "I wore that to Edison's mom's funeral."

"Oh. I'm sorry."

"She would have liked the white dress." Her shoulders drop in another defeat of indecision.

"At least all these dresses go with your necklace. Did Edison get you that, too?" I try for a way to cheer her up, and the shimmery diamond hanging off a platinum chain hanging from her neck seems like exactly the way to do that. I finish painting her left hand and start blowing on the tips of her fingers.

"It's from Dad," she says as she bites her lower lip again. "A birthday present."

"Oh. Wow," I say. A huge lump has formed in my throat. When George was only my father, he didn't even buy me gifts, because how would he have known what to get me? Sometimes he wasn't even home for my birthday. He got a promotion when I was twelve, and it sent him out on the road a lot. Sometimes he was gone for months at a time. I wonder if Chelsea truly believes George was the kind of father to me as he is for her, if she thinks it's my fault that there is a wedge between George and me.

"He's getting one for you, too, when you turn eighteen next month." She smiles and shrugs. "I'm so bad at secrets," she adds. But I wonder if she told me this because she could sense I have my doubts about George and she said this to quiet them.

"What did you do to celebrate?" I steer the conversation back to her, before she can ask me the last time George got me a present, before she can realize that for my seventeenth birthday, all I got from George was a phone call. She tells me about the fancy steak house they went to for dinner where she had lobster for the first time. Unsurprisingly, her story finds its way back to Edison.

"On Edison's eighteenth birthday he bought cigarettes. Because he could." She rolls her eyes, but her face is beaming, like she is thrilled to have license to talk about him in a *what am I going to do with him* sort of way, because he is hers. "He smoked so many that he couldn't speak. The Duvals threw him a huge party. He snuck off to the horse stables with a bottle of whiskey and tried to ride bareback through the ranch. He ended up losing the horse. I wasn't there, but I heard."

I give her a fake smile, pretending that I find this amusing, too. But I've met Edisons before, maybe not with money of his caliber, but I still know the type. Elite, but thoughtless. Rich, but classless. Your typical scoundrel. Probably handsome in a devastating, knee-knocking way. But vapid. Nothing past his eyes. Nothing in his chest cavity serving as a heart.

And I'd bet the only reason Chelsea can survive him is because she has a heart big enough for two.

Chapter 13

In the morning, Chelsea picks the peach dress. Then changes her mind and goes for the green one that brings out her eyes. And I am here to witness all this because the storm doesn't let up. The New Browns enjoy being cooped up together, hearing each other's musings, backed by the consistent noise of the rain and the wrinkling of the newspaper, the occasional laugh from the baby.

"I hope it stops raining for the clambake tomorrow," George says now that we're left alone in the living room, since Trisha and Phoebe are napping and Chelsea has vacated for another wardrobe change. The weather. This is all we have to say to each other these days. At least it's a safe topic.

"Me, too," I say, wondering if that's where I'll see Finn again. Everyone on the cove comes out for it, according to Chelsea.

"Have you ever been to a clambake before?" he asks.

I laugh. "When would I have been to a clambake?"

But that was too far. We've wandered over a land mine; we both know it. George has no idea about my life, and in moments like this, it becomes obvious.

I pretend to be done with my magazine, flipping it closed.

Chelsea takes two steps into the living room before she decides against the blue dress she's wearing and scurries upstairs to change again. By not revealing his flight arrival time to Chelsea and promising a surprise, Edison was actually promising torture. Patience is not Chelsea's strong suit.

I get off the couch and head toward the stairs, using her needing my help as an excuse to get away from George. There's a knock at the door. Since I'm closest, I answer it.

Finn is standing there wearing dark jeans, a navy polo, with his jacket shrugged off his shoulders and up over his head in a poor attempt to shield himself from the downpour. His hair is dark with rainwater, sticking to his forehead, and he is beautiful in the full light of day, more so than I remembered, even with the huge bruise on his left eye.

"You," I stammer. I'm too elated to be embarrassed by this reaction. How did he find me?

He gives me a smile that is *something*. Slightly uneasy. He's nervous, maybe?

His eyes move past mine.

"Well, invite the man in!" George calls from behind me. He gets up and walks toward us. "For goodness' sake, get out of the rain."

I barely manage to step out of the way as Finn moves around me. George opens his arms to him.

"I'm soaking," Finn warns.

"Aw, no worries. It's great to see you!" George envelops him in a hug.

I'm having an out-of-body experience. I can sense that I'm standing there, mouth open, hand still on the doorknob, staring dumbfounded. My brain is screaming at me to move, act casual, close the door at least. But I am frozen.

"You must be Maris," Finn says. He attempts to shake the water off his hand before holding it out for me.

"Yeah, this is my other . . . my daughter," George says. He steps forward with his arm out, like he's going to pat me on the back. He stops short and instead walks around me to shut the front door.

It's awkward enough that I'm able to return to my body.

"Nice to meet you," he says, reaching for my hand. His fingers give mine a quick squeeze before he pulls away.

Trisha appears at the top of the stairs, cradling Phoebe in a pink fuzzy blanket. She leans over the banister and peers down at us. "Edison, is that you?"

"In the flesh," he says. I lean into the wall to keep from falling over. It hits me like a shot in the chest, that the *something* his smile was holding when he first arrived was an apology. He *knew*. He knew that this was why we'd see each other again. Why wouldn't he have told me—why would he bother to lie? But all too suddenly, I know the answer. Because he can. Why not attempt to seduce your girlfriend's estranged stepsister under a full moon? Why not give it a go with champagne and a blanket—a blanket, for crying out loud. Why not forgo payments you owe from a high-stakes poker game? He told me himself—this is what they mean when they say you have to always listen when people tell you who they are—he said, he's in it for the *game*. The bluffing, the strategy, the high stakes. And that's all I was to him.

There's a crash from upstairs—as though Chelsea has caught wind of Edison's arrival and tried to run through the wall to get down here. There is a ridiculously large smile on his face, like he knows she's coming.

"EDISON!" Chelsea shrieks, flying down the stairs. He soars toward her, too, and they meet on the third step from the bottom. Edison catches her with one arm, using the other to hold on to the banister and keep himself upright as Chelsea barrels into him with her whole body.

I stand there silently choking on the air, watching as she kisses him, right in front of Trisha and George and Phoebe. And he kisses her back, in front of me.

"Hi, princess," he says when they break away. "Aren't you a sight for sore eyes? Literally."

Chelsea doesn't laugh at his comment. She's a mess of "Oh, I've missed you, I've missed you," and soon: "Oh god, what happened to your face? Are you okay? Are you hurt? Oh god—"

"It's okay," he says, gently removing her hands from where they were probing at the bruise. He holds them to his chest, close to his heart. "I'm clumsy, and I fell," he says. He lifts up his pant leg to reveal his bandaged ankle. Chelsea gasps. Edison smiles, seeming to adore this overreaction from her.

"I'm fine," he reassures her, spouting off a weak explanation about slick, wet cobblestone and tripping over his own *two left feet*. He's so convincing, though he has an unsuspecting audience. "And how are you?"

"Better now. Perfect now." The way they gaze into each other's eyes, I can't watch.

I've got that sickening feeling now that I know I've been wrong about everything. One of life's tricks. You can go with your gut. You can pick someone to trust. You can be wrong.

If the girls of the New Brown Family and Edison weren't blocking my way up the stairs, I would be pouring out excuses to go to my room. But now they're all moving toward me. Trisha says she's going to make us all tea, perfect for the rainy day. Phoebe bounces with delight, her hands in the air as she breezes past in Trisha's arms. Edison and Chelsea are a blob of a person, tucked together with their arms wrapped around each other. She fits perfectly in the crook of his shoulder.

"Eddy, did you meet Maris?" Chelsea says.

"Yes," he says with cheer in his voice.

"He sure did," I say.

He should be afraid of me, I think. He should be downright terrified. I know things about him he doesn't want anyone to know. What would Chelsea say if she knew her beloved Edison has actually been in town for days, that he stabbed someone during a fight over poker money, and is in possession of an untraceable phone? He let me think his name was Finn. He met me in the middle of the night with a blanket and champagne, and he kissed me back. Didn't he?

"You'll have to tell us everything about being overseas," Trisha says as if Edison has been away at war and not just at school.

"How were finals?" George asks.

Edison groans, and Chelsea rubs his back as he complains about multivariable calculus.

Trisha waves at me, motioning for me to join them from where I'm still standing befuddled in the living room. She's set out enough teacups and chairs for everyone, including me. Chelsea takes her shining eyes off Edison to look at me and call me over. The elation in her expression is like something I haven't seen since I was much younger, when excitement was bursting and I was fully sustained on fairy tales and expectations.

I take a seat in the last chair available, which incidentally puts me directly across from the happy couple and right next to George.

"It's hard," Edison tells us. "I spend all my time studying. It's such a drag." He laughs, and everyone else does, too. "You'll see next year, princess." He pushes Chelsea's hair behind her ear, then sets his hand back on top of hers. He seems to be incapable of not touching her, and I hate that I can so easily recall what it was like when he touched me. "College is not the party we were promised it would be." He winks at her. She is entranced. They all are.

"What's it like over there," Trisha says, "across the pond?" She struggles trying to fill the teakettle while holding the bottle to Phoebe's mouth. George is up in a flash, taking the kettle from her, turning on the stove, and Trisha and Phoebe are able to join us at the table. It's small. But he never did helpful things like that for my mom. Never for me either.

"Look out the window, Trisha," Edison says. "That's England." He looks at Chelsea for the last sentence. "It's all rain, all the time."

"You probably couldn't wait to get into Cross Cove for some sun, and you're greeted with this downpour!" Chelsea pouts. "You missed it by a day."

Edison nods, his eyes shifting to me for only a second, and I hate that I'd expected it, that I'd been waiting for it.

"Chels said it was pouring in London when she spoke to you yesterday and you were afraid of another flight delay," Trisha say.

This time, he is careful not to look at me as he shrugs and leans back, letting one arm rest along the top of Chelsea's chair. "I got lucky."

Edison is more charming than Finn. Edison is smooth, always engaging. His eyes sparkle with his smile. His expressions are fluid in a way that makes you forget the giant bruise on his face isn't supposed to be there. As he goes on and on about Jaffa Cakes and Hyde Park, talking basketball with George, asking Trisha about the pottery classes she's been taking, bouncing Phoebe on his knee, all the while staring at Chelsea like she's the whole universe and managing to completely ignore me, I try to see through how much of Edison is real and how much is a façade to keep his long-distance girlfriend happy, to keep her from ever questioning his devotion.

He stays and stays, past tea, past dinner, where he sliced tomatoes for the spaghetti sauce and was the first to volunteer to do the dishes. Chelsea is notably impressed, which is fitting because from what Chelsea has told me about the Duvals, you'd assume he's gone his whole life without doing common chores.

We are not sure there will be a fireworks show tonight since the rain only died down around seven and the clouds are barely beginning to pull back to show off the sky. But the routine commences, and George and Trisha snuggle with Phoebe on the screened porch, and Chelsea rushes outside.

I offer to grab the lawn chairs in case we want to sit, since the sand is wet. Anything for a moment of reprieve. Unfortunately, Edison is still under the guise of a gentleman and follows me, insisting he help.

The chairs are stored in the closet under the stairs, through a door accessible in a small hallway past the kitchen that leads to the garage. The second we're inside the closet, Edison pulls on the string dangling between our heads to turn on the light. Then he shuts the door.

Chapter 14

"I know what you're probably thinking," he says quickly.

We're so close in this closet, inches from each other. He smells different—like cologne, not the way I'm used to him smelling, like the ocean.

"I promise you don't." He starts to say something back but, *no*, he doesn't get to tell me what I'm thinking. "I'm thinking that you're an asshole." I unleash on him before he has the chance. "And a liar." He smiles at me with this Edison smile that Finn didn't have, as if I'm tossing compliments at him instead of insults. "And you don't deserve Chelsea."

That, at least, makes his smile falter.

"Fair enough."

"Why didn't you just tell me who you were?" I demand, even though *asshole* and *liar* and how he likes *the game* and his apparent need to test how far he can stretch things, how much he can get away with, explain this. *You'll see me again, Maris. I can promise you*, he'd said—and I'd thought of stars aligning. Remembering makes me feel tricked all over again. I had plans for us, and that's the crushing part—the embarrassing part. We were going to meet under the stars every night. There would be casual run-ins during the day, each one taking us by surprise; he'd find me the way I found him. And we would rescue each other, even if it was only from boredom that we needed to escape.

I'd liked that he was mysterious, exciting, *trouble*—but this was not what I had in mind.

"When you told me your name, that really tipped me off." He says this calmly like it's a perfectly reasonable excuse. "I probably should have figured it out sooner, like as soon as Chels told me she spent the day at Honeycomb Island with her family and her stepsister wandered off and made their parents worry. That should have made it obvious. But it went right over my head." He waves his hand over his head, making a whistling noise.

"You're busted either way."

The smile returns, larger this time, and he's shaking his head.

"You thought I was some random girl," I say, painting the picture for him, the same way I'm going to paint it for Chelsea, "and you met me in the middle of the night—"

"I needed my phone back."

"Twice," I remind him. "And you brought a blanket and champagne."

"Those were perfectly practical things to bring. We needed

something to sit on. As for the champagne, well, my mother always taught me to never arrive empty-handed."

"It's your own bad luck that I turned out to be your girlfriend's sister."

"It would seem that way, but it's actually good luck."

"How do you figure?"

"You don't want Chelsea to know you were out meeting me any more than I do."

"You think I won't tell her? You think I'll let her continue to waste her time with someone like you?"

"I'm going to call your bluff on that one."

I roll my eyes.

He takes a deep breath and crosses his arms. "If you tell her how you really know me, then you'll have to admit you've been sneaking out. Chels told me about you, you know. How you're sort of . . ." He pauses, at least smart enough to know to be careful with his words here. "In trouble. And you're here to give your mom a break and to get you away from some boyfriend or something. And she told me that your dad wouldn't hesitate to send you back if things became too . . . difficult. Like if he knew you were sneaking out in the middle of the night, *for example*. I also got the impression that if he thinks you're up to no good, but decides not to send you back, he'll instead spend the rest of the summer breathing down your neck. There goes your plan to have the 'best' summer."

He's completely right about why I won't tell, and that is unnerving.

"So great," I say. "You've had your fun. If this is all a game to you, you should leave Chelsea alone."

"Game? Oh no, Chelsea isn't a game. I'm crazy about her."

"You have a funny way of showing it."

He chuckles as he scratches his head. The gesture makes his elbow brush against my shoulder. He looks away quickly, so I know he noticed.

"The last thing I ever want to do is hurt her."

I scoff, even going so far as to let out a grunt so he'll know how full of shit I think he is.

"Didn't she tell you about me?"

"The boyfriend she told me about was named Edison and was supposed to be in England."

He puts up his hands. "If Chelsea knew about the poker and the way I tried to get out of paying, and that I lied to her about it and got caught up with some stranger"—he gestures at me—"who helped me escape the brutal beating that I definitely had coming, it would only wreck her summer. Turn me into a disappointment." He pauses in his sulking to look at me. "Turn you into a disappointment." I shake my head at him for the way he keeps reminding me that I have something to lose, too, should the truth come out. "Chelsea wouldn't want to date someone with a gambling problem."

"I don't know, Edison. She knows about the horse and she's still around."

"What horse?"

"Your eighteenth birthday."

"Oh, that."

My anger at him flares up again. "It's not a small thing. The horse was lost forever. It probably died because of you. When she told me about it, she was laughing. Maybe a gambling problem would make her laugh, too."

He's quiet for a second, and then he says, "Maybe."

"The sneaking out to meet me would make her less happy."

"What can I say?" he shrugs. "You were my hero, remember? And I liked spending time with you." The lie comes out of him like syrup, appealing and delicious. But it's too Edison slick and unabashed, not like a real confession.

"She would like the kiss even less." I threaten him with this, remind him of what I could let slip at any moment, as if it's still an option, like I haven't already decided not to say anything to avoid George's further disappointment, another reason for my mother to sigh and say, "*Really*, Maris? You've only been there a few days and already you've snuck out in the middle of the night and kissed your stepsister's boyfriend."

I'm more interested in how he'll respond to the mention of our kiss than I should be. I half expect him to blame it all on me, since I'm the one who took that particular risk.

"It was hardly a kiss," he says. "Nothing to worry about."

Maybe it was "hardly a kiss," but I think of the way our lips connected, his hands gripping my shoulders, then my waist. I think of how I used to chase his smile, want it, wish for it, and how his laughter made me feel like I was doing something good. He's close enough now to kiss. I allow myself only a glance at his lips. I look up and notice he has not limited himself to just a glance.

I turn abruptly to the shelf and start pulling down the chairs. He's completely detestable for a stack of reasons, the first of them being he's as good a liar as I am. That he's tricked me, shouldn't intrigue me, it should serve as a warning that I need to stay far, far away from him. He reaches over me, his arm brushing against my shoulder, to get the chair that's too high for me to reach.

Asshole is unfortunately my type. It comes with the territory of being attracted to people who are attracted to trouble or who are at least unafraid of it enough that they allow themselves to get in the thick of it.

I think of the way he brushed off his injuries so easily to the New Brown Family—*I'm clumsy, and I fell*—and how no one questioned anything he's said. He's a chameleon. And Finn was an act, too. The only real thing about him was the look in his eyes when he was running through the island, afraid he was going to die.

When I turn around holding the chairs, he's standing in front of the door, but he doesn't move. The air is stagnant in here, and he's looking at me like he has something to say. I wait to see if he'll say something Edison smooth with exaggerated facial expressions and a small laugh at the end of each sentence. Or if he'll play this more like Finn, pretending he's thought carefully about what he wants to say so much that it will sound like an admission.

It bothers me that I'll probably never know him; he's never going to share the truth with me, no matter what tricks I have up my sleeve. I was simply a momentary amusement to him. But I should be more. I saved him.

I try to press forward using the chairs as a barrier between us so he'll move away from the door. But he still doesn't step aside, and now I am closer to him than before. Much, much too close.

"Maris." I hate that it sounds like he's calling to me. "I'm sorry you have to lie to her about me. I should have said something that night, but it was so nice to just . . ." He stops to think of the right word, but he doesn't have to because I know; I was there and felt the same way—like we were letting go of something, like we were somehow freer. That's why it was a delicious secret; it felt like a world only the two of us had access to, that would've shattered if we let in other people. But he knew the whole time it was only an illusion of the night. "I don't know," is what he says instead of ending his sentence. I see a flash of Finn when he looks at me. He leans in closer, and the smell of cologne reminds me that I am not in here with Finn; I'm here with Edison. "Anyway, it won't happen again. I can still promise we're going to have a good summer." He has the nerve to smile in that cheap way. "The best."

This is Edison, full of charm and flirtation, even when he should be in trouble. Even when he messed up.

We carry the folding chairs out of the house, going quickly through the screened porch where George and Trisha sit with Phoebe, and down the steps.

The fireworks have already started as we move onto the beach grass, walking side by side. The noise from the fireworks exploding above us leaves a sharp ringing in my ears. Chelsea is dancing in the surf with her hands in the air and her eyes on the lights in the sky. She is completely herself around him now, her nerves swept up by the entity that is *her Edison.*

"She trusts you," I say to him as we set down the chairs a few feet away from her. I don't think he has the ability to feel bad about this, but I remind him anyway, as if some part of Finn is in there acting as a subconscious.

He doesn't say anything. He doesn't take his eyes off her. He just nods.

Chelsea has noticed us and she waves, but with the next bursts of color in the sky, she is back to craning her neck, her smile too big for her own good.

The sky is awash of drifting smoke and blinking stars. Chelsea rushes toward us. She says, "You guys almost missed the fireworks."

Chapter 15

It's against my better judgment that I sneak out that night and climb the hill to the half-built house. Where most people see a red flag, I see a question mark. Most see Do Not Enter and simply walk by; I think, *Why not? What could be so bad?* And I push past the sign to meet my demise.

But I couldn't sleep and couldn't stop thinking about him and the way he'd fooled me.

I don't know why he would be here. I am clearly the fluke—the collateral that happened to him by accident that he has to contend with before he can enjoy his great summer with the girlfriend he chose, the one he speaks to every night before bed, time zone difference be damned, to sustain their distance for the majority of the year. The one who came to his mother's funeral, who sees through the birthday bullshit with all the whiskey and cigarettes and the lost horse, and would probably laugh off a gambling debt, too, especially when his family seems like they could easily handle it for him.

I wonder if there's any part of him that's ashamed of the trouble, embarrassed about his near-death experience. Sometimes it is humiliating to get in over your head. When you're experiencing the rush, you don't anticipate the potential for failure and how it will affect your pride.

Just like I can't predict the crushing blow of humiliation I'm about to feel now, when I get to the vacant house and realize he's not there, that he'll never be there again. Finn is a lie and Edison is a disguise.

As I'm walking up the dirt path I see light coming from the top floor. And then I see him. He's standing angled against the window opening, the tarp pulled back, the lantern sitting on the ledge. I step behind a tree and shut off the light glowing from my phone. He alternates between looking out the window and checking his phone for the time.

Is there possibly anyone else he might be waiting for?

I stand behind the tree awhile longer, watching him. I am there for almost forty-five minutes, and he stays, he waits. No one else comes.

I decide not to show myself. He's proved to me in more than one way that he's not good. I think of Chelsea dancing in the surf under the lights and her desperately happy face when she saw him today. There are too many reasons to stay away from him and only one reason to see him.

I try to ignore that this feels like a victory, walking away knowing that maybe I wasn't the only one who wanted something. That maybe he shared a part of himself with me that night, the way I did with him.

When I leave, I can't see him in the window anymore. But I know he is still there, because of the light from his lantern.

The thing is, I am not good either.

Chapter 16

The next day, the sun is out in full force, the sky clear blue and vivid—a welcoming scene as we head to North Point Beach for the clambake, where the end of Main Street meets the ocean in the form of an expansive beach. Today, the docks are full, and the water is dotted with anchored boats. Boats next to boats next to boats. Everyone is here, whether you rent one of the houses along the water or have a mansion in the cliffs. Because who can tell the difference when you're sand-smeared with ocean mist in your hair and scarfing on butter-drenched seafood.

Chelsea is walking on air. She's off the boat first, jogging as fast as her wedge sandals can carry her, trying to find Edison and the Duvals.

The beach is crowded with people and lawn chairs and beach umbrellas, food vendors, and paddleboards and kayaks for rent. The air smells like suntan lotion and sizzling butter.

At first, we can't find them, but then they appear, toward the back of the beach, higher up than the rest, under a blue-and-white-striped canopy, sitting on an outdoor living room set. The canopy is a clean, bright spot on this crowded beach. It looks out of place and perfectly in place at the same time.

Edison is leaning against the back of the couch with his arms crossed. When he sees us, he puts on a smile for the ages, stands up straight, and opens his arms.

"You made it!" He motions for us to come under the canopy, out of the sun.

The moment we enter their canopy, I can feel it, the air getting drier, cooler, the ocean smell fading, replaced with that of basil and pineapple. A true testament to the magic of money, the extravagancies of wealth. It's made them different already.

There are four Duval men, including Edison, all tall with broad shoulders and those gray-brown eyes. Edison is by far the youngest and the scrawniest, with his lean muscles that never seemed ropy until he's standing next to the others. There is a woman sprawled out on the chaise longue in a large hat and oversized sunglasses.

Chelsea and Edison make the introductions since it's the first time George and Trisha are meeting the Duvals. Both sides tack "We've heard so much about you" onto their greetings. When they say this to me, I know they are being polite.

The Duvals are strong in their stance and in their handshakes. They have full-toothed smiles and unwrinkled clothes and deep, earnest voices.

Oswald is the oldest. He has dimples still prominent against his aging skin, heavy with wrinkles and sunspots. Even I can tell that when he was younger, he was of the devastatingly handsome, knee-knocking variety.

"Please pardon Eddy's appearance," Oswald says, brushing sand off Edison's bare shoulders and handing him the white polo lying on the back of one of the chairs.

Instead of putting it on, Edison rolls his eyes.

This surprisingly makes Oswald smile.

Warren is Oswald's son. He has graying hair like Oswald's, but a full head of it, as well as a finely trimmed mustache. He speaks in a tone that reminds us we are outsiders.

"Any friends of Edison's are friends of ours," says Warren. He smiles a practiced smile. "All the more people to keep an eye on Eddy, troublemaker that he is." Warren's eyes find Chelsea when he says this, and she beams back at him, laughing lightly like this is an inside joke—Edison getting into that playful sort of trouble he gets into.

"Clumsy is more like it." Oswald chuckles, too.

Sepp Duval is introduced as Oswald's grandson instead of as Warren's son. He's older than Edison, everything about him more progressed, from the hair on his chest to the definition in his shoulders, but his face still has a youthful glow. Sepp inherited Oswald's dimples and has hair blonder than any of the others'. He doesn't say anything, not even hello. His interest in us has faded, and he is looking out at the crowd in search of something more amusing. He flags down a passing beer cart, grabbing two.

Chelsea sheepishly bends forward, waving, trying to meet the eye line of the woman on the couch. I can tell by the shakiness of Chelsea's smile that she is nervous about getting this woman's attention.

"My wife, Karen," Warren intercepts, since we're all looking at her now.

It takes two pats on Karen's shoulder and Sepp speaking for the first time, saying, "Mother. Mother, the Browns are here," before she seems to notice there are people trying to talk to her.

She takes off her large sunglasses to reveal hooded eyelids smeared with shimmering bronze shadow and says, "Pleased to meet you." At least, that's what I think she's said. It's hard to understand her because she's slurring. There's an empty martini glass resting in front of her. Warren stands at the stainless steel drink cart in the corner of the canopy, mixing her another. Karen's lips are very full, her cheeks prominent, her skin radiant, and she is beautiful. But her eyes look aged and wise, as if peering out from a mask of who she wants you to see.

I try to fit Edison into this picture as Warren and Karen's son, Sepp's younger brother. But I remember Edison's mother is dead, and I wonder if it was she who was related to this family and there was once an authentic Duval woman.

"I bet you're happy to have Eddy back for the summer," Oswald says to Chelsea.

Sepp lets out a sharp laugh. "Look how he comes back to us—*literally* beat up by life."

"You made it a whole year. I'm proud of you, kid." Oswald pats Edison on the shoulder.

"Now's your chance to be worldly," Warren says to Edison. His eyes squint almost shut when he smiles. "Get it out of your system now before the demands of the real world catch up to you." The way he laughs is almost threatening. Edison frowns, like this shift in the conversation makes him uneasy. "We can only have one Sepp in this family, after all."

All the Duvals share the same low chuckles over this, except Sepp, who rolls his eyes and shakes his head.

Warren leans our way to explain, though despite this inclusion, it still feels very much like it's their world here; we just happen to be standing under the canopy holding it. "Sepp spent the winter visiting some of our business partners in Spain and the last two months in France doing god knows what. Next month, who can say?"

"I handle all the international affairs," Sepp states, a defensiveness in his tone.

"Right," Warren says, "whether that takes you to Cannes for the film festival or Pamplona for the running of the bulls, or wherever the supermodels are congregating, you 'handle it.'"

Sepp says something to him in French. Then something else in Spanish. Thus proving his point, I guess. Oswald starts speaking French, and he and Sepp banter back and forth for a while.

"Not this again," Edison says, laughing. Now it seems Warren is the annoyed one. They all get a turn. It's like a dance.

"I was only asking Sepp if supermodels did in fact *congregate* and how one knew where to find such gatherings," Oswald says. When Oswald's dimples make an appearance, it's like a reset button, dissolving all the tension between the Duval men.

Chelsea asks Sepp if he's going back to finish his degree after the summer's over, and Oswald laughs.

"I graduated last year, thank you very much," Sepp says.

"Congratulations on your useless degree," Warren says, shaking his head. "A world history major. What a brilliant excuse to spend four years abroad."

"And what was your excuse for majoring in philosophy?" Oswald asks Warren.

"To have something to talk about at dinner parties other than the cement business. As riveting as it is."

"That's your livelihood you're insulting," Oswald says. The dimples reappear in one of his magical smiles.

Chelsea notices the break in tension and leans in to ask a question. "You're still majoring in business, aren't you, Eddy?"

Warren and Sepp laugh heartily. The Duval men are either annoyed at their life's situation or laughing at it. It's blissful in a way, and it comes with having money, I can see, but in this moment, I understand the appeal of the Duvals. They have no real troubles. There's something lax and infectious about being around this kind of laissez-faire atmosphere, like we're breathing it in and we can rest assured that no one here will be talking about anything too serious or taking anything too seriously. Only shallow problems are welcome here.

"Hey," Edison says. It is his turn to be irritated. "Someone's got to worry about actual business practices, haven't they?"

This gets another roaring laugh out of Sepp and a proud nod from Oswald.

"We still can't believe how Edison got so lucky, meeting you," Warren says to Chelsea, a quick and obvious subject change. She puts her hand over heart, in thanks to Warren.

I check to see if Edison is looking at me. He is pointedly staring at his toes. I feel powerful in a sense, knowing that he went to meet me last night, that he waited for me. We both know the truth: the real luck for him was me being there on the island.

Chapter 17

As the afternoon presses on, and we start mingling with others on the beach, people are more curious about us now that they've seen us come from the Duvals' canopy. We meet men with gold watches and women with diamond earrings and other people my and Chelsea's age, who are wary to be outright friendly but also polite enough to appease their parents. The people here are out to flaunt, and now we are no different.

"George Brown, head of sales, Goodman Pharmaceuticals" is George's official title, the way he introduces himself to everyone he meets. Some have titles like George's; others are like the Duvals and their names say everything you need to know about them. Trisha, Chelsea, and I are wife and daughters. Chelsea gets to assert her title as a future college student and, of course, the girl-friend of Edison.

On my second plate of seafood, I lose sight of the New Browns, who are not in the Duval canopy or under the beach umbrellas we set up closer to the water. I notice them in the surf, posing for a picture, George holding Phoebe with his other arm around Trisha and Chelsea, as one of their new friends—the family of Bryce Steward, VP of finance, Astley and Associates—takes their photo. Edison stands behind the camera making faces to get Phoebe to smile.

I plop down in the sand, right where I am, which is a fine spot because I'm not infringing on anyone else's area and am not in the way of one of the volleyball games going on or in the path that leads to the fire pit with the food. I feast on my plateful of lobster and clams, crab legs and corn, watching as people try to navigate their paddleboards over the waves, children collect seashells along the shore, the New Browns act like a perfect family, and Edison plays the part of the perfect boyfriend.

Sepp finds me twenty minutes later, sitting in the sand, hunched over with butter dripping down my chin. I saw him coming a mile away and didn't move because I thought he wouldn't see me. Guys like Sepp—older, pretentious, worldly, even if his experiences are confined to only the privileged slices of life—never tend to notice someone like me.

"How's it taste?" He falls ungracefully beside me, impressively managing to keep his own full plate upright and his beer from spilling.

The state of my face, covered in butter, and my nearly empty plate should make the answer obvious, but Sepp stares expectantly.

"It's perfect," I say.

This makes him laugh, low and breathy. "Nothing is perfect," he says. I wish I could see his eyes through his Wayfarers so I'd know how far gone he really is. Instead, all I can see is my own hardened expression staring back at me.

Sepp is quiet, so I add, "This food is the exception."

He nods again, smiling this time, and leans forward to take a bite of freshly dipped crab, letting his plate catch the butter.

Chelsea and Edison are walking in the sand. They're several feet away and the shore is crowded, but they stand out. Their smiles. Her laugh that is part shriek. The way he rushes at her and carries her fireman-style into the water.

"Look at those two," he says, shaking his head. "So in love. Do you believe it?"

"Believe what? In love?"

"That *they're* in love." He nods toward the ocean, where they are running hand in hand out of the water.

"I believe she is."

Sepp laughs. He points at me with a crab leg. "I like your honesty."

I feel a flash of pride for reading Sepp the right way, knowing he'd like straight answers.

"Why did you ask me about them?"

He pushes his sunglasses up the bridge of his nose with the edge of his thumb to avoid touching them with his butter-drenched fingertips. "To hear your answer."

"That sounds like . . . a test."

His smile gets bigger.

"All of life," he says, pausing to take a sip of beer, "is a test."

"Well, did I pass?"

He laughs quietly to himself again, watching me. "You knocked it out of the park."

There's something deceiving about Sepp, a loose disposition that seems careless but at the same time like he's seconds away from snapping. I look back to the shore, where Edison and Chelsea are sitting shoulder to shoulder in the sand, gazing out at the water.

"Have you ever heard the saying *Fake it till you make it*?" he says. "That works, by the way." There's a stillness to him as he sets down the gutted lobster tail he's moved on to and looks at me. "It works every single time."

"Thanks for the advice." Sarcasm laces my tone, and for a moment, I think I've offended him. He leans back a little as if to get a better look at me.

"You know, you seem pretty harmless."

"Thanks?" I shrug. "I am pretty harmless."

"That's not what I heard."

"Have you ever heard the saying *Don't believe everything you hear*?"

Sepp laughs. "Maris," he says. There's a moment of us slurping up the last of our seafood before he continues. "I think we're going to be good friends."

He's probably easily impressed because he's been drinking, but I take the compliment anyway and clink my lemonade against his beer when he holds it up for a toast.

We sit there looking at the view, listening to the chatter around us, both of us too full to talk.

It's peaceful, until I spot a familiar face meandering through the crowd. There's gauze and bandages taped carelessly around his neck. Cuts on his forehead. A bruise on his chin. The knuckles on his right hand are purple. I rub the sun out of my eyes as he gets closer. He's looking straight ahead, dressed as nicely as everyone else in a white button-up and khakis. His collar is popped and open to make room for the bandages. His hair is combed back, and he's completely clean of dirt. But I recognize him. Broad shoulders. Clear blue eyes. Wide-set mouth. There's no doubt in my mind. He's the man from the island, the one they called Archaletta.

"What are you looking at?" Sepp asks.

"Nothing." Now my eyes are scanning the beach for Edison. For the other men that were with Archaletta that day. Maybe they are here to confront him. Maybe the run-in will be an accident.

I find Chelsea, but she is alone, making her way toward Trisha, who is sitting under the umbrella with Phoebe.

"Let me take your plate," Sepp says, dumping the shells from my plate onto his and stacking them before he stands up.

I stand up, too. I decide I should find Edison, to warn him, at least, even if part of me thinks he deserves to have these lies come crashing down on him. But maybe no one deserves what might happen if Archaletta sees Edison here; if he's still angry, still out to get what he's owed. Undeniably, I can't help but think, *What would he do without me, if I'm not there to stop the bad thing from happening?*

"Where are you going?" Sepp asks.

"Just around," I say, shrugging. His interest is jarring. It's probably due to all the beer he's had that he finds me amusing enough to want to keep tabs on. "I'll be somewhere on the beach. Just need to stretch my legs." Too many excuses, but Sepp doesn't seem to notice.

"Okay, then," he says, nodding at me once more and giving me a sideways smile as he moves toward the area with garbage cans.

I don't spot Edison, but I see Archaletta. He seems to know exactly where he's going, though he's stumbling a little, like maybe he's been drinking. That's not a great combination—anger with the lowered inhibitions of alcohol.

He weaves past the food, past the canopies sitting atop the flatter part of the beach, past the Duval tent, where there is no sign of Edison. Past the white balloons tied to the posts marking the start of Main Street. He's headed toward the place where Main Street merges into a roundabout, like a driveway to this beach.

Maybe this is good riddance and he's going to catch a cab back to wherever he came from. He reaches the roundabout and crosses.

I do hear it, that useless voice in my head saying maybe it's best not to follow him; it's best to leave Edison to solve his own problems, his own lies. But I think of the one true thing I know about Finn and Edison: the look in his eyes, how afraid he was of Archaletta that day he thought he was about to die. And I cross the street.

Chapter 18

He passes the shops, strolling casually, though not walking a straight path, hands in his pockets, glancing at the window displays. And then he dips into an alleyway past the ice cream shop.

Even only a few steps down the narrow alley and I feel the isolation of it—the noises from the clambake already falling away, the coolness of the shade, the smell of sizzling butter replaced with the smell of rotting fruit and decaying seafood from the trash bins. I watch as Archaletta lets himself stumble farther down the alley; it seems to be getting harder and harder for him to walk. He pauses to lean against the wall and digs his phone out of his pocket. He drops it immediately and nearly topples over as he bends down to pick it up. When he finally does look at the screen, he lets out a noise that is half-moan and half-laugh. He shakes his head and turns, his back against the wall. His expression is sad, but he's still making that noise like he finds something funny, and every once in a while a smile breaks through his expression.

His head turns my way quicker than expected. His eyes widen, and I know it's too late for me to duck behind the trash bin between us; he's already recognized me.

"They were right about you," he slurs, struggling to lift his arm as if it is too heavy as he points at me.

"What are you doing here?" I ask. I shouldn't be afraid of him, knowing he can barely walk, but my hands are trembling, and my voice comes out shaky, too. "What do you want?"

This makes him laugh that strange sad laughter again. I can see the blood seeping through the bandage on his neck; he is dripping in sweat, his hair wet from it. When he rolls to face me, his eyes are heavy and red, like he's very drunk.

"You tell me," he says, shaking his head. "Hey." His voice turns serious. "I get it, you know? All that money. Who could stay away?" He breaks out into a chuckle that makes his whole body shudder. "I couldn't. I couldn't." His laugher turns to a violent cough, and as it subsides, he lets his eyes focus on me. "It's a curse, though; I hope you know that."

He lifts himself up off the wall and stumbles toward me, faster than I thought he was capable of moving.

"I'm going to tell you something," he says, taking a step closer as I take a step back. His breath is sour. He reaches across the bin, and his fingers dig into my arm. I try to jerk out of his grasp, but this only makes him pinch me harder. "I am not the dangerous one," he says in a loud whisper, his expression getting darker. "You should run."

The second he lets go of me, that's exactly what I do.

Chapter 19

I run until I am back down Main Street, back to the beach. My hands are still trembling, and my heart is beating like it wants to break through my rib cage. My arm is still hot from where Archaletta grabbed it. I try to rub out the feeling of his hand clamped around my arm.

I try to shake the sound of his voice from my mind. *They were right about you. I am not the dangerous one.* What was he talking about? Drunken ramblings that came across like a warning. But Archaletta was the one in over his head. He was the one who tried to ambush Edison on the island by bringing two of his friends. He was the one who tried to beat him senseless to get him to pay. *All that money. Who could stay away? I couldn't. I couldn't.*

I scan the beach for Edison. The Duvals' canopy is empty.

The sun is getting lower in the sky, and people are coming to the beach to enjoy the last moments of sunshine, gathering with their families, setting their lawn chairs so the arms are touching, sharing beach towels, getting as close as possible. The New Browns are all bunched together on a beach blanket. George is in the middle, with Phoebe on his lap, each of his arms around Trisha and Chelsea. They lean into him. If I were to join them, where would I fit?

I continue walking down the beach, looking for Edison, for Sepp, for anyone else.

I send Trevor a text. *I miss you.*

I miss you, too, beautiful girl. And a second later: *Come over.*

This is what I forget sometimes. I only ever matter to Trevor when I'm there in front of him. There *for* him. He didn't see past the girl who came when he called and didn't shy away from doing the things he wanted to do. He never saw the parts of me that existed when I wasn't with him—the parts of me that had to pay for what I did when I was with him.

At least when someone lets you down, you can stop expecting things from them.

I keep walking along the shore, weaving between the flocks of people also enjoying the sweet spot of the wet sand where the tide comes in. There are still a few people in the water, floating or standing or gliding past on their paddleboards, shadows against the yellow and orange sky. A few feet away, I see Karen standing in the water, her long macramé dress getting drenched at the bottom. She is staring out at the sky as if it's going to tell her a secret.

I wade out next to her. She doesn't acknowledge my presence, but I don't mind. It feels less lonely watching the sky change colors with her next to me.

The sky finally turns gray, and I feel my phone vibrate in my pocket. A text from George telling me to meet them at the Duval canopy. I send my reply quickly.

"We should head back," Karen says, her expressionless voice startling me. I wasn't sure she'd registered it was me standing next to her. She's still looking straight ahead, but then she turns to me. "They'll be wondering where we are."

I nod. But she is already wandering out of the water. She waits for me on the dry sand before she starts walking again and keeps my pace as we retreat to the Duval canopy.

Chapter 20

The Duvals are wearing with the day. They have all returned to the canopy by the time Karen and I arrive. Sepp is passed out on the couch. Oswald already went home, Warren tells us.

"Past the old man's bedtime," Edison jokes. He is standing behind the couch, pacing slightly. He seems the most awake, but also like he's depleted. Like this is the last of his energy burning off before our eyes.

The New Browns look ready to go also, Phoebe passed out in George's arms, their beach bags packed, the umbrella folded.

Warren starts going off about the food. Apparently, their chef is better. We'll see tomorrow, he promises.

"I imagine we'll be seeing you on most days," Warren says. This captivates the New Browns, and they lean in wearing wide eyes and wider smiles to listen to Warren's summer plans for them. Helicopters to the north islands. Taking out the yacht, the sailboat, the Jet Skis. Drinking Jamaican rum and eating nothing but the freshest seafood. He even mentions some elaborate party they'll be attending in Maine, the private jet more than ready to accommodate us, and he'll happily make a call to get us added to the guest list.

Edison nods along. But he is only part Edison now. Part of him looks distracted, like the boy on the island.

I go over to the stainless steel drink cart in the back corner of the canopy, brushing lightly past Edison when I walk by. I take my time pouring myself a glass of water, wondering if he'll take the hint and join me here. I've taken three sips before he finally does.

"Did you see him?" I say in a quiet voice.

"Did I see who?"

"Archaletta."

Edison doesn't say anything. He brings the glass he is holding to his lips, even though he hasn't filled it yet. Then he laughs. "Why would you ask me that?"

"Because I saw him on the beach. A few hours ago. I tried to find you, but—" I debate telling him that I followed Archaletta to make sure he didn't have his friends with him and because I thought there was a chance Edison might need my help again, even though Archaletta seemed way too drunk to be of any harm to anyone. But I don't want him to know, embarrassed suddenly that I went to any trouble for Edison, especially now that he's laughed at me.

"You tried to find me?" He smiles.

His smugness right now is unbearable; I don't know what I was thinking—I grab my water and turn to go.

"Wait, wait." He puts his hand on my back, keeping me there, and with the other hand uses the tongs to place ice in my glass as a cover for why we're still there. "I'm sure you didn't see Archaletta." He waits for me to meet his eyes. "It was someone else." He nods his head slowly, like he's waiting for me to agree—he wants me to nod back.

I don't do what he wants. "Archaletta said something to me."

Edison is quiet.

"Do you want to know what he said?"

Edison takes his time filling the glass he was using as a prop. He turns around so he's leaning against the cart and he's facing the Duvals and the New Browns where they sit under the canopy. He takes a long drink of water.

"Look at them," he says. I turn around so we are standing shoulder to shoulder with our backs to the drink cart. "Don't they look happy?"

I know what he's doing. He's threatening their good time, telling me I could ruin it if I keep pushing him on this. Destroy Chelsea's happiness, shatter all the plans the New Browns have made with Warren for a summer full of Duval luxury. It's meant to remind me that if their vacation is ruined, mine would be, too. It works.

I slowly sip my water as goose bumps rise on my arms.

I watch as Chelsea's eyes meet Edison's from the far end of the canopy. She blushes as he smiles at her. I smile at Chelsea, too. She waves at me, so I give a small wave in return.

"The stuff that happened on the island, the thing with Archaletta, it was honestly nothing," Edison says, his voice ripe for the summer, loose and carefree. "I fell in with the wrong people play-ing poker, and that's all. I'm sorry you're so bored you have to make all of this into something bigger than it is."

He lifts off from the drink cart and goes to join the New Browns and the Duvals.

A few minutes later, we're all saying our goodbyes, our see-you-tomorrows. Edison walks us to *Vienna*, carrying one of our beach bags, and helps us all into the boat. He leaves no extra glance for me, no subtle squeeze of my hand as I step off the dock.

Maybe I do that, make things bigger in my head. The cliff I jumped off, others were jumping, too. It was a known spot along the river. How risky was it really when so many had been there before I had and survived? Still, I'd held my breath on the way down as if it might've been my very last seconds alive. Trevor wasn't even that much of a risk; I knew entirely what I was get-ting with him, both the good and the bad. I didn't love him enough to make losing him hurt the way losing someone you love is sup-posed to hurt.

So maybe it was only a fight over a poker game, Edison being flaky about what he owed, Archaletta ambushing him, Edison stabbing him in self-defense. I can't make sense of what Archa-letta said to me in the alley, but maybe it doesn't matter anyway and they were simply ramblings of a drunk person.

I sit near the front of the boat as we ride back so the wind is right on my face and I can see all sides of the cove.

A kiss can be blown out of proportion, too—I know that. But not the lantern light I saw last night, the boy from the island wait-ing for me to meet him.

Chapter 21

In the morning, Edison stops by for breakfast, bringing with him freshly baked croissants, French roast coffee grounds, and steaming cinnamon-pecan buns, so we get to start the day with a taste of the Duvals' personal chef without even leaving the beach house.

In the afternoon, we take *Vienna* across the cove to the Duvals'. The Duvals have two docks at their private beach. It's an expanse of white sand sitting several feet below their house. Their beach is at the end of the north side of the cove, segregated by the sharp walls of the cliff, making it only reachable by boat or from the Duvals' estate by a long staircase etched in the side of the cliff.

Edison and Sepp wave us over to the dock on the far right and help George tie up the boat. Over breakfast, Edison had said that we didn't need to bring anything except ourselves, but we still brought our towels and Phoebe's diaper bag and a portable play-pen that doubles as her traveling crib. This appears to be excessive of us. The Duvals have everything we could want or need—lounge chairs and sun chaises, a towel valet with fluffy cobalt towels that match the several beach umbrellas already propped up around the beach, food, and beverage carts. There is even a shaded play-pen set up for Phoebe and enough sand toys to keep her occu-pied for days. Entertainment comes in the form of badminton and volleyball, paddleboards, surfboards, large tubes and inflata-bles for floating, snorkel gear, Jet Skis. It is everything Warren promised at the clambake and more.

No one asks what we think of all this. Because to them, it's normal. A beach of amenities. A beach for losing track of time, for floating through the afternoons fueled by the freedom of hav-ing no real agenda.

We take the Jet Skis out first. Edison carefully helps Chelsea slide on her life vest and tosses mine to me across the sand, where it lands at my feet. It came off ruder than he must've intended it because he rushes over to help, but Sepp beats him to it, picking it up before I get the chance, shaking off the sand, and holding it while I slip my arms through.

"This isn't really a two-person job," I say.

"Oh, I know that. But it's all about the optics."

"So you look like a gentleman and I look helpless?"

"Exactly that." He reaches over and yanks on the strap in front of my life vest to secure it tighter. Edison watches a few feet away; his head snaps in the other direction when I meet his eyes.

We circle the cove on the Jet Skis and take a lap past North

Point Beach and the lighthouse. I love all this speed and freedom, the easy handling of the Jet Ski and the spray of the water. Sepp leads us, but I cut corners and race in front of him once in a while to keep the *optics* balanced. He laughs like he knows what I'm thinking.

We are as vibrant as the sun when we return to the Duval beach, except Edison, who turns methodical as he puts away the life vests and wipes down the Jet Skis.

A white-and-navy boat pulls up to the dock. Oswald stands and points to it, and Warren rushes over to greet them.

"Sepp." Edison nods toward the boat.

Sepp notices it, says, "Oh shit, they're early," and jogs over to meet them with Warren.

A guy and girl seeming about Sepp's age walk up the dock to the beach. The boy chats with Warren, and Sepp keeps pace with the girl. He stands very close. The two new guests are in their swimsuits, and take nothing from the boat with them, like they knew this beach would have whatever they could possibly need. After spending five minutes with them, it's apparent why. They are the same breed as the Duvals, wealthy enough to assume that a private beach will come with essentials and extras.

The introductions they give us are formal: Michael and Katherine Ellis, children of Richard and Linda Ellis, of Ellis Exports. George excites at this, familiar with the company because of the work they do with Goodman Pharmaceuticals. Oswald is surprised that George has knowledge of the export business the pharmaceutical company uses since George is in the sales division. George seems to take this as a compliment and explains he is familiar because of the higher-ups he knows who work in logistics.

Michael and Katherine's maternal great-grandfather was a

famous Korean poet, who George claims he's heard of even though I've never seen George read poetry in my whole life.

Katherine keeps her long dark hair back in a bun and has an infectious smile that seems to have even rubbed off on Karen. Sepp calls her *Kath*. He helps her put on her life vest, glancing at me with a smirk as he does so, though this time the scene doesn't at all portray Katherine as helpless, so much as it makes Sepp look like he's needlessly doting on her.

Michael stays for only a quick drink, a few slices of flatbread, and a story about how he got the scar on his left knee falling off a table during an Oktoberfest in Munich.

George is still talking about how nice it was to meet them when Michael is speeding away and Katherine is making her second lap around the cove on the Jet Ski with Sepp.

This is what impresses George, I guess. The Duvals, the heirs of the Ellis fortune. Chelsea readjusts her hair for the third time in the last five minutes, and I wonder if she is also impressed with Katherine, if it has her feeling insecure.

"You look great," I say, passing her on my way to the paddle-boards, her hands fussing with her hair again. I don't look back to see if I've helped her to quit worrying or not, but as I'm walking my board out to the water, I see Edison taking her hands from her hair and weaving their fingers together as he leans in for a kiss. Probably a much more effective way of boosting her confidence and making her stop obsessing about her hair.

I paddle out past the shore, leaning into the waves as I drift forward.

Chelsea and Edison ride the same paddleboard. She sits in front, waving to me as they glide my way. They slide up next to me, and we all sit down, rest our paddles over top of the boards, bobbing up and down with the waves. Chelsea talks about how beautiful it is, the sun sparkling on the water, the bold blue of the ocean in the distance.

"It's like living in a postcard," Edison says, a stolen line from that night we met at the half-built house. He doesn't look at me when he says this, but a small smile forms on his lips, like he's sure I noticed. What did I think the summer would be like if he was Finn and our only tie to each other was from meeting on the island? Nothing like this. Certainly not this extraordinary. Even still, the memory of that fantasy gives me a sharp hit of longing for that boy I thought he was and how I thought we were going to be together.

We retreat back to the beach around the same time as Katherine and Sepp do and raid the food cart for crab and avocado wraps, caprese poppers, and watermelon slices—items that are refilled throughout the day by the Duval staff, who swiftly appear and disappear before we can catch their faces or anything distinguishable about them. They are the magicians of the beach. Anything we could want, they make it manifest before us. The towel valets are always full, the sun chaises always brushed free of sand, the cushions always dry. There is always a full pitcher of cucumber-infused water and never any dirty dishes lying around.

Edison flops down between Chelsea and me, sitting in the sand, not even bothering with a towel, not caring how hot it is or that it sticks to his wet skin. The sand on the Duval beach is white and soft, like maybe they'd had it brought in. I'd put nothing past them.

Kath and Sepp sit together on a towel. Her hair is down now, long and dark and damp and wavy. There are smatters of sand clinging to her legs, and she doesn't care enough to brush them away. She and Sepp start speaking French to each other; whatever they're saying has them cracking up. Of course, *this* is who Sepp Duval entertains at his family's beach.

I can sense the pressure Chelsea might feel to be a certain kind of girl worthy of this kind of outing. She squints uncomfortably against the sun, even under her shades, and takes careful bites of her watermelon so the juice won't drip down her chin. Sepp and Kath seem so in sync, sophisticated in the same way, with so much to say to each other and in more than one language. And here she is, with the new sister she doesn't quite know how to talk to and the new father who's all too impressed by everything that is considered normal to the families on the cove. Edison at the very least is still trying to distract her from all that. Today, he is Edison at face value. He is only Chelsea's rich boyfriend with an easy smile, who laughs like he knows he's charming. But this is what makes her happy.

Sepp's margarita is done quickly, and he's on his way to get another, asking Kath if she's ready for her second, though hers is not even halfway done. A glare from Oswald stops him before he gets a refill, and he veers off his path to the cart, asking if anyone is interested in playing badminton instead.

Chelsea and Edison play against Sepp and Kath, who win and then play against Warren and George. After their second victory, Kath tags herself out to let me in—she's thoughtful, too. Sepp and I win, and I lose track of the teams after that because we keep switching. There is one odd person out, but it creates a flow in the game, the way we all rotate person by person, so our teams are always changing, but each person keeps track of the games they won. In the midst of this, I've become competitive, downright obsessed with collecting the most wins. It feels like we've all become this way, enthralled in the game, cheering when our temporary team wins, and hyper to get back in after we've been tagged out.

I like all the excitement. I like that we're all yelling and that time is moving both quickly and slowly and that every second counts. I like that when I'm on Edison's team and I dive in the sand to make a play, he yells, "You've got it!" and, after I've made a successful hit, will swoop down to help me up and hold my hand in the air as a display of victory. I like that he doesn't let go right away. I like that when I'm on George's team he gives me these big double-handed high fives, and he genuinely looks proud of me.

When it comes down to it, the four of us with the most wins play in the final game—George, Sepp, Kath, and me. George is quick to pick me as his partner, and it makes me smile, even though it is an obvious pairing given the four of us.

"I don't know how you lost. Your backhand is incredible," Edison is saying to Chelsea on the sidelines.

"I haven't won a single game," she says.

"Give yourself a break. You're new to sand sports. I promise, after this summer, you'll be ready for badminton domination. By next summer, you'll be undefeated." This makes her smile. With Chelsea, much of what Edison says is in the spirit of encouragement. And talk of the future. One day and someday. A lot of promising.

For the final game, George and I shuffle and splinter in the hot sand and beat Kath and Sepp by four points.

"I'm new to sand sports, too." I bow in victory, opening my mouth so they can tell I'm winking even though I have sunglasses on. They all like it when I'm sassy. And it gets a careless laugh out of Edison. Though George is the one who laughs the loudest.

"Maris hates to lose," George says after I let him hoist me into the air to celebrate. George says it, so therefore it's true about me, his daughter remade, someone he likes, the girl I'm becoming in his eyes.

"I'm not accustomed to losing!" I can give him what he wants.

More laughs all around, especially from George.

Here in the sun, on this make-believe beach, I pretend that I'm a radiant girl with a contagious smile. Sassy and hilarious and a jokester. Someone who transforms regular conversations into inside jokes. A good daughter. George pretends this is what I am, too.

Chelsea and Karen join Trisha under a beach umbrella. They build sandcastles, then let Phoebe knock down the towers with her hands. They smile at me as I walk past them.

I stand for a while in the ocean, the water up to my waist, letting my palms skim the top, staring out at the houses dotting the beach on the other side of the cove, the side that is flat, the side where the sand isn't as soft. For as much as I liked that there was no weirdness with George, that we were happy for the moment that I was the daughter he always wanted and he was the father I used to dream he would be, I feel a tug of sadness. That pesky reminder that he isn't usually that happy with me and whatever was between us during that game could all dissolve when we return home, out of this paradise.

Here is an idyllic backdrop to be the perfect stepsister best friends that Chelsea dreamed we could be, to get along with her the way I was getting along with George. But I can't stop thinking about Edison's smile, his hand lingering on mine, the few stolen glances.

I take a deep breath. And then I start to swim.

I don't stop until my arms are tired and I can hardly breathe.

Chapter 22

I lay myself out to dry on the Duval dock, which is made of a gray material that looks like wood but feels like wax. I run my fingers over it and smile when there are no splinters.

After a few moments, I hear footsteps coming from the shore, and soon Chelsea is lying on her back next to me. She is dry now, too, and her hair has settled into wild beachy waves that keep falling in her face. Edison sits on her other side, letting his feet dangle over the edge.

"Dad is still gloating from his win." She calls him *Dad* so easily.

"That's George," I say. "He loves winning." I don't know if

that's accurate, but it seems like something that must be true of everyone.

She frowns slightly at hearing me call him *George*.

"He was having so much fun. I love when I get to see that side of him, and he can really let loose. Isn't he the best?"

The silence when I don't answer her stretches on for the length of five waves hitting the dock.

"I hated growing up," Chelsea says to the sky. I wait for her to treat us to another set of stories about the father she never got to meet, the one-bedroom apartment she had to share with her mother, the lights being turned off every other month when they were late with payments. But when I look at her, she's wearing a small smile. "When I was in sixth grade, George told me that life would get better one day and that it would keep getting better. He was right. He's always right."

My whole body flashes hot with anger. When Chelsea was in sixth grade, I was in sixth grade, and George was still mine. I still had a family back then. I'm not stupid enough to think that Trisha's pregnancy was a result of only one sexual encounter between Trisha and George, but I didn't realize he'd replaced us long before I thought we needed replacing. I knew he wasn't happy with my mother and me. I have a lifetime of evidence—missed dance recitals, the long, exasperated sighs, the yelling, the general disinterest in anything we thought was fun, from the movies we loved to our favorite place to eat out. When he took that sales job that kept him constantly traveling, even though I was young, I knew it had more to do with us than work. I knew he was running from us. But I didn't know he'd already found refuge with them, that he'd given up that fast on us. When we traveled with him to the town where Trisha and Chelsea lived, George's current home, the trip with the cheap motel and the fortune-teller neighbor—he had already found them. When he left me for hours, sometimes not coming home until after eight, sometimes staying gone past midnight, was it because he was spending time with them?

"It's too hot," I say, standing quickly—too quickly, because my erratic gesture brings Edison to his feet and has Chelsea sitting up.

"I can get you some water," Edison is saying.

I am trembling but frozen in fury on this damn dock with Chelsea and her stories that could break my heart.

But I could break her heart, too, I think. There's a thudding in my chest that reaches my ears. *Oh, why not?* Why not abolish this perfect day, let the New Browns see all the ways I despise their happiness? Burst this bubble they're in thinking I'm acting better, that it's doing me some good being out here, and tell her all about Edison and the sneaking out, the champagne and the blanket, the kiss that I will gladly blow out of proportion just for her.

She stares at me, her expression full of uncertainty, like she can see it—the monster in me trying to escape.

I open my mouth, ready to tell her everything I really wish, everything that would peel away her happiness about George and Edison and me. But I'm cut off by a splash. A blast of water hitting the side of my face and then filling all the space around me. I break the surface in time to see Chelsea scrambling to stand up, saying, "Eddy, why did you do that?"

He is next to me in the water, pushing his wet hair out of his face.

"Sorry," Edison says, not even trying for sincerity. "I thought Maris looked like she could use some water."

She stares at him, shaking her head. She would definitely be rolling her eyes and smiling, except she's worried that I'm upset about being knocked into the water.

"Are you okay?" she asks me.

I nod. The water has stolen my tears and washed away my anger. My head is clear. The monster is in its cage. I don't want to hurt her; I don't want to be isolated. I don't want to ruin this summer for them or for myself.

Edison stares at me, trying to read my reaction.

I have a horrible thought: I'm glad he's here.

I slap against the water, sending a sizable splash right in his face. Chelsea laughs, exultant now that she knows I'm not mad about being pushed in the water.

I splash him again. For having it so easy.

He wipes the water out of his eyes again, and this time when he looks at me, he nods. Like he knows. Like he could tell I needed to be stopped, the way I could tell on the island that he needed me to stay.

"Let's race," I say.

"Maris," he says so quietly I don't think Chelsea can hear him above the sound of waves hitting the dock. "We don't have to."

"Come on." I send a final big splash his direction and kick off toward the shore. "I hate to lose, remember?"

He shakes his head. Edison's smile sprouts on his face. "Fine. But you won't beat me."

He lets me win.

Chapter 23

We eat dinner on the Duvals' grotto surrounded by tea lights, the smell of charcoal and the sound of our laughter crisp as the night's air. The ocean is far below us, but we can still hear it roaring.

After the meal is over, I wander to the edge of the grotto, where Sepp is leaning against a brick retaining wall that holds up a row of round hedges for the garden on the other side. Kath left right before dinner, and the second she was out the door, he downed two margaritas and hasn't let up since dinner.

"Hey," I say.

He is already part gone. When you have money and no real responsibilities for the day, I guess there's no harm in being listless and drunk the way he is.

"Kath was nice," I say.

"Glad to have your approval."

"She seems like the type that gets everyone's approval."

"That, she is." He stops to examine me, pointing and saying, "You don't miss a damn thing, do you?"

We both turn at the same time to the sound of Edison and Chelsea laughing. Maybe we're both thinking that she is also the type that gets everyone's approval. Not a red mark on her record. Nothing to be held against her but naïveté.

But Sepp didn't drink the way he wanted to, the way that would get him lost in his own head, until after Kath was gone. Has she seen him like this, peeled back and reckless and sloppy, and overly impressed with himself? Is she lucky that he hides this lesser part of himself from her? Or does it leave her in the dark, and it's a type of dishonesty that deceives her?

I always thought you let the people you care about see your rough underbelly, that they are the ones you are supposed to be able to trust with the things you are ashamed of. Maybe he lures her in with his charm and class, and once he feels like she's chosen him, he slowly lets his demeanor show?

I can't help it—I wonder if this is how it happened with Trisha, when she met George, when she decided she loved him. If she fell for him before she knew about us, if that's why it was easier to look past it. If that's how it worked with Chelsea, too, welcoming a new father figure into her life. Look how well it worked out for them.

"Let's play a game," I say, motioning for Edison and Chelsea to come over. They hesitate, not hiding that they are unsure of me. I don't mind being unpredictable to them. I don't mind that they are guarded around me.

Sepp sighs, like this idea exhausts him.

The Duval garden is a maze. Tall round shrubs sectioning off the different varieties of flowers and trees and helping to secure the tea lights strung above, illuminating the allotment. This garden is for hiding, for getting lost.

"What's this game?" Sepp says.

"Hide-and-seek, except different."

"Riveting." Sepp rolls his eyes, and I elbow him.

"One person hides and the rest of us try to find them. If we see them, we join them in their hiding spot; the last one to find the hiding place loses."

"A nursery game," Sepp says, laughing to himself.

"I think it sounds fun," Chelsea says.

"What does the loser have to do?" Edison says.

Sepp and I are both quick with the suggestions. He says, "Take a shot of that god-awful moonshine that the governor gave Oswald." I say, "Jump into the cove naked."

"Like some sort of punishment?" Chelsea sounds concerned.

"No one has to drink moonshine." Edison laughs.

"All right, all right." Sepp nudges me. "Since you thought of it, you'd better be the one to hide first."

I enter the garden alone. I move past the blue flowers bundled the size of baseballs and past tall trees with white flowers hanging, leaving the ground a snowy mess of petals. I go all the way to the end, until I'm near the edge. By the hedging of lilacs at the end of a row of tall and perfect-pink flowers. I scoot under it and lie flat on my back and stare through the branches up at the night sky. There aren't many lilac blooms on the bush, but I can still smell the sweet scent stronger than the thick smell of soil.

I lie there looking at the stars, waiting for him to find me, like I know he will.

Chapter 24

Edison wanders over slowly. He stops for a moment before he squats to get a look at me.

"Do I really have to crawl in there?" he says, but he keeps his voice quiet, and when I scoot up to make room for him, he's on his hands and knees sliding through the branches.

We're closer than we were in the closet. We're enveloped in a shadow, out of range from the light of the moon and twinkling tea lights lining the garden.

"How did you find me so fast?" It took him less time that I imagined it would. "Did you cheat?"

"This is one of the few hiding spots with somewhat of a view."

"What do you mean?"

He motions to the other side of the brush, through the tangle of branches, where on the opposite side of the cliff, the ocean and sky stretch on for miles.

"It's better in the daylight. Or during sunset."

"I'll bet."

"Not my first time hiding in the garden," he says with a smile.

I imagine a younger version of Edison, running around here. That night at the half-built house, he'd told me his first time here was when he was thirteen. "What were you hiding from?"

He smiles, keeps his gaze looking forward. He doesn't say anything.

We hear Sepp before we see him as he takes heavy steps over to us. He peers through the bush.

"Oh god, how are we all supposed to fit?" He breaks branches as he climbs in with us. "That was a major oversight in this game of yours, Maris."

He situates himself between Edison and me. He pulls his knees to his chest and holds his drink close.

"The point is that with more people hiding in one spot, the easier they will be to find."

"Oh, is that the *point*?" Sepp says. "I'm sure this is exactly what you had in mind."

"Leave her alone, Sepp."

"Maris can take it, can't you, Maris?" He moves to look at me, and his drink spills down the front of his shirt. He curses. "So what are we going to make Chelsea do for being so terrible at this game?"

Chelsea finally walks over to this part of the garden. We watch her white sandals move slowly our way. We stay still, ready for her to see us. She is about to turn around, when Sepp reaches out and grabs her ankle. She screams, but her surprise turns into relief when we all come out of the bush, and she joins us in laughing.

"Does this mean I lost?" she asks as our laughter dies down. Her eyes are wide, scared for what we will make her do.

"It's okay," I tell her. "It means you get to hide first next time."

But there isn't a next time because Sepp refills his drink and is too sloppy to play, and George and Trisha are worried about wearing out our welcome, even though the Duvals promise that's not the case and will never be the case. The dinner table is gone from the grotto, only there for us when we needed it, and now replaced with patio furniture. We walk down to the boat, and the beach is empty, nothing but sand and ocean, like we hallucinated the whole day. All traces of the afternoon, here and gone, so fast. We are quiet as we return to our reality, our home without a garden, with rough sand and tall grass. Thin walls and dishes that wait for us to clean them and put them away. I close my eyes, and I can't wait until tomorrow.

Chapter 25

The next morning, Edison comes across the cove to see us. He is the bearer of chocolate croissants and bad news. Today, he has errands to take care of in the town. Today will not be a day at the beach like yesterday.

Chelsea beams. She does not hear the bad news that we aren't getting another afternoon of Duval-style luxury. She only hears opportunity to learn more about Edison, same as I do.

"What errands? You're going into town? Can we stop by the Duval offices? I've never seen them. I would love to see them." It doesn't take long for her to convince him that we should go, too. His insistence that it's boring does nothing to hinder her; for once, we are on the same page, where the thought of not spending the day on their luxurious beach makes me want to do something new instead.

Edison paces himself on the boat ride back, never turning up the speed. It's obvious from the rigid way he's standing and in the way he forces a smile whenever Chelsea looks at him that he does not want us with him.

He leaves us in the foyer for a good forty minutes while he changes, and he comes back in a casual suit, navy and brown.

The second we exit the Duvals' mahogany front door, he has his jacket off, balling it up before he tosses it in the back seat, like he doesn't intend to put it back on.

Cross Cove isn't as far from civilization as it seems—the very definition of close but removed. As we exit the freeway, the trimmed and tidy city presents itself. Just the way I remember from the other two times I visited George, once for his wedding, a second time to meet Phoebe when she was four months old. It was around Christmas; the town was snow-covered and dreary. The cold made everything quiet and still, and I remember thinking how I would have liked it if I'd been there under any other circumstances. Phoebe scared me to death, so small, so fragile, so innocent, but responsible for all the combustion in my life. I remember looking at her, thinking about how Phoebe had her whole life ahead of her. She is just beginning. She doesn't know. She can't suspect what will come, what joys, what horrors. She is lucky and she is tragic all at once.

I watch Edison's eye in the rearview mirror as he stares hard at the road as though it is going to disappear from under us any second.

We turn off a busy street and move farther and farther away from the buildings and parking structures, and soon we are taking turns onto narrower roads with stop signs instead of stoplights, and sidewalks cracked from the roots of the giant trees that stand in front of the small homes, complete with shutters, symmetrical windows, and pitched rooftops. As we continue on, the houses grow older, less cosmetic, and more overrun with ivy, and weeds and tall grass growing out of control. These houses have character, my mother would say. They have chipped paint, siding patched unevenly with mismatched material, crooked drain pipes, clutter on their porches, old easy chairs and discarded satellite dishes. These houses are boxed in by short, rusty metal fences. We pull into the driveway of a shabby light green duplex with a little steeple roof over the shared porch that's got one railing made of metal and another made of wood. Weeds have chaotically found their way down the cracks in the driveway, making it bumpy, like riding over grass.

Chelsea turns to Edison. "Where are we?" Her voice is somber, which sounds especially strange on her. "This is the errand you had to run?"

Edison nods. "Picking up a package."

"A package? From who—"

He's shaking his head, so she stops talking. He glances at her, and I can see from his profile he is giving her a smile. He taps his fingers to the beat of the music playing low in the car, but his eyes are like ice, stiff and vacant.

"Should I come with you—" Chelsea starts as Edison hastily gets out of the car.

The door slams shut when she's mid-ask.

She turns in her seat to shrug and flash me the flattest smile I've ever seen, like reassuring me that it's fine the way he stormed off is the same as reassuring herself.

Edison's left the car on, so I roll down my window. There's a solemn mood here, even though the sun is shining and the birds are chirping. I can hear the faint noise of children laughing in the distance, and the air smells like summer barbeque.

Chelsea and I watch as Edison walks up the porch steps. He goes to the front door on the right side and knocks gently. The woman who answers it has short gray hair and wears a long smock. She hugs Edison when she sees him and doesn't let go for a long time.

She disappears inside for a moment and comes out with a large manila envelope. She's shaking her head, like she's apologizing, as she hands it to Edison. She takes out a handkerchief and pats her eyes. He is giving her the same forced, sad smile he gave Chelsea on our way over here.

I notice a mailbox settled next to the sidewalk. It's a regular brown color, sitting on a brick perch. But there's a label on the side in large metal letters, and even though some of them have turned orange with rust, I can still read them.

FINN.

"Where are we?" I say, even though Chelsea doesn't know either—but now I'm starting to piece it together. The mother he lost. How he only started coming to Cross Cove when he was thirteen, when the Duvals have had a house here since before Sepp was born.

"What's Edison's name, Chelsea? Edison Duval?"

She shakes her head, her eyes finding the mailbox, too. "Edison Finn."

"Is this his . . . this is where he grew up?"

"I don't know," Chelsea says. She seems scared to admit this to me, to herself, too, maybe. Edison isn't a Duval, and he did not grow up like one. And she has no idea where he really spent his childhood. She's face-to-face with all that he's hidden from her. But he's brought her here now to see; he's brought us both.

I'd pictured Edison coming from pristine, sterile mansions, all with echoing foyers and grand staircases. All fully staffed. All large enough to get lost in. Chelsea must've, too.

Edison gives one last hug to the woman before he comes back and slides into the driver's seat. We are quiet in the car. Sitting and not moving. Edison stares at the package in his lap.

"It's from her?" Chelsea says, examining the package. "And it came this week?"

He nods. "It doesn't make any sense." He breathes out. "This is why they say the post office is the most inefficient branch of government." A joke is what he's after. A break in the raw tension cracking through the stale air of the car.

But Chelsea stares at him with big, careful eyes, like she is too afraid to respond.

"Maybe we should roll down the windows, get some air," she finally says.

He needs to laugh, I think, remembering the way I set his laughter free on the island. He needs laughter, not air, not comfort— he needs a brief escape, to be pulled out of this moment and whatever is making him so subdued. And even as good a liar as he is, he cannot do it by himself.

"Are you going to open it?" Chelsea asks.

Edison stares at the package. He licks his lips, like maybe he'll answer her any second.

"What do you think it could be?" Chelsea says.

He shakes his head. He puts his hands on the package, then puts them on the steering wheel, and then returns them to the package.

"Are you afraid it's a bomb?" I say.

I wait. A half second of Chelsea's mouth falling open in mortification. A half second of Edison's eyes in the rearview mirror, stunned and striking all at once. And then I hear it. His rich laughter haloed in relief. Chelsea finally joins him, giggling politely, though the concern never leaves her eyes.

Without another word, he tears open the top of the envelope. He peers inside, and I hold my breath. I see Chelsea is holding hers, too. There is no flinch in his expression. No sign of a smile, or a scowl; no glimmer of emotion whatsoever.

He sticks the envelope on the floor in the back seat behind Chelsea and starts the engine. Chelsea asks him something as he's backing out of the driveway—something small, something about the weather. I glance down at the floor where the envelope is resting. It is addressed to Edison Finn. The return address: from Francesca Finn at Sacred Hearts Hospital.

My eyes find his again in the rearview mirror. Goose bumps form on my arms; I look at him and I can feel myself dissolving.

Chapter 26

The Duval office is in a regular brick building with glass doors. As it's been explained to me, they have an office at their quarry, where the cement is made, and an office downtown for doing business. We glide up eleven stories in the elevator before we reach the top floor and are greeted by pretty marble floors and gray chairs, a glass desk with a white computer and a red vase holding aqua-blue stones. The woman sitting behind that front desk sits up straighter as we approach. Tall windows line the wall behind her, showing off the city and casting the glow of sunshine over the office. No one else is here, and it's a smaller office than I was expecting, seemingly with enough desks sectioned off behind the reception area for about fifteen people or so. There are two hallways right off the entry, each leading in different directions, where I imagine the more private offices are.

"You're late," the woman behind the desk says to Edison. She takes off her headphones and picks up her phone, saying, "He just got here," into the receiver. Now that we're at her desk, I see that she is munching on cheese balls and her computer screen displays a paused episode of *The Bachelor.*

"Late?" Edison says.

Sepp comes bursting in from the hallway on our right.

"Where the fuck were you? Didn't you get my messages?"

He flashes Chelsea and me a quick smile in place of a greeting.

Edison shakes his head, takes out his phone. "I don't have any messages from you."

"Not on that phone," Sepp says, then, with a quick glance toward Chelsea and me, adds, "Your work phone."

"They're here?" Edison says, a hint of panic in his voice.

"They fucking blindsided me, and I've been stalling them for over thirty minutes," Sepp says, talking low. Edison sighs.

Chelsea has turned to the wall, studying a painting of a landscape, like she's trying to give them privacy since it's obvious we're the intrusion here. I try to do the same, taking out my phone and pretending to check my own messages. I hear familiar voices coming from down the hall.

"Hey, can we get this over with or what?"

"We've waited long enough."

I look over my shoulder and see them lingering in the hallway, half hanging out an open glass door. They are exactly as I remembered them. Mid-twenties, with faces that are clean and shiny, but still with a cut here and a bruise there, if you know to look—and I do. The one who on the island was wearing the red hat now stands there in a brown suit, his chestnut hair slicked back, his green eyes scanning the lobby and stopping on me. He elbows the shorter guy, also from the island, also in a suit, the bruises on his knuckles more pronounced than the bruises on his face.

"We're coming, we're coming," Sepp says, walking back toward them.

Edison notices the direction of my gaze. "This way." Edison stands directly in front of me, a hand on my shoulder, encouraging me to turn, his eyes pleading.

Once I've turned, he puts a hand on my back, the other on Chelsea's, as he leads us down the opposite hallway, telling us, "This shouldn't take too long," and, "The break room is on the right. I'll come get you when our meeting is over. Help yourself to whatever you want."

I have a million questions on the tip of my tongue as he shuts the door and secures us in the break room. At least Sepp is with him. At least he's not alone with those two and Archaletta, if Archaletta is there with them and I just couldn't see him. My stomach is in knots wondering what's happening down the hall, but Chelsea smiles as though hers is full of butterflies.

This is an adventure for her. She's imagined him here, working with the Duvals, and now she gets to see it for herself. A dream coming true, the picture of her future getting more and more real. I want to think she's silly, to be filled up by the extravagance, but then I taste the coffee, and it is a dream. The croissants are fluffy and the chocolate in them pure heaven, like the kind Edison brings over.

We find a table by the windows and look down on the town, out at the blue sky.

"His last name isn't Duval," I say, giving up on beating around the bush. I want to know everything about him. "How is he related to them?"

"He's not." Chelsea says this like it's an admission. "But he is in all the ways that matter," she says, talking fast, her tone more defensive than I've ever heard it. "They love him, and he loves them. He's not a charity case just because his mother died and his father's been in prison since he was two—he was a part of their family even before his mother died. They don't treat him like an outsider, because he's not. He's one of them. They've known him for a long time, and they knew his mother, Franny."

A family bound by something other than blood. This is how it's always worked for her.

"They're his family," she repeats. "When he brought me home to meet his family, his mother, we went to the Duvals' home. Because that's more of his home than anywhere else has ever been." She seems insistent on this, and that says to me that she is ashamed, and the things she's ashamed of have to do with secrets Edison kept from her, too. Not knowing where Edison resided when he wasn't at the Duvals', not ever knowing where he grew up. I wonder if she'd ever thought to ask or if he avoided these kinds of questions, instead showing her only what he thought she would like to see.

I think of his worried face in the driveway, his fingers turning white clenching the package.

"Why is he still getting mail from her?"

"I'm not sure."

"What was she like, when you met her?"

Chelsea doesn't ask why I'm so curious. There's this thumping in my chest, a single track in my mind that only wants more information about him, like a craving; like he's mine to know about. Chelsea has the keys to the doors I'm locked out of.

"She was . . . she had plans for Edison. I only met her that one time for dinner with the Duvals. She seemed really happy to meet me. She told me she had heard all about me and was glad Edison had someone like me in his life. After she died, he was heartbroken."

"How did she die?"

"She had a rare blood disorder. She was perfectly healthy until one day she wasn't. She was barely in the hospital for a day before she died."

The more I know about him, the more I can peel away at who he is and separate all the dimensions of him that are what he wants us to see instead of what is really there.

"He's okay, though," she tells me. "He left for school right after she died, but he told me he was getting through it. And the Duvals took care of everything—hospital bills, putting her things in storage, the funeral. He's still sad about it sometimes, of course. But he's okay; he really is."

I nod, trying to decide if I believe her—if I think he's truly let her see any of his real sadness; if I think he's let anyone see, unless they stumbled onto it by accident.

Chapter 27

Sepp and Edison retrieve us from the break room about forty minutes later. They are both smiling. Sepp wants to celebrate. He's holding a bottle of tequila and a bottle of champagne.

"A successful meeting," Edison explains.

Chelsea is innocent chic. "You sold a lot of cement?"

This makes Sepp laugh manically. He swigs directly from the tequila bottle.

We order delivery from Sepp's favorite Chinese restaurant and go on the roof to eat it. The view up here is preposterous, stretching out for miles. Steeples and mansard roofs poking through a sea of full round trees. The sunset turns the sky purple and orange. Sepp is still elated, and none of us can keep up. He opens the champagne bottle and lets it spray everywhere, so there's hardly any left to drink.

He screams into the open sky. He whoops and cheers. He shouts, "This is it!"

"Over here," Sepp says, taking my arm and moving me to the other side of the rooftop. Chelsea follows closely, curiously— probably protectively also. He positions himself in between us when we're a few feet from the edge and swings an arm around each of us, letting his hands dangle over our shoulders. The bottle of tequila knocks against my elbow. "Isn't it beautiful?"

Chelsea and I exchange a glance—Chelsea covers her mouth so she won't laugh out loud. Edison joins us, standing beside her.

Sepp drops his arms from around our shoulders and gets closer to the edge. He leans against the railing.

"Come get me—I dare you!" he shouts at the sky, his voice ripe with excitement. "I dare you!"

Edison shakes his head at Sepp, laughing, so we'll know not to listen to him. But I always listen to Sepp, because I don't think Sepp says things for no reason.

I move slowly toward the edge of the roof so I'm shoulder to shoulder with him.

"Maris—" Chelsea's abrupt warning trails off into nervous laughter. She's afraid. She thought Sepp didn't care about anything, especially not about the Duval business, but here he is, looking like he's just been spared, celebrating like he means it.

I hold on to the railing; maybe that will calm some of Chelsea's fears.

Sepp leans against the barrier and faces me, the wind dusting up his hair as he points to me with his bottle-holding hand. A teardrop of tequila glides down his chin after he takes a sip. His face puckers like he's no longer enjoying it. "Eddy's always been lucky. And me, well, I've always been invincible." He holds out his hands, standing up all the way, backing up like he's showing me his kingdom. "I bet I could fly right off this roof." There's something so sad about him right then, even as elated as he seems.

I remember feeling like that, like I could inhale the world and hold it in my lungs; like if I felt that invincible, then who was to say I wasn't. I was good at tricking myself.

"Take it easy," Edison says to him.

"Grow up." Sepp turns on his heel, downing another drink for the ages. "I own this world, and this world owns me!" he yells, leaning forward and letting the railing hold him up at the waist.

"Be careful!" Chelsea calls.

"I'm invincible!" he screams. It's a feral noise. Chelsea reaches for Edison, but he is walking toward Sepp.

"We know," Edison says. His voice is calm, soft. It works, and as soon as Sepp is close enough, Edison tucks an arm around him and pulls him away from the edge. He starts toward the door, and Sepp goes with him. Chelsea and I follow closely behind.

"I'm invincible, and you're the luckiest bastard alive," Sepp tells Edison, when they're stalled in front of the door, but in that moment, he is looking right at me. He swivels in Edison's arms, putting a hand on Edison's cheek, like he's steadying his face, so they're looking right at each other with their matching eyes. "I'd do anything for you. And I have, haven't I?"

Edison nods slowly.

Sepp smiles; his eyes are shiny. "And now we will be unstoppable."

Later that night, after we've finished dinner and the sky is dark,

Edison and I find ourselves alone at the elevator in the dark office, waiting for Sepp and Chelsea to get out of the restrooms.

"I saw who you were meeting with," I say. *It seemed like another ambush*, I don't add.

He motions to his face. "Still conscious, no fresh bruises."

"It went better than the last time."

"It went exactly how it was supposed to go." That's all he says.

"Sepp seems relieved."

He nods. "We both are."

"You don't have to worry about them anymore, then? Or Archaletta?"

Edison looks to his feet, takes a quick breath before he answers. "No, not anymore."

Chelsea comes back, and moments later, Sepp joins us so I don't get to ask if they paid the guys from the island or if Archaletta was there, too.

"All in a day's work," Sepp says into my ear, leaning against the wall of the elevator as we travel down to the lobby.

"Selling cement?" I say, knowing I shouldn't reveal that I know anything else.

"Putting out fires." He smiles. He holds out his hands. "Look, Maris, no burns." He laughs. For a second he turns serious and his eyes half close as he looks down at me. "I earned every ounce of that champagne." Then he's laughing again.

This must be how the Duvals handle problems. They are solved fast and celebrated hard.

Chapter 28

The next day Chelsea and I sit blindfolded in the back of Edison's boat, holding hands as the wind cuts at our faces. In the cargo are our overnight bags. The Edison charm convinced George and Trisha to let us go in the first place.

Chelsea peppers him with questions, trying to guess where we're going, and he finally lets us take off our blindfolds.

We are surrounded by ocean, no shore in sight. This makes Chelsea overjoyed—*Where are you taking us?!* And I am the same, but keep my excitement under wraps.

It starts as a small speck, and soon we're upon it, its sandy base stretching out before us—an island.

"That's it," he tells us with a smile, Chelsea's arms around his neck as he steers.

It's small; we can see the curve of it. It's like Honeycomb Island in the sense that it's sandy on the edges and full of shrubs in the center.

Oswald, Warren, and Karen are on the dock to greet us, along with the owners of the island: the Smiths.

The Smiths—Gloria and Renee. Older women, one in silk, the other in linen, wearing matching six-carat diamond wedding rings. They're in the business of construction and property development and have nurtured a friendship with the Duvals for decades. Their yacht is anchored next to the Duval yacht. It is bigger.

Sepp and Kath arrive shortly after we do in a red speedboat. Sepp greets the Smiths by kissing them both sloppily on the cheeks. *The wives*, he calls them.

We have a quick lunch of caprese sandwiches on the deck of the Smiths' yacht, and then the parasailing boat arrives.

Chelsea and I go together. We're strapped in the harness, smiling so hard with anticipation that our cheeks get sore. The boat propels out in front of us, and we shoot higher and higher into the air. My heart races as the world opens up beneath our feet. The trees on the island get smaller and smaller, and I can see shadows moving under the ocean. I close my eyes and concentrate on the wind on my face, the occasional feeling of weightlessness, and pop them open, getting a rush from how distant the ground is, how far we could fall, afraid to miss any of it.

Chelsea screams at the top of her lungs. A happy sound. And when we land in the water, she has this gigantic smile on her face. She goes again with Edison and comes back with the same smile.

"It was like flying," I tell my mother on the phone afterward, sitting in the outside area of the upper deck on the Duvals' yacht, watching Chelsea and the Smiths and Karen and Kath hover around the chocolate fountain inside, dipping in strawberries and shortbread.

After I hang up with my mother, I take the stairs down to the main deck and see the Duval men through the glass doors. They stand in a huddle talking. But I can't hear them. It's quiet down here and shaded. I'm tired from the parasailing and the heat, and I am enjoying this reprieve, so I stretch out my legs and ease back on the padded bench facing the back of the boat.

There's a commotion behind me. Footsteps and loud voices and the sound of a door sliding open.

"Stop telling me to calm down." It's Edison. "This was never part of the deal. And you promised me I didn't have to stay."

"It won't be too much longer," Sepp says. "The first part is done. We did exactly what we were supposed to do in that meeting."

"Then I should be able to go. You don't need me for the rest," Edison says.

"Yes, we do, and you know very well that we do," Warren pipes up, his voice booming with anger.

"You never told me it would go on this long."

Warren snaps, "I don't know what's gotten into you today, Eddy—"

"Warren." Oswald tries to cut him off with a warning. "Come back inside. Let him have some air."

"Well, he knows how it works," Warren says. "He can get far away from us and Cross Cove and everything that he hates as soon as all this bullshit is over."

"It's going to be okay, Edison." Oswald's calming voice is the last thing I hear before the sound of the door sealing shut. Next comes a sigh I recognize as Edison's.

I slouch lower in my chair and in doing so knock my phone onto the floor, where it lands with a thump. So I have no choice but to sit up, let Edison see that I've once again been exposed to the parts of his life he tries to hide. To my surprise, Sepp is still with him.

Edison shakes his head, then shrugs, defeated. He wipes his hands over his face like he's too tired to make up an excuse. Behind them, lingering on the stairs, is Chelsea. I wonder how long she's been there and if she heard the Duval men fighting like I did.

They notice me looking past them and follow my gaze behind them, to the left.

Edison's hands drop, and his face falls. Chelsea leans into the railing, like she wishes we didn't see her. She frowns when she notices me, like it somehow is worse that I've heard it, too, a flaw in Edison that would be easier to ignore if there was no one to witness it. No secrets on this yacht. Big and expansive, but we are all too close and drawn to each other, and nothing is safe or sacred.

"I don't know how to be here," Edison says to her, like he's begging her to understand.

"Careful," Sepp says to Edison. It sounds like a warning.

"Without her—" He breaks off, shaking his head. I think he means his mother, even though that wasn't what the fight was about at all, and the most troubling part for Chelsea about what she overheard isn't whether or not it's hard for Edison to be back because of the painful memory of his mother; it's that the reason he's in Cross Cove is wrapped up in the Duvals' business. They insisted he be here and that it has nothing to do with her. "At school, it was like I was on a different planet. It was easier."

"I'm sorry it's not easy for you to be here," she says with a forced smile, tears lurking. "I'm sorry things aren't better."

I follow Chelsea to the upper deck, where Kath, Karen, and the Smiths are lounging and drinking white wine. Edison follows her, too. She smiles at all of them, but it never reaches her eyes, and I can tell by the concentrated wrinkle in between Chelsea's eyes that she's trying to sort out some of what she's heard. Her disenchantment is more apparent now that we're surrounded by everyone else, all of them smiling, laughing, relishing in this day, carefree as ever.

"It's hard to be back, princess, that's all," Edison says, leading her away from everyone and over to the deck railing. He gives her a smile that is so Edison I wonder if she's comforted by it. Or if now she can see through it.

"I understand," she says quietly. He kisses her then, quickly at first. The next kiss he gives her is slow and delicate. He kisses her to quiet her. To reassure her. To promise her.

It's a kiss that leaves me with a hollow feeling in my chest. There's distance in the kiss. It is just lips. Just hands. It is only for show. With pieces of perfection chipping away, I can see the force in their sweetness. He pulls back, and our eyes meet over her shoulder. He seems surprised to see me there, watching, and looks away fast, keeping his arm around Chelsea as he steps to stand beside her so his back is to me. After a few minutes, they are whispering and laughing, and Chelsea is smiling as though she never stopped.

But it's too late. I am thinking what I am not allowed to think: he would be different with me.

Chapter 29

The Duvals and the Smiths. With their large diamonds and their larger boats and their fresh seafood delivered and prepared and served to them with a side of yellow wax beans and arugula. Their private islands and designer champagne and parasailers.

We're here with them so this is all ours for the day, too. But I can feel it now, how this is borrowed time. There's splintering under the surface that money does wonders to cover up.

After dinner, we enjoy a walk on the beach. It's a calm day, the sun is fading, the wind is sparse, the water tepid. Karen sprawls out on a lawn chair, wearing her bikini, soaking up the last of the evening's fading sun. Warren has joined Sepp and Kath, where they are attempting to make a fire. Edison and Chelsea are leaned up against a fallen tree trunk with their feet in the sand.

Oswald's smiles are the warmest I've ever seen, and he gives them freely to the Smiths as the three of them walk, shoes in one hand, champagne in the other, spilling over sometimes when Renee talks with her hands or Gloria bumps into her when they encounter uneven sand. I walk next to them, and they let me.

The Smiths and Oswald are talking about things I cannot imagine, private island parties and house seats at the symphony and charity galas to save polar bears. Shoes that pinched all night. The cliff-side structure that wouldn't support a hot tub. Like the first time I met the Duvals, I find these non-problems relaxing, and I sink into that place of envy thinking about what life would be like if these truly were the only troubles that existed. Except now I know they're not. Money and beautiful homes and long stays in Europe can't fix the way it must feel for Edison to return to a paradise that's missing his mother; it only serves to help him run away, gives him some semblance of temporary denial, and creates a distraction, and looking around, nothing familiar like the desert, I can see that appeal too, even if there are daggers beneath the surface, easy to reach if you let yourself remember.

The money and the ease, the ability to escape, must comfort Chelsea, too, enough that she can overlook everything she doesn't know about Edison and that she rarely gets to see him. I look back at the two of them, still sitting in the sand, legs crossed and facing each other, smiling as they talk. I wonder if I would be able to ignore all the things about him that I might never know and if the desire to dig deeper, to know more—everything—and to insert myself into all the parts of his life, hidden and open, would ever lift away, and I could simply exist with him like she does, happily accepting whatever he tells her as truth.

"Those two," Oswald says, noticing my gaze, taking this opportunity to pull me into the conversation. "Nothing as delightful as young love."

"The first time I fell in love, I was seventeen," Renee says. "It was awful at that moment, but in retrospect, it was so beautiful."

"Have you ever been in love?" Gloria smiles at me like she expects me to have a delicious story.

There were many things about Trevor that I loved. But I knew beyond a reasonable doubt that I was not happily or madly in love with him. I knew it in my gut, in my bones, in my heart, and in my head.

"I don't think so," I say.

Gloria laughs. "You would know—trust me, honey."

"The people who are supposed to come into your life will," Oswald says. The fortune-teller had only talked about letting people go, accepting and embracing their leaving, and it's refreshing that Oswald's focus is about bringing people closer, embracing them as meant to be there. When Gloria laughs again, he says, "What? I truly believe that." And then he is laughing with her.

"I do, too," says Renee. "I mean, look at Gloria and me—what are the chances we visit the Chinati Foundation on the same day and are part of the same tour? It was definitely fate. We were always going to be a family. It was . . . inevitable."

"Yes, yes, I completely agree. It's like what happened with us and Edison. We didn't find Eddy; Eddy found us," Oswald says. He turns his attention to me, even though we're all listening, curious. Gloria says, "Remind me of this, again."

"His school was a few blocks from the quarry," Oswald continues. "He wandered into the woods one day, wanted to watch the machines and the workers. He was always there, hanging around, such a spirit to him, a love of the noise, the surrounding forest, the destruction, the things the quarry made, all that crushed stone. We adopted him, you could say. Gave him odd jobs. Something to do after school before his mom got home. And Franny, well, she was special. It was gracious of her to let us into her son's life. And we're better for having known her."

Gloria is wiping away a few stray tears on her cheeks. "That poor boy, losing his mother like that. I'm glad he has you all."

Oswald says, "It was as though we didn't know a piece of our heart was missing until it arrived." He puts his arm around Gloria. "He is the most determined person I know. Strong, too."

To me, Edison is a cluster of characteristics, specialized traits changing with wherever he is and who he thinks he needs to be.

Does Edison feel about the Duvals the way I feel about the New Browns, like I'm standing on the outside even though everything about them seems welcoming? Does he get the sense that there are conditions, the way I do, despite how nice the New Browns are? Does he feel an allegiance to his mother, the way I do to mine—thinking of her every time he gets close to belonging somewhere else, remembering where he came from, what he lost?

When it gets dark, we all put on another layer of clothing and we gather around the fire for s'mores. Slowly people disperse, going to bed, and soon it's only Sepp and Kath and Chelsea and Edison and me. Kath is busy on her phone, talking to her cousin, someone else Sepp seems to know, as he called out, "Tell that brute I said hi," when she first answered. Chelsea and Edison stand on the opposite side of the fire, pressing their hands against the heat. I can't hear what they say to each other over the crackling of flames and the beating waves of the ocean and the sound of the wind thumping through the trees.

"Are you happy?" Sepp asks, nudging my toe with his.

I don't mean to, but I glance at Edison.

Sepp laughs a little, following my stare, and I don't like that he's noticed. "You know, Edison tells me everything."

"Are you happy?" I say, turning the question back on him, curious what it could mean if he knows about Edison and me, and wondering if Edison really does tell him everything or if Sepp only thinks he does.

"Of course I am." He laughs again.

Kath is off her call and motions for Sepp to go back to the yacht with her. He doesn't keep her waiting.

"Sepp," I say. I don't continue until he turns around. "There isn't anything to tell."

He puts his hands in the air, like a surrender. He smiles and says, "Whatever you say."

Chapter 30

Chelsea and I are put in a spare room on the Smiths' yacht, since all the Duval rooms are taken. The waves make sloshing and plopping noises when they splash against the side of the yacht. Chelsea is completely exhausted from the day and falls asleep right away. I can't sleep. I'm anxious from my fingers to my toes and too awake wondering about what Sepp said to me about Edison telling him everything.

I hear footsteps on the dock. Maybe I was listening for them. I go over to our window, barely level with the dock, and he's there, crouching down, like he knew I'd be looking for him. He motions for me to join him outside.

He stands at the end of the dock, in front of the speedboat we took here. On my way over to him, I remember when I first got to Cross Cove and he was never where I was looking. Now it's as though I wished him to be there, so here he is.

"I was going to take the boat out," he says when I reach him. "You can go with me if you want."

I glance at my feet. "Why would I want to come?"

He is alone now. I could ask him about the fight I overheard earlier today on the yacht deck or about that meeting with the men from the island at the Duval office and what kind of deal he and Sepp made with them. There's so much I don't know about him, and I can't seem to shake the curiosity.

"Because." He shrugs. "You wanted to know how fast this boat can go."

There's a thrill I get being around him, too, and I like that he seems to understand something about me.

There are many reasons I should not be out in the water alone with him, most of them having to do with how much I want to go.

"Come on," he says, bending down to pull the boat closer to the dock. The breeze ruffles his hair. "You'll like this—I promise."

He holds the boat steady as I climb inside. He hops in after me.

The motor hums to life as Edison starts the engine. We drive out into the open ocean. He turns on the boat lights when the island and the yachts and everyone sleeping soundly in their beds are far behind us and cranks up the speed.

"Stand up here," he says, talking over the motor. "Next to me."

I do as he says, and when I'm close enough, he takes hold of the sleeve of my sweatshirt, positioning me beside him.

"So how fast *can* this thing go?" I say.

We drive farther out, until there's nothing but a dark ocean and a star-filled sky on all sides of us, like we're in space, only this boat to hold us.

"Ready to find out?" he shouts, not really asking a question, but I'm saying, "Yes," all the same. The boat kicks up another notch, flying faster over the waves.

I feel bursts of terror and happiness and anticipation, all at once—a good feeling, combined with that thrill of familiar excitement. When I grip onto the edge of the windshield, Edison's smile widens.

A grunt of the engine, a shift downward, a sudden boost, and we're shooting forward. We cut through the water so fast my ears buzz. The wind whips us with such a force it stings. But he was right. I do like this. Plunging through the air, I'm not thinking about anything except the wind on my face, the spray of the water, the adrenaline pumping through me, and how it all makes me feel invincible, like I'm outrunning death or daring it to take me now.

Edison's face is lit up in a way I've never seen before. He lets out a cheer, and I try to do it, too, but when I open my mouth to shout, nothing but giddy, vivacious, roaring laughter comes out. Over the growl of the engine and over the crashing of the waves and the hiss of the wind, I hear Edison laughing, too. I hold on to the top of the windshield and tip my head back as the air swirls around me. The dark ocean could be the sky, and the sky is on fire, the stars are all shooting as we charge past them.

This is the kind of rush that makes you forget everything except for the moment. I can feel so many burdens peeling away from me already, the resentment I feel for a family that formed without me; how the more I get to know them, the more I want to be a part of it but don't know if I ever will be because of the frustration my father feels toward me and the disdain I feel toward him; the fear that I carry with me like a constant—being scared to die, but much more scared of not living; terrified of the way I feel about Edison and how he might feel about me; unsettled and desperately intrigued by whatever he's withholding, and worried he might be hiding from me the way he's hiding from Chelsea. The stack of things I regret, everything that happened when I was with Trevor—I can push that all away and let it lift off with the wind.

This is flying, and this is falling. This is soaring. This is danger and freedom and not caring. This is letting go.

He slows our speed gradually until we come to a stop. The waves glide under us, rocking the boat.

"That was—" I stop talking because I'm holding his hand, clutching it so tightly in mine and I didn't mean to. I don't know when this happened. I let it drop. He smiles at me like he knows why I cut myself off.

"I do that sometimes—come out here at night and go as fast as I can," he says, slightly out of breath like I am from the excitement. "It scares the hell out of me but somehow makes me feel better."

"That was amazing." My heart is still racing from the ride. And from the way he's looking at me right now, like everything he's afraid of and everything that saves him is mirrored in my expression. *This is how you're going to do it*, I think. *This is how you really get to the deepest parts of me. This is how you make me fall for you, relentlessly and irrefutably.*

He shuts off the lights on the boat so we can better see the blackness and the stars. "We're surrounded," he says. A rogue wave jostles the boat, knocking me toward the edge. I reach for the windshield to keep from toppling over, but he already has his hands on either side of me, holding me steady.

"I'm afraid of the water at night," I confess. He's slow letting go of me. "It's so dark and you can't see what's underneath."

He turns the boat lights back on because it's part stunning and part terrifying to be out in the middle of the ocean like this, with the only other lights millions of miles away, burning up in the sky.

"I dare you to jump in," he says quietly, staring at the water like he's not actually daring me, he's daring himself.

At first, I laugh. But I'm still buzzing from the ride, still a little out of breath, still feeling magnificent, invincible. And it feels so good to let go, forget that I'm mad at families that give you everything except for that undefinable thing you really need, forget about this obsession and want I have for him when he doesn't belong to me because he doesn't belong to anyone.

"All right," I say, moving to the edge of the boat.

"All right?" He doesn't seem entirely convinced, even when I ditch my flip-flops and take off my sweatshirt.

I don't let myself think too much as I place one foot on the ledge of the boat and push off, hurling myself into the water.

Edison shouts, "Wait—don't!" but it's too late.

I crash down and sink deep—that's what it feels like—but I only have to pump my legs a few times to break the surface. Edison is on the side of the boat now, kicking off his shoes and tossing his sweatshirt and tumbling forward, landing with a splash beside me.

"Why did you do that?" he yells at me when his head pops out of the water. He's mad, maybe afraid, but I am surging with electric happiness and absolute pride—like I conquered something. He sees my wild smile and starts to laugh.

"That was completely reckless!" he says. I don't know if it's because a wave has pushed him or if he swam here on his own, but he is right in front of me, suddenly so close. "And really brave."

What I'd always wanted to be.

I lie on my back, floating, letting the coldness claim me. I give in to the waves. I let them carry me and every problem, every secret, every burden I've been holding close for the past few years. He does the same thing, and we lock our hands, so if we roll away with the ocean, we won't lose each other.

We don't stay in the water very long. When Edison says, "We should get out," I take his hand and let him lift me into the boat. I use one of the blankets he's pulled from the hutch and get out of my wet clothes as quickly as he does; we both have our backs turned as we strip until we are in nothing except the blankets. I follow his lead and hang my wet clothes on the windshield and over the side of the boat. Then we are laughing, and I still don't know where we are or if it's possible to go back.

Chapter 31

We are shaking as we sit down side by side on the bench seat, borrowing body heat. We are happy. Even if we aren't supposed to be.

We should go back. I know we should, and I feel the first buds of real betrayal as Edison slouches farther in the seat and I bring my knees up and curl them to my chest. My blanket slips off my shoulder, and Edison pushes it up. I let myself slide against him, so our arms are pressed tight together. The blankets are the only barriers between our bare skin. I like the feel of him close, so I lean into him, shutting my eyes, waiting until the fresh sting of guilt has passed before I open them again.

Maybe he doesn't have a choice either, being out here with me like this. Maybe it's like Renee said about some things being in-evitable.

Or maybe it's not that complicated and he is simply a bad boy-friend, a liar, an asshole, this is a game to him, and this is another one of my sorry excuses to bring more excitement into my life.

He rubs his hands together, then puts them to his mouth to warm them.

"My mother always said that motorcycles were dangerous because that much speed is freeing, but you're gone before you even have the chance to remember what you're running from."

I want to ask him about the fight I overheard on the yacht and why he wants to go away. If he pretends to be running on nights like this. If it means anything that this time he took me with him.

"That's why she liked roller coasters so much." His face when he talks about her is the face of the boy I first saw on the island—a face that couldn't hide a thing.

"My mother always says, 'Living fast means you crash hard,'" I tell him.

"Are you close with your mom?"

"Not the way I want to be. I've told her too many lies."

"Why?"

"What do you mean, why? Because I wanted to do things she wouldn't've approved of; because I didn't care they were things I shouldn't have been doing." But that's not the whole of it either. Edison waits for me to continue, like he knows there's more to my lies to my mother than I've admitted, because he knows there's more to me. "I lied because I didn't want her to worry. I knew what I was doing was wrong and I didn't want her to know; I didn't want to be another problem in her life. I didn't want to be another reason she couldn't get out of bed."

"You lied to protect her."

"Yes. But it was selfish, too. If she didn't know what I was doing, she couldn't stop me. But now I don't know if she'll ever really trust me again."

"Trust is earned, right? You'll get it back."

"I hope so. I bet you never lied to your mom."

"I never had any reason to." He shrugs; his shoulder brushes against mine. He smiles. "She would have liked you."

I think his mother is always there lurking in the back of his mind.

"Tell me about her."

And he does. He tells me about her laugh, so loud it used to embarrass him at the library. And she was always starting knitting projects and never finishing them, so their living room was an array of half-finished blankets and scarves, hats with holes at the top, socks without heels. He tells me how she used to whisper in his ear before he fell asleep. *Be strong*, she told him. *Great things will happen*, she assured him.

I'm about to tell him he's lucky, but she's gone, so I don't say anything.

"What was Sepp saying to you, by the campfire?" he says. "You know you really can't trust anything Sepp tells you."

"He asked me if I was happy." I don't tell him the other thing Sepp said, about how there are no secrets between them, and how I lied and told him there was nothing to know.

"Oh." I can hear his smile before I see it, the way he breathes in like he has to prepare for them. That's one of the ways I can tell which smiles are real and which ones are Edison showing off. I wonder how long I've known this about him. I wonder what else I've learned by accident.

"And what did you say?" he says. "Are you happy?"

"I'm happy right now."

He stares straight ahead because looking at me suddenly isn't safe. "Me, too."

This admission, mine and his, is overwhelming. I adjust, putting on my sweatshirt and letting the blanket slouch around me. He does the same. We settle back into the seat, still closer than we should be. He looks at my hand, resting too close to his, and he takes it. Carefully, he flips it over so he can see the cut on the side of my wrist. He traces it slowly.

"You didn't know who I was and you split yourself open for me."

"Reckless," I remind him.

"Brave," he says. He gives back my hand, and I wish he'd take it again.

"All for nothing, right?"

"Not for nothing."

"It was only a poker game." And this was only a boat ride and our kiss at the half-built house was nothing and the fight he had with the Duvals was about his dead mother. He touches his cheek, where the bruise has started to fade and is a shadow around his eye, as the lie settles around us.

"Sometimes I really don't know how I live with myself," he says quietly.

There's a pit in my stomach; I hope he's not talking about me, the two of us, together alone when we shouldn't be. I let my eyes fall shut for a second, blinding myself briefly to all the beauty in front of me—the night sky, Edison.

He slides down even farther in his seat, even closer to me. I let my head lean against his shoulder and feel his cheek lightly press against my temple.

And then, because I'm really being brave, I tell him, "I wish things were different."

"Me, too," he says. He turns his head so it is no longer leaned against me. He's quiet. I lift my head off his shoulder, sensing the shift. We should've taken back all our secrets, but instead, we've given ourselves even more to hide.

I think of what Sepp said to me at the clambake about honesty and faking it and if I believed Edison and Chelsea were truly in love.

"Are you in love with her?" I don't know if asking him is brave or if it's only selfish.

He leans forward and rests his elbows on his knees. "Don't."

"Why did you bring me out here—along for this?"

"Because I knew you'd like it," he says, his voice turning dark. "But you didn't have to come." The guilt is getting to him, coming out as anger, directed right at me. As he continues, I'm growing furious myself at the way he's shifting the blame. "You didn't have to meet me to return my phone; you didn't have to help me on the island."

"Excuse me, I thought I was saving you!" I yell, my fury compounding back at him.

"You are!" he says in a sudden outburst.

He rubs his hands over his face and leans back.

He didn't say, *You did.* He said, *You are.*

What I want to tell him is that maybe he's saving me, too. In the simplest and smallest ways, like pushing me off the dock before I could explode on Chelsea for things that weren't her fault, for taking me out here, knowing I'd like it, that I'd need it. But maybe he pushed me off the dock to save Chelsea from the awful things I was about to say; maybe he took me out here because he knew I'd say yes. He would never invite Chelsea to do something so risky like this. She would be full of warnings; she would care about being safe. He brought me on a precarious boat ride because he knew I'd like it, that I might even shout, "Faster, faster!" I plunged into the ocean because I was afraid of it. And he came in after me.

"And now," he begins, shaking his head before he continues. "Now we have to stop, okay?"

He grabs his wet shorts from where they are hanging against the edge of the boat, and even though he slides them on under his blanket, I still avert my eyes.

He stands up and walks to the front of the boat, like he's going to drive us back as fast we drove out here.

"I know you came to the half-built house the night I found out who you were. I know you waited for me."

I watch his shoulder tense before he turns around. He looks at his feet, like he is ashamed.

"I don't expect you to be with me the way you are with her," I say, remembering what I wanted that night at the half-built house after I'd boldly kissed him. I'd wanted mystery and excitement, but I'd also wanted him to myself and a secret for myself. "After this summer, I go back to Arizona, you go back to England, which is where you really want to be anyway, right?"

When you fully exist in the moment with someone, you don't have to worry about the next day or even the next hour and definitely not the next year, I'm thinking. But I want him to admit what he feels for me.

"The thing about Chelsea—" He stops for a second, like he knows probably nothing he can say will do justice to the ways he's betrayed her—how we've both betrayed her. "I want to be with her." He turns back again, leaning forward against the steering wheel. "I don't have a choice," he says. He doesn't look at me when he continues. "Chelsea has met my mother. If I end up with someone else, they won't ever know that part of my life. And that doesn't feel like a future I'd be able to live with. I can't even fathom it."

When he finally does look at me, I give him a single nod. If I talk, my voice will give out. There's nothing to say to this. It doesn't matter if Chelsea is better for him, or if he wants me more, or if I understand something about him that no one has in a long time, or that he understands me. He chose her for a reason. This is something I'll never be able to give him.

"We should go back," I say.

"Before the sun comes up," he agrees. "Before anyone notices we were gone."

But Sepp is there when we get back to the dock, sitting on the deck of the Duvals' yacht, under a dim light, wrapped in a coat and blanket, drinking out of a mug, which he salutes to us as we come in.

"It's fine; you don't have to worry about him," Edison tells me. Maybe because Sepp already knows; maybe because Edison has a lie ready to tell him. Maybe because Edison's secrets live with Sepp and Sepp is good for them.

I sneak back into Chelsea's and my room, changing into dry clothes and putting my wet clothes in a separate compartment of my overnight bag. I crawl into bed and close my eyes and wish for sleep to come swiftly. But it doesn't.

I wake up in the morning to a blue sky and a breakfast buffet, everyone smiling like it's a new fresh day.

It doesn't matter, I think, if what he has with Chelsea is forced or if he's hiding a part of himself from her that he lets me see. It's the same as Sepp and Kath, how he keeps the best parts of himself for her, because she's worth it. For Edison, I am mostly the person he wishes he'd never met.

As we load our bags into the boat and get ready to head back to our reality at the New Brown beach house, I try to pretend that what I'm feeling, this pit deep inside of me, isn't heartbreak.

Chapter 32

Chelsea and I spend most of the rest of the afternoon, after we get back from the Smiths' island, out on our beach shared with other families staying on this side of the cove. It's scarier on this side. George and Trisha don't let Phoebe play in the bare sand; they put down a blanket. They don't carry her into the water with them either, too scared of rogue splashes because this side of the cove is prone to hasty boat activity.

There's a tiredness about Chelsea, and I can't decide if it's a sadness of sorts, maybe left over from overhearing Edison's argument with the Duvals, or if she simply wishes that after Edison dropped us off, he didn't go rushing back to the Duval estate. She wears her heart on her sleeve—and her discontentment. The two of us are lying with our heads at opposite ends of a large tube we found in the garage and pumped up with a bike pump, our bodies parallel.

She's very quiet as she stares up at the blue, blue sky.

"I'm waiting for Edison to tell me he loves me," she says finally. "He's never said it."

Chelsea thinks I am safe. And I wish I were someone she could trust—a sister to share in her distress or at the very least sympathize with it.

"I'm waiting for him to tell me a lot of things, actually." She crosses her arms.

"Like what?"

"That wasn't the first time I've caught him fighting with Warren and Sepp. About a week after his mother died, I overheard them arguing about Edison leaving for school. I never asked him about it, but at the time, I thought the fight was because he didn't want to leave. But now it seems he can't wait to go back. It almost sounded like he didn't want to come to Cross Cove this summer at all. But that's not what he said to me. All year, he told me how great it would be, us together here. And now he apparently hates being here? He told me not to worry and had all these reasons to explain himself. Mostly he said it was in the heat of the moment and he's missing his mother a lot, so I can't ask him about it again."

"You can ask him about whatever you want."

She is quiet for a while. "I don't think I'm supposed to ask him. Whatever it is, I don't think he wants me to know. If he would just tell me he loves me, it would be easier. It would be the only thing that mattered."

I flip on my side so I'm facing her. It rocks the tube.

"Love doesn't erase everything. It doesn't fix everything. It doesn't make lying okay. It doesn't make unforgivable things forgivable."

She stares at me, a look of pity in her eyes. "Yes, it does, Maris."

"They're only words," I say, lying back down.

"But I need him to say it," she says. "He's everything I've ever wanted. And I'm not talking about the money."

"I know that, Chels."

A group of Jet Skiers pass, leaving behind waves, and the water tosses us back and forth. We stay still, without the energy or the capacity to try to steady ourselves, and not caring if we topple over.

We don't capsize. The waves temper out as quickly as they rushed us.

"I bet he'll tell you soon." I believe it. He isn't going to let her down.

"I hope so," she says.

There's a closeness I feel for her. A longing. I want all her dreams to come true. I don't want her to be disappointed. I don't want to ever be the one to disappoint her. And I get the feeling she wants all my dreams to come true, too. I can't help but wonder if it's possible for us to be close, the way she wants—if maybe we already are. Without even really trying. Just because.

"You know what might make you feel better?"

"What?"

"Ice cream." A sweet and simple solution, one that Chelsea will love.

"That place downtown?" She sits up on her elbows.

We paddle to shore with our hands, splashing each other as we go, laughing as we struggle to roll the tube up the shore. We bolt up the stairs of the deck, a race, excitement in our sprints. We hear the doorbell in the distance. I am hoping it's not Edison, but I can tell by the way her eyes light up that despite everything he hasn't told her, she's hoping it is.

George is standing at the front door. It's not Edison on the other side. It's two men in suits, with badges. And while everyone is surprised that it's me they're here to talk to, I am not.

Chapter 33

Luke Archaletta.

He's a bartender at a dive bar in a city a few hours north of Cross Cove. He's twenty-eight. He's someone's son. And now he's missing.

Detective Nevada and Detective Diya are sitting with George and me in the living room, sipping tea Trisha brought out with a tray of biscotti. I can tell she is nervous by the way her fingers clench around the tray as she sets it down on the coffee table. Chelsea and Trisha take Phoebe upstairs so they are out of the way, but I know they are listening.

The detectives are very kind, saying, "We're so sorry to bother you," acting both like they are only doing their job and also as though they think that questioning me will be meaningful to their investigation. It's a tactic, I think. I expect the first few questions they ask will be questions they already know the answers to.

They produce a photo of Luke Archaletta. He looks younger, smiling, all clean-cut in a blazer. Except his hair is lighter, much different from the dark mop he was sporting on the island and the last time I saw him in the alleyway. I don't say anything about the photo; I don't react. Detective Nevada places another photo of Archaletta in front of me, this one looking much more like the man I knew to be Archaletta, hair dark and scraggly.

They ask if I've ever seen this man before. I say yes and listen to the sound of the leather squeaking as George shifts uncomfortably in his chair.

According to the detectives, no one knew what he was doing at Cross Cove. His father didn't know he'd left town. And Luke Archaletta lived alone. His cell phone was found in his car, parked in its usual spot in front of his apartment, which was above the bar where he worked. The last call he placed was for somewhere called the Dragonfly Inn, located in Cross Cove on Main Street. But the owners of the inn don't recall ever seeing him.

The detectives don't know what he was doing in Cross Cove. But they do seem certain that he was here.

"A few witnesses saw him at the annual summer clambake," Detective Nevada says. "According to our timeline, you were probably one of the last people to see him that we have record of."

I know they can't really prove that.

At my silence, Detective Diya takes a notepad out of his shirt pocket and flips through it. "We have an eyewitness who claims he saw you and the missing person talking behind the Big Scoop Ice Cream Parlor." He stops fumbling with the pages. "Luke Archaletta isn't his real name, but that's the name you know, isn't it?"

"He never told me his name."

"So you have spoken to him?"

I try to gauge how I should appear right now. Irritated or off put or relieved. Mostly, I am curious how they knew to come here, how they found me when I've never vacationed here before. "Someone identified me?"

"Relax," Detective Diya says. "It's our job to track down people flagged by eyewitnesses." They are both quiet then, waiting for me to continue—waiting to see if I'll change the subject again. I wonder if this made them suspicious.

"He was very drunk when he talked to me," I say. "He came up to me out of nowhere, and I couldn't even understand what he was trying to say to me." A lie, but mixed in with enough of the truth that it won't be called into question because I'm sure the other eyewitnesses noticed Archaletta swaying as he walked.

"And in the alley, at the clambake, was the only time you'd ever come into contact with the missing person?" Detective Diya taps the photo in front of me. "This man."

I look down, hearing the sounds of Detective Nevada's pen scribbling and of George cracking his knuckles.

I think of Edison on the island, so sure he was about to die. I think of that middle-of-the-night swim in the ocean and his speedboat that will never be fast enough. I think about his dead mother and all that she wanted for him. He told me to stop saving him. But he also admitted that I was in fact saving him.

"Yes," I say.

The next question they ask is completely predictable. "What were you doing in the alleyway behind the ice cream parlor?"

"I was following a cat." There's a certain rush that comes with lying. I think a lot of people probably don't like it—the racing heart, the sweaty palms, the fear of being caught. These are the things that made lying worth it for me. All that buildup and anticipation wondering if you'll get away with it.

No one questions this even if they think it's strange. The detectives leave, slipping me their cards, telling me to call them if I think of anything else, and they thank us for our time.

Chelsea and Trisha come down the stairs the second the front door closes, demanding to hear the story from George and me, despite them having heard for themselves through these thin walls.

"I thought you hated cats," Chelsea says after we've rehashed it.

"No, I don't—I don't hate them." Except she's right. "Why do you think that?"

"At Christmas, you said you didn't go near them after one scratched you when you were fourteen."

"You remember that?"

"It was only a few months ago." Back then, I said very few things to her. I can't recall anything we talked about, only that I avoided her. I wonder if George remembers the day I decided I hated cats. He was out of town when the neighbor's cat scratched me, but he heard about it when he got home. I had an obnoxious blue bandage on, and I made him look at the red lines carved into my skin.

"I felt bad for this cat. He looked hungry." This time, she believes me.

Chapter 34

Edison comes over for dinner that night. I listen from my room as the New Browns greet him; so much excitement. He reminisces with Chelsea about the Smiths' island, the parasailing, the exquisite food, while George and Trisha ooh and aah at the descriptions.

It's dusk when I finally go downstairs, the itch to see Edison getting stronger. I don't see him. The New Browns are together in the kitchen. The windows are framing a pink sky, and the room is lit up, giving everyone's skin an otherworldly flush. A family, smiling and laughing in the hue of the sun's rays.

Edison emerges from the bathroom off the living room and notices me before they do. I feel embarrassed, which I didn't expect—like he not only knows how I lied to the detectives for him but he also knows why I did it and how I feel about him. He told me to stop saving him. What if he thinks it's pathetic, the way I can't help it?

He breaks out a classic Edison smile and announces to the New Browns, "There she is," and they all look up with bright faces like they are happy to see me. They beckon Edison and me into the kitchen.

George is seasoning and pounding the ground beef, shaping it, grilling it. Chelsea and Trisha are chopping and stirring and saying, "We need more salt." George is named the official can opener. Edison and I are the taste testers. Trisha wipes the stray hairs out of her face as she leans over a stove that's on full throttle with boiling and steaming pots. Phoebe laughs in her high chair. Edison moves around the kitchen. "This looks amazing, smells amazing!" His small talk is superficial, but it's what they all want. He is tasting the mashed potatoes. He is seasoning the green beans. He is full of compliments and jokes. He brings up the party in Maine that the Duvals are taking us to next week, both building it up and talking it down—*It'll be epic, but these parties are way over the top; the guest list is phenomenal, but it's so crowded*—and this gets Trisha and Chelsea on a tangent wondering what they should wear. Edison promises he'll be able to help, promises they'll be stunning no matter what—so many promises rolling off his tongue.

When it's all ready, we pass around the food. We talk over the sound of chewing and silverware clanging against plates and Phoebe's shrieking with her small baby voice. The food is delicious. It's better because we made it. I wonder if this is what it's like all the time, being a part of the New Browns, and if I'll ever get used to it, if I'll ever forget how different it is from the life I've had with George before.

When our plates are nearly empty, we talk about our dreams.

"Paris," Chelsea says. "I want to stand in the shadow of the Eiffel Tower and stare up at it, straining to see the top, craning my neck, almost falling over backward—being so startled at its size . . . that's what I dream about. Seeing this thing that's so overwhelmingly large and marvelous."

When she describes it like that, it becomes my dream, too.

"I'll take you sometime," Edison says, reaching for her hand, his voice as soft as a pillow. Just like that, he's hijacked the dream.

"I'd like to go to Paris," Trisha pipes up.

"Then you'll come, too!" Edison beams a smile at her.

"And after Paris," Trisha says, "how about we head farther east? I dream of Dubai—"

"You're certainly not going without me," George says, a twinkle in his eye. "And while we're moving east: Thailand, we must go to Thailand."

"Ah yes—I dream of those beaches." Edison lifts his glass of iced tea and clinks it with George's glass of red wine.

"And then to Australia!" There are stars in Chelsea's eyes, fireworks in her voice.

"Ah yes, ah!" George is so excited he's been reduced to sighs. "And for all this travel, I wish for a sabbatical."

The near rhyme makes us all crack up with easy, what-the-hell laughter, triggered by anything, like a trap waiting to be set off by the wind. Even Phoebe is squealing wildly, trying to keep up. Can I stay here like this, having fun with them, even with Edison's hand on the back of her chair, even though I can't stop being mad at George, even as Chelsea lives in some kind of make-believe world where no one was left behind when she got her wish for the perfect dad?

"What do you wish for, Maris?" I feel George's hand on my shoulder; it tenses the moment the question mark is final, and lingers, nervous and unsure, clutching to keep me in the moment, make sure I know that things are going well and if I pop out of this picture of perfection, the colors will swirl together and everything will turn brown. He's afraid of my wishes, I think. And he's right to be.

Edison moves in his chair, making a loud creaking sound, and I stare at him. He really is beautiful.

"I wish for no more rain the rest of our vacation," I say.

George exhales, Trisha smiles, and Chelsea is nodding in agreement.

"But where do you want to go?" Chelsea asks. "You're the only one who didn't name a place." My eyes are magnets to Edison's. He didn't pick a place either. He's only the wish-granter, a genie, and the New Brown Family is lucky enough to possess the lamp. They think he must have no use for wishes.

"If you could go anywhere . . . ," Trish encourages.

"To the moon," I say, thinking of that night on the lot with the half-built house and how the sky was so stunning and vast.

"Make it Mars," Edison says, and everyone's silence turns into crisp laughter.

Chelsea's cheeks turn pink, flushed from being held in a smile for so long. I wish I could look at George and see a hero instead of a disappointment. I wish I'd met Edison's mother. I want to be the one he feels forever connected to for knowing his past. I even want those too-short designer dresses he buys for her. I want everything Chelsea has.

We get up to put our dishes away, and after starting the dishwasher, Chelsea pulls Edison out on the screened porch. I can

194 • Alexis Bass

hear the faint sounds of laughter, then silence. In the quiet, I know they must be kissing.

It's different this time, the way I'm feeling. This isn't just obsession. It's madness. It's hopelessness. It's corroding me. Jealousy is a sickness, but this feels rotting. I excuse myself and walk quickly upstairs, pushing open the window to my bedroom, closing my eyes against the breeze. It makes me miss Trevor and the way we both owed each other nothing because we were bound together by our selfishness. A sadness settles over me knowing I could never go back to that now, that it would never be satisfying again. The same way I can't go back to telling myself that George wanted to be happy with my mother and me, now that I've see how George acts with the New Browns, how easy it is for him to be thoughtful and the kind of father I always dreamed he would be.

I don't know how much time has passed when they start calling for me. The pie is ready to serve.

The New Browns are divvying out slices, laughing about who gets the biggest piece and how much whipped cream to use. They start to reminisce. They go on and on about something I wasn't there for, something I won't, can't, will never understand. All these precious pieces of their lives that thrive without me. I'm quiet this time when I join them, and I stay that way as we eat dessert.

Edison does catch me alone, like I'd hoped he would, when it's the two of us in the house, the last ones outside to see the fireworks, his hands full of extra chairs, mine carrying the sodas. I don't know what to say to him or if there's anything worth saying. I protected him, and maybe he won't know; maybe he shouldn't. Maybe he does, and is that somehow worse, after he'd said I should stop?

"Chelsea told me about the detectives," he says, his eyes looking out the window, watching the New Browns as they walk to the beach. I feel panic rise in my chest, because maybe he'll think that I told them the truth; maybe he'll be mad. But then he says, "Thank you."

I thought I would be afraid of this, too—of him knowing what I did for him, even when he'd told me not to, even when he'd told me the reason he'd picked Chelsea and the reason he wanted to stop having any more secrets between us. But right now, I feel light with relief, a surge of hope because maybe he knows now that there are things he can trust with me that he can't trust with anyone else. Suddenly, I don't care about how big my lie really is, if he knows where Archaletta is or what happened to him.

The fireworks are starting, and Chelsea is waving at us from the sand.

I want him to understand that I am safe, that I can hold all his secrets and that I want to.

"There wasn't any poker game," I tell him so he'll know that there are things I already figured out about him, that he can't lie to me anyway.

He bows his head and adjusts the chairs in his hands; he opens the door but he doesn't move to go through it.

"Meet me tonight," he says, and the door falls closed behind him and he's walking quickly down the stairs and through the brush.

On the beach, we set up the chairs, but no one sits in them. The New Browns are too elated from the evening, ripe with delight. Even Phoebe insists on kicking her legs as George bounces her up and down.

We spend the next fifteen minutes standing in the rough sand, staring at the colorful explosions in the sky.

Chapter 35

The half-built house is dark when I arrive a little before midnight, but the front door is ajar. When I walk in, I see light coming from around the corner. He has two lanterns set up, one on the floor, one on the counter in the kitchen, where it juts out to form a breakfast bar. A few of those small white use-in-case-of-emergency candles are scattered on the counter, dripping wax onto the granite.

Edison is leaning forward, peeling the dried wax from the counter.

"You're going to tell me the truth?" I ask. "The reason I lied? The truth about what happened on the island?"

He takes a large breath and stands up straight when I walk over to the opposite side of the counter.

I wait to see if he'll be honest with me at last.

"They weren't supposed to know I was there," he says. "I was there because I was spying on them. They weren't supposed to see me. That's why my boat was hidden."

"Who are they?"

"I don't know." He continues quickly, knowing that answer wouldn't be enough. "I mean, I didn't know who they were that day on the island. There were people making threats, so I asked to meet them. I was only trying to see who they were. But they saw me and . . ." He pauses to catch his breath. "Luckily, you did, too."

I have more questions; does he know what happened to Luke Archaletta, does he know he was a criminal; what was he saying to threaten Edison—a protective nature is suddenly conjured in me as I remember how he could barely walk, barely talk. But across the counter, Edison is looking at me like he's grateful, like he's about to say something else, something more meaningful than thank you, because now he is finally admitting the danger he was in on the island. He doesn't say anything, but he moves slowly from around the counter, toward me. My heart starts to race as he gets closer. "You take a lot of risks," he says. "That day on the island, jumping into the ocean that night. Why is this?"

He's close enough to touch now, and I don't remember the last time I wanted someone this intensely, if I ever have. "You're one to talk." All I can think about is how badly I want this gap between us to disappear.

"Okay, sure." He smiles. "But it seems different for you. It's like you go looking for it."

Every time he says something that makes it evident he can see through me, I feel all at once vulnerable and exposed, but in a way that doesn't make me feel ashamed. I want him to see more, to see all of it, all of me. "I'm afraid of regret," I say.

"That's all?"

"What do you mean, that's all?" I hold my breath. He's so close that when I look up at him, I have to lift my chin slightly to see his eyes.

"But it goes both ways," he says. "You can regret doing something as much as you can regret doing nothing."

I meet his eyes and watch as his gaze travels down to my lips.

"Not in my experience," I say.

He puts his hands on my face and studies me. I grip his sides, the only way to hold myself up, because I know his kiss is coming, and I can already tell this is the kind of kiss you can never be ready for.

It's not like the first time his lips were against mine, brief and sudden, surprising and sneaky—this kiss has been caged up, screaming at us for days, begging to be let out, and now it floods us. My hands travel to his hair, and his find their way around my waist.

"This makes things complicated," he says quietly, not letting go of me.

But I'm shaking my head. "Things were already complicated," I say, really thinking, *Things were worse before, when you kept me out.* I lean forward and put my mouth against his, and he must be able to feel the urgency in my lips because he kisses me back the same way—like the world is ending, like we'll be dead tomorrow, like this is all we'll ever have.

It's not the right thing to do, kissing him like this when he still belongs to Chelsea. But it feels like the only thing we can do, as though us being together like this is our sole inevitability.

We leave when the candles have burned out. He walks me to the street, giving me one last kiss before I go. I turn to him and say, "Hey, Edison, who threatened you?" *There were people making threats*, was all he said.

He smiles at me like I haven't even caught him off guard, but maybe he likes that I tried. "No one."

My whole body hums as I walk back to the New Browns' beach house.

That day at the fortune-teller's room, when I listened from the other side of the bathroom door, I heard her talking to a woman who thought she was dying. "There are red dots on my legs," the woman said. "It has to mean something." The fortune-teller didn't ask to see her legs; she didn't ask if the woman had been to the doctor—she was supposed to know these things after all. She waited a long time before she responded, but when she finally did, her voice was firm. "Do whatever it takes to feel completely alive," she said. And that was all the woman needed to know; so that was the end of the session.

Chapter 36

We go to the Duvals' beach the next day, after Edison comes over bringing the best almond croissants and French roast coffee. There's not a cloud in sight, and the weather is hotter than it's been all summer. The water feels like heaven.

I like that when Edison yawns, I'm part of the reason. I like that when he leans back on the dock to let himself dry off, really relaxing, it's because he can rest assured knowing I've covered for him. I like that he'll casually brush against me as he walks to the food tray. I like that when he looks anxious and glances at me, I know it's because he's impatient for the next time the two of us can meet alone.

I like him with me in the shadows and everyone around us in the dark.

Chelsea is completely herself, all happiness and generosity. She is the only thing that ruins this for me. But I try to justify it. *You stole George from me*, I think, trying to dampen the guilt I feel every time she beams at Edison, every time she puts sunscreen on my back or reminds me that we could have inside jokes if we wanted to, bringing up the day we went parasailing as we stand with the water up to our necks in the ocean.

I swim back to shore and take out the Jet Ski again, zooming away from her as she watches with her hand against the sun. I weave around to the back side of the cove, where I am out of the way of the passing boats but can still see the whole scene happening at North Point Beach and the lighthouse. Sepp rounds the corner and pulls up beside me.

He turns off his Jet Ski so he is floating like I am.

"It's fucking hot out," he says, leaning over to splash his legs with water. Katherine Ellis didn't join us on the beach today, and while Sepp didn't get completely smashed, there's something looser about him. He curses. If he's not interested in something, he ignores it, politeness be damned. He's more carefree; he's lighter. He's more himself.

"I don't think you really like Kath," I say.

"Oh no?" He laughs. "I like Kath a lot, actually," he says, undoing his life vest and letting it fall open. He rolls his shoulders. "She's one of the good ones."

I groan a little at this comment, and he chuckles.

"But you're not *you* when you're around her."

"I know—I'm better."

"But you're lying to yourself and to her. You don't do what you want when she's around. You don't let her see you get drunk. You don't let her see that your humor is sort of dark. You even stand differently, and you definitely talk differently."

"You mean because I speak French?"

He laughs, and I frown, since it is very clear he is laughing at me.

"Oh, come on," he says. "You're projecting your feelings about Edison and Chelsea. This is very textbook, Maris, and you should be ashamed to be so transparent."

This shocks me, and my mouth flies open, though I guess it shouldn't since he did warn me that Edison told him everything. I kick water at him, but the splash doesn't quite reach him.

"Don't be mad," he says. "There might be some things too personal for Eddy to share, but I haven't come across anything yet."

"So now you're judging me—that's great."

"Me? Never. Glass houses, Maris. Glass houses." He pushes his hair back from his eyes. "It does seem like it could potentially be a big mess, though."

"It won't." I shake my head, maybe too quickly to really be believable. "Plus, it doesn't matter. After the summer, I'm going back to Phoenix and he goes back to school, and he'll keep seeing Chelsea because that's who he wants to end up with, and everything will go back to normal."

"Now who's lying to herself?" He starts his Jet Ski and speeds off, tipping his head back to laugh. "And way too slow!" he shouts, turning to see if I've decided to chase after him. Of course I have.

The New Browns and I return to our side of the cove midafternoon. The Duvals are having dinner downtown with friends, and sometime after they are done, Chelsea, Trisha, and I are to meet Edison and Karen at a boutique to try on dresses for the party in Maine.

The wait stretches on after we eat, too early at six, since the Duvals' reservations probably aren't until seven thirty, which is the time we ate dinner with them on their grotto. The TV is on, but the jokes and the laugh track are only background noise, as no one is watching it. Chelsea is constantly checking her phone. Trisha keeps reapplying her lipstick. George sighs whenever he looks at his watch.

"Should we play dominoes while we wait?" I ask. A New Brown pastime. But their hesitation tells me they are more interested in the ritual of waiting, letting their patience stretch and snap.

I go into my room and change into shorts and a tank top and my running shoes.

"Do you have time to go for a run?" Chelsea asks, glancing at her phone again.

It's almost eight. The Duvals have probably just finished their salads, ordered their second round of drinks. The New Browns are happy to let life revolve around the Duvals, and I get it, how much fun they provide, and the money, what it can buy, what it gives us, and how it's improved our summer. But I can't stay inside with them anymore, waiting for Edison to summon us downtown.

"I won't be gone long," I say. They let me go without another word.

Chapter 37

I take a different route on my run. This time, after the hill behind the New Brown beach house, past the half-built house, past the Victorian mansion on the corner, I take the road to the left that carries me out of the residential area and toward the downtown strip. This road is lined with tall, overgrown grass and large trees on either side. There is a more direct path from the New Brown beach house to downtown, a road that is nicely paved and land-scaped. But according to the map, this direction not only has less traffic, it also has a better view from the top, before the decline toward downtown.

The neighborhood is well behind me and out of sight. I'm al-most halfway up the hill, when I see two figures coming in the opposite direction. I recognize them only by their silhouettes in the dim evening light, not only because of their height difference but because they've been there in the back of my mind since I saw them on the island, and since I saw them in the conference room at the Duvals' office.

I'm debating running the other way, but something about them seems different. They do not look rough, like they did on the island and at the Duval office. Now they are matching in dark jackets and unmarked black hats. They walk with confidence and good posture. They're still several feet away from me when they make a sharp turn straight into the row of billowing trees along the other side, and they disappear into a cloud of darkness. I take a few more strides forward, until I reach the long tree that's grown randomly on my side of the road, and hide in the shadow of its thick trunk.

A few seconds later, a light appears, the glow coming from the open doors of an SUV. The two of them glance around, like they are making sure the coast is clear. Then they pull off their jackets to reveal white button-down shirts with dark red vests. They talk quietly as they remove their vests. The taller one takes off his white shirt entirely, while the shorter one only undoes the top few buttons. Next, they both remove their belts and swap them with holsters. I crouch lower into the shadows as I watch them slide their guns in place and put on their jackets.

They climb into the SUV and after a few minutes, its engine starts, its lights come on, and it drives out of the trees and down the hill. The windows are tinted and the license plate is unmarked.

Trevor and I used to be able to spot cops disguised as civilians, about to raid a bar for underage drinking, a mile away. They were always the guys dressed in colorful shirts, like they were staged to appear carefree. Their shoes usually gave them away—practical and too new. They also held themselves a certain way: they were too confident, they were too observant, they stood up too straight, establishing a sort of dominance. The argument was they weren't necessarily trying to hide. But they did take some time to settle in before they brought out their badges and started approaching people, and in that time, they always seemed to give themselves away to us, the people who knew to look out for them.

That's what I'm thinking as I continue on my run, how I wonder what Trevor would make of what I saw. And if that's what I should believe, even if it doesn't make any sense. Because if they were the police, what were they doing with Archaletta that day? And if they were undercover, what does that mean for Edison and Sepp and the disappearance of Archaletta? What does it mean for me, since I lied?

I stay on the path, follow it downtown, too keyed up to even bother stopping to admire the view at the top of the hill. The road winds parallel with Main Street, and I take it, jogging along the back sides of restaurants and bars and shops, on this road that's only use now is for entrances to parking lots or to get to the freeway without the hassle of Main Street traffic. A couple servers come outside to smoke, a boy and a girl, both wearing white shirts with dark red vests and black pants. I cut right, off the road, and wander down the strip, all lit up, peering in windows, all around me the sounds of conversations and laughing, the air thick with the scent of sizzling butter from the restaurants and the smell of salt from the ocean. All the fancier, five-star restaurants have servers in nearly the same uniform. Crisp white shirt, dark red vest; crisp white shirt, black vest; crisp white shirt, hunter green vest.

Wearing that would help them blend in down here.

The problem is both undercover cops and criminals have cause for hiding in plain sight.

"Maris, Maris!"

I swivel around to see Chelsea waving at me. She's with Trisha and the elation on her face would indicate that Edison has summoned them down here.

"We couldn't get a hold of you, but you're here now—it's perfect timing."

"Perfect timing," I say as she rushes toward me.

The three of us walk toward Faye's Boutique. The confusion of what I saw is on a loop in my mind, making everything else faded and fuzzy, as it sinks in with every step I take and I feel the full burden of what it could mean if undercover officers were on the island and in the Duval offices.

As we enter the boutique, I am almost as anxious as Chelsea to see him. Except underneath my nerves, there is that layer of anger that's been set on fire since the last time I saw Edison. There's still so much he's keeping from me. And I don't know what he knows, or what he doesn't, or what else he's hiding, but it's too late, because I've already lied for him. I lied for him the way I would lie for Trevor, but with Trevor at least I knew the entirety of what I was helping to cover up.

This feeling of unease only worsens when he greets us, charming and welcoming as ever, the way everyone likes him.

Chapter 38

Faye McMann is a close personal friend of the Duvals, according to Edison, which is why she's invited us to her boutique after hours to peruse her collection for the party in Maine this weekend. Faye isn't there; she's in Milan, *of course*, but we are greeted by her favorite sales associates and personal stylists and tailors, according to Edison. They have a cheese-and-charcuterie board set out for us as well as champagne.

Despite the story of Faye doing this favor for the Duvals, I think it's really their subtle way of making sure that we're properly dressed for the party—letting us know that even our most formal formalwear won't be acceptable for this party, where gowns and tuxedos are the expected attire. The shop has white floors and walls and is impossibly stark. There are rows and rows of dresses, black and white and red and pink, some sparkly, some silky, some long, some short. Too many dresses to choose from. With Chelsea's indecision, we may be here all night.

Karen has already begun and is standing in a long navy gown on the fitting platform in the dressing area, admiring herself in the full-length mirrors hitting her from all sides. Sepp is there, too, toting his own bottle of champagne, serving himself whenever his glass runs low. He helps Edison, whose job after we've picked out our dresses is to snap photos of us in our favorites to send to George, so his opinion counts even though he stayed behind to be with Phoebe.

I try on a red silk dress for fun, since I've already decided on the long black dress with a subtle ruffle around the neckline and pockets in the folds at the waist. I peek out from behind the curtain and shake the drapery of the dressing room next to mine.

"Chelsea? Can you help me with this zipper?"

There's no answer. The whole dressing area is empty. I hear the sound of someone clearing their throat. Sepp is leaned against the wall on the opposite end of the room.

"Karen went to the counter to pick out jewelry. They all followed. We've lost them to shiny objects. But I can help you with your dress."

I step out from my dressing room and wait as Sepp sets down his champagne bottle and glass. I hold my dress against me as he slowly zips it up in the back. He offers his hand to walk me toward the center of the dressing area and onto the fitting platform.

"I don't like it," he says.

"Tell me what you really think," I say.

"It's too delicate. And definitely too red."

"It fits well," I say, letting my hands glide down my sides. He watches me but is quick to look away.

"Silk reminds me of bedsheets," he says, walking over to retrieve his bottle and glass. He stops by the tray to get a glass for me and starts pouring.

"I'm not supposed to drink while I wear the merchandise."

He brings me a full glass anyway. "I won't tell."

I take a slow sip, careful not to spill. Sepp takes one long drink and nearly finishes his glass. I like Sepp like this, loose and predictable. Unsuspecting.

"Remember the night we were all at the Duval offices?"

He shrugs his left shoulder. "It wasn't that long ago, was it?"

"The last time we had champagne together?"

"Did anyone actually get to drink any of that champagne? It sprayed everywhere. My hangover the next morning was very clearly a tequila hangover."

"What were we celebrating again?"

He holds up his half-empty bottle and his almost-empty glass. "When are we ever not celebrating?"

I pause to take another sip. "Who were those guys you met with that day? I saw them through the glass doors. They looked too young to be important."

"Hey, they're older than I am, and I'm pretty fucking important."

"They were important enough to spray champagne. Drink half a bottle of tequila."

"They weren't that important," he says. "They only thought they were. Such big heads on those guys."

"Takes one to know one," I joke.

Sepp doesn't laugh; he's too busy tipping back his head, polishing off his glass.

"So who are they?" I say.

"Just a couple of assholes looking for their lucky break." He pours himself another glass, almost overfilling it, catching it right in time. "Why?"

I shrug. If Edison told Sepp about meeting me behind Chelsea's back, did he also tell him that I was there on the island? Sepp watches me carefully now, like he is still waiting for a proper answer.

"Will you help me out of this?" I step off the platform and push aside my hair, giving Sepp access to the zipper.

"If I had a nickel for every time someone asked me that."

I roll my eyes as he frees his hands and lets down the zipper.

Edison enters the dressing area carrying an assortment of hangers, holding them high so the dresses don't drag on the floor. His eyes widen for a moment at Sepp standing so close to me, my bare back peeking out from the opening in the dress. Sepp walks over to help him untangle some of the hangers and spread them out in Chelsea's and Trisha's dressing rooms.

I disappear behind my curtain to take off the dress. There's a knock on the wall. I clutch the dress to keep the front from falling and pull back the curtain an inch.

Edison holds out a long silvery dress. "Chelsea saw this one and thought of you."

I take the hanger from him and let the dress dangle in front of me to get a better look at it.

"Are you sure?" This dress is stunning. It is sparkly without being overstated. It's brilliant in the way it catches the lighting. It's made of material that looks heavy but feels lightweight. Why wouldn't she want this one for herself? Why would she see something this beautiful and think it belonged on me?

He nods. "She said she thought it was perfect for you."

I am still too stunned to speak.

"It's going to look great," he says, giving me a small smile with Edison's charm behind it before he shuts the curtain.

"That's the one!" Sepp yells when I come out wearing the dress. Trisha and Chelsea make a big fuss, clapping, having me twirl, taking dozens of photos for George. Chelsea waves over one of the sales associates and asks her to bring out shoes that will go with the dress.

"What dress are you getting?" I ask her.

"I can't decide," she says. "Surprise, surprise." She shows me the three she is debating between, and I have her try them on again. I ask the sales associates to get her shoes. I clap when she comes out, guilt surging inside me as I help her weigh her options, suggest hairstyles to go with each dress, ask her which shoes she prefers. Acting like a sister doesn't come natural to me the way it does to her. And being kind to her now feels incredibly deceiving. I don't like this kind of lying.

When we leave, Edison hugs each of us goodbye. He lingers a little in front of me, scanning my face like he's searching for something. I wonder if he can tell that I'm keeping something from him. Or if he's so used to holding a veil over the truth that he doesn't know to look for lies in other people.

Chapter 39

The Duvals send a car in the morning to pick us up and take us to their private jet. Unsurprisingly, there is a runway for private planes not too far outside of Cross Cove. The car pulls up right next to the plane on the runway, and the Duval staff loads our luggage.

The Duvals are already settled in, along with the nanny they hired to stay with Phoebe during the party, Rosie, from London. "Like Mary Poppins," Sepp jokes, not caring that no one laughs until Rosie does, giving us all permission. George and Trisha warm to her and her vast knowledge of sleep training and her fifteen years as a nanny to the duke of some European country I've never heard of, and her last ten years spent with a family in Zurich that relocated to New York, and her degree in childhood development from Kingston University.

It's a short ride, barely an hour. Up and then down. Fast and full of luxury. Large leather seats that recline with extended foot-rests. A full drink cart with finger foods I can't pronounce. I enjoy it, all this fuss. Chelsea has a glass of champagne and turns so giggly Trisha gives her a stern look. It makes her sit up straighter, and a worried look spreads across her face, like she thinks she might have embarrassed herself or been as obnoxious as Sepp without having the privilege that comes with being Sepp. I smile at her, and so does Edison, a subtle reassurance, but the glow doesn't return to her face until George winks at her and mouths something that I can't make out but has Chelsea looking like herself again, because George knows exactly what to say to make her feel better.

There are two limos waiting for us when we land, one to take me and the New Browns and Rosie to our cottage, the other for the Duvals and Edison. The Hanover Estate is large and vast and full of private residences. Warren explains that a limo will pick us up in a few hours to take us to the location of the party.

The limo drives us through what looks like a narrow country road, except we glide smoothly over it like it's freshly paved. We arrive at our cottage, with a vaulted ceiling and gas fireplace, and enough rooms for us all to have our own, even Rosie, who will be staying across from Phoebe's room, where there is already a crib and a changing table and shelves full of picture books. Our cottage is backed up against a forest, but we are still high enough to see the view of trees that move into a valley that stretches for miles. It's decorated like a rustic cabin, full of plaid and exposed wood.

Chelsea and I put on our makeup and take turns curling each other's hair before we get dressed.

There's an undercurrent of excitement running through me, as we talk about the possibilities of the night, what the party might be like. We try to imagine it; we don't know where to begin. The limo picks us up right when the sun starts to go down. Phoebe is already asleep when we leave. Our limo driver is wearing a white mask. We all stop in our tracks when we see him, thinking it's bizarre, but then he lets us know that our masks for the masquerade are inside the limo, courtesy of the Duvals.

"I had no idea it was a masquerade," Trisha says enthusiastically.

This is an adventure first and foremost. The anticipation builds within me, and I am as excited as Chelsea.

We sort through the masks. George's is the most obvious. A black mask to go with his tuxedo. Chelsea chooses the lavender mask matching her dress, with a white flower stemming off the right side. Trisha opts for the mask made of white lace, and the metallic lace mask is for me. Just like that, we are all in costume. With our faces hidden, we could be anyone.

We ride down a smooth path barely wide enough for two cars. The hedges are right up against the left windows for the beginning part of the trip. And soon, we are careening through a plush green valley, with tall and thick oak trees that make outlines against the fading sky. We move through an area thick with trees, casting a dark shadow over us.

Light appears ahead, streaming from the towering house in front of us. It's expansive, with large columns and shutters, standing atop an enormous brick staircase.

We arrive at the same time as another limo, and the Duvals' limo is directly ahead of ours. They are waiting for us in their matching black suits with matching black masks. Karen's dress is long and gold; her mask is made of thread so thin it looks like little golden wires.

Edison takes Chelsea's arm, and Sepp offers me his.

There is a delicious thudding in my chest, a fluttering in my stomach, as we finally move up the stairs, and I get closer to finding out where we are going.

Chapter 40

The security to get into this party is intense. We are funneled through a line, bumped up a bit by one of the men in maroon working the door, seeing Warren and understanding who he is enough to let him skip ahead of the line, but all the same, we must show ID, get checked off two lists, have our handbags searched, and have a metal detector wand scan our bodies. The women behind us talk about how the entering procedures are a pain but that this isn't nearly as bad as attending an event at the White House. Her friend counters, saying the royal wedding was much more of a hassle. The woman adds, "At least we know it's safe here."

Inside, the foyer is grand with mountain-high ceilings and

creamy marble floors and a chandelier that's made of small slices of crystal. It is as crowded as Edison said it would be. There are so many black suits. So many dresses that sparkle. Everyone's faces are half-covered, decorated in masks to match their clothing.

I almost fall backward, looking up at a floor-to-ceiling Renaissance painting of an angel and a man wrapped in an embrace. It's not only exquisite, it's large and looming—overwhelming in its beauty.

Sepp sighs. "You're easily impressed."

He smiles at a group of passing girls dressed up in red, white, and blue, shiny like a firework. They walk right past Sepp to gush over the painting. "My best feature is half-covered," he says, gesturing to his face, aware that I witnessed the subtle rejection.

"So take it off."

He laughs at me like I've said the most ridiculous thing.

An orchestra plays music with foreboding undertones, music for ambiance, not for dancing. The lights are turned low. All the rooms are open in this house and nothing is off-limits, and behind the different doors are a variety of personal delights, from magicians to tarot card readings. Some of the rooms look like they are out of an art gallery, with ropes to keep people from touching the paintings. There are many people, too many to keep track of, and I notice the party guests are not greeting each other mindlessly. No nodding to be polite, waving and smiling from across the room. Every interaction is with intent, because no one knows who anyone else is with these masks, unless they know who they're looking for. I can spot Sepp in the crowd, the way he stands, the golden mess of his hair, Karen flashy in her dress, Trisha and George, who always have their arms linked and are always laughing too hard, smiling too wide, and Edison, who stands too tall and is forever straightening his collar, messing with his hair. He hardly leaves Chelsea's side. She is easy to place because of her smile and the handsome man on her arm.

"And how did you two meet?" is the standard question Chelsea and Edison get lobbed anytime someone learns they are a couple. It's strange to me that the people the Duvals can recognize even with their masks on are still perfectly happy to make small talk with us, the masked acquaintances. It's no mystery why George looks as happy here as he did on his wedding day. Simply being here, we are presumed to be important.

Edison and Chelsea have an answer ready, one that makes people put their hands over their hearts and sigh and smile and wish they were young and in love again.

"We were in the same line at a café getting coffee. I noticed her right away."

"And I thought he was so cute, but I am so shy."

"We were at the registers at the same time, next to each other, and we both ordered a chocolate croissant."

"The cashiers were so funny! Mine was saying I should have it, and Edison's said he should have it. And finally it was decided that Edison technically ordered it first. They offered me a complimentary regular croissant, which is not the same at all. I was ready to storm out of there."

"She must've thought I was such a jerk, taking that chocolate croissant. But there was only one left."

"But then he caught up to me as I was leaving; he apologized and said he wished he'd been smoother with his plan but that that had been his way of buying me the chocolate croissant. And then he asked if I'd like to sit with him. We talked for three hours straight and made plans to have dinner the next night."

It's cute, and sort of clumsy, with that requisite sweetness that comes with meetings that didn't go as planned on the first attempt and the romantic gestures that make up for it.

The three of us wander the party, we get too full on lobster fra diavolo and baklava, and later, as we stand with a group clapping as a magician makes a stack of cards disappear into a glass of water, Sepp taps my shoulder.

"Boring," he says, lending me his arm and leading me out of the room.

Sepp waves down a passing caterer, grabbing a martini off his tray. He offers me the toothpick full of olives, and I take it.

"Isn't this supposed to be the best part?"

Sepp says, "I never eat the garnish."

"Of course not; that would be tacky." We smile at each other as I bite off one of the olives.

"I know you think I'm a pretentious asshole."

"More like an incorrigible bastard."

"And that you don't understand my relationship with Kath, or what Edison is doing with Chelsea."

"Isn't the answer to all these questions simply that you and Edison are both great at lying to yourselves about what you really want? You can't reconcile what you actually want with what you think you should want." I eat another olive. "It's so textbook, Sepp; you should be ashamed."

He taps me on the nose. "Nothing is ever that simple. Though it'd be nice if it were." He swirls his martini and hesitates before he takes another sip. "But some people can be scared away. And you have to be careful."

"Sepp, you're not as scary as you think you are. And why do you want someone who scares so easily?" But I know he means that someone could be scared off by his drinking and cursing, his ego and his dark sense of humor, thinking these traits are red flags that make him undesirable.

"I don't know—some people are worth it." His comment is flippant, but his face drops like he realizes immediately he said the wrong thing and that I took his comment and applied it to Chelsea, implying Edison feels she is worth it, but doesn't feel like that about me. "Maris, that's not what I meant."

"It's fine," I lie.

He shakes his head. "Not all of us can be with whoever we want." He shrugs, and there is a heavy sadness to him lurking there even as he tries to pass it off.

I want him to tell me what he knows, confirm that I was important enough for Edison to tell him about. But I am not one of the good ones, and that is evidenced in the fact that I want Edison even though it would hurt Chelsea, that I am determined not to care about sneaking around, and I let the secret of it thrill me. I know he's lying to me and to her, and that doesn't stop me either. I enjoyed how much I didn't care with Trevor, so the pain of what he did could somehow never really reach me. It's not the case with Edison. I feel every blow with him. But it is a relief to feel something.

"Maybe I'm as bad as both of you."

He stops and turns toward me, sighing and letting his shoulders drop. "Is this a party or a pity party?"

I laugh.

We meander into another room with walls covered in paintings. Katherine Ellis stands with her father and brother. The Ellis men are tall with silver masks to match their ties. Kath notices Sepp and excuses herself. She joins us behind a velvet rope, where we are pretending to admire a painting of angels whispering to each other in heaven.

"That's one of my favorites," she says. She's wearing a pink sleeveless gown and a mask made of the same material.

"I'm terrible with art," says Sepp. "But I know something beautiful when I see it." He, of course, is staring at her and not the painting when he says this.

She laughs, placing her hand lightly on his shoulder.

"Everyone here looks the same to me all dressed up with their faces covered," Sepp says. "But my eyes found you the moment I walked in the room."

She smiles. I think if we could see her cheeks right now, they would match the pink of her mask. She answers him in French, and he speaks back to her in French, and I take the hint that this must be flirty banter that they don't want me to hear.

I leave the room and walk down the hall. I spot Edison a few feet ahead of me. He isn't with Chelsea or one of the Duvals. He's alone. I try to catch up to him, but he is walking very quickly. He ducks down a corridor, an offshoot of the main hall, and goes through a large oak door, then down a flight of stairs. I follow him. The walls on either side of us are intricately carved, and the banister is made to look like tree branches tangled around a post at the bottom of the stairs. The sounds of voices echoing from the party get quieter and quieter, and I cannot hear them at all by the time I reach the bottom of the stairs. There are only a handful of other people down here, all seemingly knowing exactly where they are going, before turning in to one of the rooms. Some of them close the doors.

Could people be doing business here—at this party? Maybe this party is more than networking and showing off, and the point is not to see and be seen the way George seems to think it is, and all that glitz is a cover for the real business that happens behind closed doors.

Edison seems to know where he's going. Maybe we could meet down here, somewhere, just the two of us.

He runs into Warren, stopping more abruptly than I expected, and I step behind a grandfather clock to hide myself. I am only a few feet away from them. I can't make out what Warren is saying, but I hear Edison say, "I'll get him now. We're in room seven."

Warren nods and walks in the same direction as Edison, away from me.

The only yearning stronger than my desire to catch Edison alone is my curiosity to know what goes on behind the closed doors in the sublayer at a party like this. And what Edison is doing down here, who he is meeting.

Now that I know to look for numbers on the rooms, I can see them clear as day etched carefully in the wood carvings. The 7 is shaped like a tree branch with leaves sprouting from it and a bird perched on the top.

I walk in slowly. It's a dark study, full of cherrywood and black leather and claw-footed furniture, with tall shelves packed full of books and antique statues. Faint piano music pours through the speakers mounted in the corner of the wall, and there are candles lit. I look around for somewhere to hide and spot a closet at the end of the room. Honestly, I think twice about going inside, but then I hear the Duvals' voices getting closer, Edison saying, "This way, this way," Sepp saying, "Slow down, slow down," and I don't hesitate to duck into the closet.

I am wedged inside next to musty-smelling jackets and boxes

of books and a file cabinet and a safe. I leave the door open a crack, just wide enough for me to see what's happening on the other side of the room.

The Duvals and Edison pour into the room all at once. Warren is straightening his jacket. Sepp is pushing his hair back. Oswald adjusts his bow tie. They all take off their masks.

Edison says, "Stevens should be coming any second," and checks his watch.

Barely a moment later, a man in a navy velvet jacket and matching mask enters. They greet him with handshakes as the man slides his mask up into his thick head of brown hair. He is older, maybe Warren's age, and has a hazy look in his eyes.

"Nice grip, Stevens," Sepp says.

"That's Senator Stevens to you, punk." He moves to ruffle Sepp's hair, and Sepp ducks out of the way. Stevens is thrown off balance a bit by this, like maybe he has enjoyed several cocktails throughout the night.

"Take it easy," Warren says.

"It's a party," Stevens says, laughing.

"Shall we begin, Senator?" Oswald says.

"First tell me the bad news," Stevens says. "The kid with the recording?"

"Taken care of," Sepp says.

"Jesus Christ, that greedy bastard almost gave me a heart attack. And his little helpers? Did you pay them off? Bet that wasn't cheap." The senator is slurring a little.

"They've been taken care of, too," Oswald says. "Nothing for you to worry about."

"What about the thing with Ellis?" Stevens says.

"Ellis's shipment has been confirmed. We're set, when the time is right," Warren says. "I hope you realize, without us, this could have been very bad for you."

"Don't fucking start with me, Warren," Stevens says. "What's bad for me is bad for you, too; don't pretend otherwise."

Oswald speaks. "So you'll meet with the Smiths? There's an opening in their schedule in August to discuss the upcoming project—"

"Oh yeah," Stevens says. "You know I'm always good to meet with them. Introduce them to whoever. Sign whatever."

"Their proposal is very smart," Oswald continues. "It's going to make you look good as well. Bringing in all those jobs, building infrastructure this state needs—"

"Yeah, yeah," Stevens says, leaning against the desk. "And I bet it requires millions' worth of cement, too?"

"It's beneficial all around—" Warren starts, but Stevens doesn't seem to be paying attention anymore and cuts him off.

"I get reelected, you get rich. Fine, fine."

None of them nod or agree with this, but they all exchange glances, as though they are silently judging Stevens for being so drunk and free with his words.

"And what about that other guy?" Stevens snaps his fingers like he's trying to trip his memory. "You know—the other guy on the recording. The Goodman Pharmaceuticals guy."

"We're keeping him close," Oswald says.

"How close?"

"Edison-is-dating-his-daughter close," Sepp says.

Oswald puts up a hand like he's stopping Sepp from continuing. Panic rises in my chest.

"We don't foresee him as a threat," Oswald says, "but we'll do what's necessary if he does anything to give us doubts."

"We can't have him getting arrested, spilling his guts to cut a deal," Stevens says. "I hope you're covering your bases on this one."

"You know we always do," Warren says.

"Because if he even seems like he's going to cause us a whiff of trouble, I want him taken out."

They nod—all of them.

"He's here tonight?" Stevens asks.

Edison looks to the floor. The Duvals stay quiet.

"Well?" Stevens spreads his arms in a giant shrug. "There are girls hanging around Edison, one in particular—I figure that's her?"

"Come on, Stevens, there are always girls hanging around Edison," Sepp says.

"This place," Stevens says. "If there was ever a place to get rid of him, it's here." He wiggles his fingers. "Where the walls don't talk." He bursts out laughing.

I have to close my eyes and brace myself next to the door to keep from falling forward.

"We're prepared, of course," says Warren. "But it's not going to come to that—not yet anyway."

"But it's pretty convenient that he be here," Stevens says.

"His boss is in attendance tonight," Oswald says. "He belongs here as much as any of us."

My chest constricts.

Stevens groans. "Ugh, those fucking pharmacy guys and their lobbyists are always up my ass."

"Very well. I think we're done here," Oswald says.

"Thank god," Stevens mutters.

I have one chance before they all disperse, and I take it. I hold my phone up to the crack in the closet door and snap as many photos as I can of them before they put their masks back on and walk out of the room. These are the people who were discussing whether or not to eliminate my father and now I have proof of them together.

Edison stays after they've all left. He takes care in wiping down the door handles and tabletop with a cloth he's pulled from the inside of his jacket. I debate confronting him, but how am I supposed to trust him now? I need to get out of this room, keep an eye on George—my thoughts are interrupted by a loud dinging sound. A text from Chelsea. *Where are you?!* Edison freezes like he doesn't believe that he's really heard something. Then she calls and my phone rings loud and obnoxiously until my shaking hands finally get it to stop.

The closet door flies open, and Edison is standing there with his mouth agape.

Chapter 41

"What the hell are you doing here?" Edison says.

"Why were they talking about George?" I have a lot of questions about what I heard, but this is what comes tumbling out of my mouth first.

Edison puts his hands on his head and steps back muttering, "Jesus Christ." His expression is aghast and his hair disheveled. "Were you following me?"

"What the hell was that?" I demand.

He glances behind him to make sure the door is still closed. I watch him take a slow breath in and stare at the floor. He doesn't know what to say to me now that the dust has been kicked up over the things he's hiding—everything they've all been hiding. I watch him grab at the back of his neck and adjust his collar while he tries and fails to think of a lie.

"What am I supposed to make of that?" I say, and when he looks at me with a stern glare, I can see the frustration building in him, and I wonder for a moment if I should be afraid to be here alone with him, in a place where *the walls don't talk*.

"We can't discuss this here, okay?" he says. "I'll come get you tonight, after the party is over, and I'll tell you whatever you want to know."

"You'll tell me everything?"

"Yes." He starts toward the door and spins around when he notices I haven't followed him. He waits.

My voice trembles as I speak, asking the only question I need answered before I'll let him leave this room. "Are they going to be okay? Is George and—" I want to say *my family*, but it still doesn't feel like I have the right. "Tell me they're going to be okay. Nothing bad is going to happen to them—tonight or ever?"

"Nothing is going to happen to them," he says immediately, sounding firm, but I can still hear the desperation in his voice, and see it in his eyes, like he's worried or scared, maybe both, that I won't believe him. "I promise. It's going to be fine. As long as you don't say anything about what you've heard. Can I count on you?"

I nod. "Yes, okay."

We exit the room, and then I don't leave his side all night. We stay near Chelsea and George and Trisha, too. Edison seems to understand why it's important for me to be with them and why my trust could be broken if he were to disappear again during the party.

We spend the rest of the night in the ballroom with the tall windows and the stone floor, where a livelier band plays popular songs from the last four decades.

Edison and Chelsea sway to the music, their arms around each other on the dance floor. His smile looks so distant, and hers doubles in size, like she's trying to compensate for this. Or maybe it means she is too happy to even notice. I think of what Sepp said earlier: not everyone can date whoever they want. I don't think it's a coincidence that Kath is the heir to Ellis Exports and that the Duvals mentioned them in that room with Stevens.

We have to show our IDs when we leave the party, and get our names checked off another list. They search our purses again and wave the wand over us. The limos are lined up and waiting, and traffic moves slowly. George and Trisha are drunk and giddy; Chelsea is over the moon, too, talking a mile a minute about what a great time she had. But she tires out quickly and falls asleep with her head on George's shoulder before we reach our cottage.

Chapter 42

Chelsea wakes up for only a few minutes, after we arrive at the cottage, to brush her teeth and put on her pajamas. George and Trisha also go straight to bed, but I still wait a little while, lying in the dark over my covers before I text Edison to let him know that the coast is clear for me to leave.

Alone in the silent dark house, my thoughts start to sort themselves out, leaving behind the panic I'd felt after what I'd heard and giving me some clarity. They all seem to be connected, George and Senator Stevens and the Duvals and the Ellises; their ties to Stevens are of the business variety, while whatever ties them to George and the Ellises is covered up by personal relationships.

It's nearly an hour after we returned, about 1:00 A.M., when I finally text Edison. He'll have answers or he'll have more lies. But when the choice is to stay away or to pursue the possibility of the truth, regardless of the risk, I am always guilty of making the same choice.

He writes back: *Come outside.*

I pull a sweatshirt on over my pajamas and slip on my running shoes. I walk out the front door because the bedrooms are on the other side of the house and this cottage doesn't have thin walls like the New Brown beach house. I follow the path past the driveway, to the street. Edison steps out from the bushes to meet me. We don't say anything as we walk a few feet down the road until we reach the golf cart that he rode over here. He drives us down the narrow road. Edison has a map, but he seems to know where he's going. We ride for about five minutes before we reach a small cabin with the porch light on and a rocking chair out front.

"This is where you're staying?"

He nods. "Just me."

We open the door to reveal one spacious room with a wall for a kitchen, a small sofa and two chairs around the fireplace making up the living room. There is a desk in the corner, and a bed along the far wall taking up most of the space.

It's warm inside, thanks to a fire brewing in the fireplace.

The exhaustion is plain on us both, Edison constantly rubbing his eyes, me yawning every few minutes. We sit together on the sofa in front of the crackling flames.

"Do you believe me that nothing bad is going to happen to George?" he says.

"I don't know. How am I supposed to believe anything you say now?" Now, or ever again.

"But can you at least trust me that I would never let anything happen to George, or Trisha or Chelsea? And I won't let anything happen to you either."

"Maybe I could trust you if you sorted out some of the other lies." He's told so many I wonder if I'd be able to untangle them. And what makes me think he'll tell the truth now? Just because I feel like he's the first person who's ever really seen me? Just because I felt like I was that person for him, too? But it's not enough to trust him after what I overheard, no matter how badly I wish I could.

"What do you want to know?" he says.

I don't know what to ask first, so I start at the very beginning. "What were you really doing on the island?"

"I was hiding." He alters his answer. "I was *supposed* to be hiding. Someone was sending threats to Stevens. He's the senator who was in the room—" I nod so he knows he doesn't have to explain. "Someone was trying to blackmail him with an incriminating recording of him—something from years ago. We didn't know who was behind the threats, so we made arrangements to meet him. We said we'd pay for the recording. Archaletta didn't know who he was meeting either. Which is probably why he brought his friends—other criminals interested in a payday who would back him up—even though Archaletta was supposed to come alone."

"They're all criminals?" I say, thinking of the unmarked van and the disguises.

"Archaletta wasn't even his real name. And the two men he had with him aren't upstanding citizens either, from what I've seen of them."

It's a good sign that he's at least told me the truth about Archaletta's fake name, matching what the detectives told me.

"Why were you the only one who went to the island to meet him?"

"It wasn't really going to be a meeting. We just needed to see who showed up. I'm not a Duval, and if people don't know the Duvals well, they don't know who I am."

The text message on Edison's phone when I found it on the island had said, *What did you see?*—I remember.

"But Archaletta did know who you were." Goose bumps form on my arms remembering the way they'd called his name in the forest on the island, the terrified look on Edison's face.

"Yes. And they spotted me right away. Archaletta tried to get information out of me. He wanted to know how he could get paid for the recording. I wouldn't talk, and that didn't sit well with him. I saw the knife strapped to his belt and managed to pull it. You know the rest."

"What happened to Archaletta?"

"No one will ever find him."

"He's missing, Edison."

He nods. "He's a criminal and he's missing, and his friends have what they asked for, and the recording is no longer a problem, and that's all you need to know."

"That's why the other two from the island came to the Duval offices?"

"We thought it might be safer, talking to them at the office. Negotiating with them wasn't a problem. Everyone has a price."

"You and Sepp aren't afraid they're going to use the payoff against you?" I think of what I saw on my run—the hidden SUV, the disguises, the guns.

"There's always that chance. But our deals are hard to resist."

"Why do the Duvals care about protecting Senator Stevens?"

This is the easiest part for me to work out on my own based on what I heard, but I ask him anyway, hoping he'll tell me more.

"The Duvals and Stevens have an arrangement. He helps us and we help him. It's a trade of secrets. I don't know all of them, and I think it's better not to know." He stares at the roaring fire, the flames reflect in his glassy eyes. "Some secrets are traps."

"What else do you know about it?"

"Too much." He sighs. "Enough that I'll never get away."

"Get away?"

He waves his hand, dismissing this.

"What does any of this have to do with George?"

Edison shifts so his arm is resting along the back of the couch and he's closer to me. "George is on the recording with Stevens. I've never seen it; I've never seen it because it's not necessary for me to know what's on it. All that matters is that it's incriminating somehow for both of them. It could easily destroy Stevens's career—probably George's too—if it got out."

"Why does Archaletta have this recording?"

"I have no idea." I'm starting to get the impression Edison is on a need-to-know basis when it comes to the affairs of the Duvals. "But it's convenient timing, coming at Stevens with this kind of blackmail right as he's turning into a political powerhouse. People are starting to recognize him." He turns so he's facing me. "That's why we had to keep George close. In case Archaletta figured out who he was and tried to blackmail him, too. Or tried to use him against Stevens. We were never going to hurt George."

I watch the fire when I ask the next question, and try to ignore how my first instinct is to hold my breath, waiting to hear the answer. "How did you really meet Chelsea?"

"We were looking into George Brown. We thought the best

way to get to know him would be through his daughter. We had her followed and knew she loved to go to the café in her neighborhood every Sunday morning for a chocolate croissant. We needed to make sure George wasn't a threat, that he wasn't being pressured to talk. We needed a reason to know him, to be close to him, while we secured the recording from Archaletta."

I feel the most shameful stroke of relief hearing this, knowing that nothing between them is perfect, because none of it is real. He's given Chelsea manufactured happiness and artificial affection, and it's not fair that he's standing in her way of finding the real thing. Maybe nothing between Edison and me is real either and I'm only getting closer to him because I've seen and heard too much. I've lied for him on more than one occasion and maybe he thinks the price for my continued silence is middle-of-the-night meetings and secret boat rides. On the boat he'd pushed me away and then after I lied to the police, he met me at the half-built house. He set up candles. He asked me about regret. He kissed me.

I lean back, away from him, feeling tricked again and it's just as bad as the day I learned he was Edison and Finn was a lie. He senses the shift and turns toward me. I sit on my hands, in case he tries to grab one, in case they try to reach for him. I turn my head so I can't see him—so he can't see me—in case my face shows how hurt I am.

"It's not over yet," he says. "The recording, the payoff, there's still some stuff to take care of to make sure it's really never going to touch Stevens, or George. Otherwise—" His hand gently touches my arm. "Come on, you know if it were up to me, I wouldn't be with her."

I let myself look at him. He's closer than I expected. He sees something in my expression that makes his hand drop from my arm. "You said you had to be with Chelsea because she'd met your mother, and you could never be with someone who didn't know that part of your life."

"It was a lie."

"Exactly."

"Come on," he pleads. "You know why I told you that—because we were getting too close." He brings his hand to my face but is careful about touching me. He lets the tips of his fingers graze the hair that's come loose from my ponytail. "Remember what you told me," he says quietly, "about the reasons you lied to your mom."

To protect her. That's how he'd defined it and I'd agreed. Even though it was selfish, it was also to keep her away from the trouble I was getting into; things I didn't want her to know, because I didn't want to hurt her.

"How am I supposed to believe that?" My lip trembles. I'm scared of how much I am ready to let myself go, to let myself trust at least that confession from him.

"I told you all of this so that you would know the truth about what you heard at the party and what you saw on the island. So you would know what you lied for and that there's nothing for you to be afraid of," he says, his hand returning to my shoulder, moving up the side of my face, so I can't turn away from him again. "But you have to believe me about how I feel about you. It's why I told you all this. It's why I won't tell you anything else."

My eyes fall shut and I feel his breath on my lips before he kisses me so gently and hesitantly it's like he's still waiting for me to tell him I believe him. I don't tell him this, but I do kiss him back, turning the soft kiss into something that's fierce and electric.

Is this what it means to exist in two worlds; trusting him enough to let him press his mouth against my lips, my neck, along my collarbone, lift my arms so he can remove my sweatshirt and my tank top, lie on the floor with him, skin to skin, letting his weight shift over me and believing him when he says I am safe and he wants to protect me, while having no faith that he's given me all the information I should have and his confessions aren't still muddled by lies and ulterior motives, hiding a bigger, much worse secret?

I don't tell him that right now, with him, like this, is the closest I've ever let someone really get to me, and it's not how it was with Trevor, or how I ever dreamed it could be—like the sum of me is wrapped up tight, rolling between his fingers, and I know that even though he could, he won't crush me. But he's looking at me like he knows; like he feels the same way. I don't tell him that there are some lines I can't let myself cross, even though my betrayal is already deep and unforgivable, but he never reaches for my shorts, the way he did my shirt, and when the fire starts to die and the darkness closes in on us and the electricity between us surges stronger, he moves away, takes a blanket from the sofa, and lies down behind me so my back is pressed against his stomach and his arms are around me.

I shift so I can see him. His smile is beautiful. It is everything. It is the moon and Mars and Dubai and the beaches of Thailand and the top of the Eiffel Tower.

I watch as he slowly closes his eyes. My eyes fall shut, too.

I want nothing else, not a single thing in this godforsaken world, except to lie here with him, listening to his breathing getting deeper and slower. A forbidden and buried thought comes to the surface: I could die right now. Happily.

And another: I'm in love with him. Madly.

Chapter 43

We wake up right before sunrise. The sky is hazy with the glow of the sun and the birds are chirping as he drives me back to the New Browns' cottage.

The morning light illuminates our surroundings and the beauty is overwhelming. The lush green trees and the golden valleys that stretch for miles. Everywhere the Duvals have taken us, it's been astoundingly picturesque. But at what price? So much beauty, but what does it cost? How many lies? How many secrets? How many bruises and backdoor payoffs?

And how does this kind of life sustain itself?

"Edison?" He slows the golf cart and looks at me. "What would your mother say?" He turns away, his eyes full of worry. "If she knew," I add.

He stares ahead as he drives us forward. "She said, 'You're going to have a beautiful life, my boy.'"

I sneak in through the front door, and Rosie is in the living room with Phoebe, who squeals when she sees me. I'm ready to blurt out lies about having gone on a morning run, but Rosie picks Phoebe up and takes her into the kitchen, not acknowledging me at all.

The plane ride home is full of quiet cheerfulness; the New Browns and Chelsea already nostalgic for last night, because it was packed with enough memories for an entire summer. The Duvals are all relaxed. Oswald smiles that smile I used to think of as re-setting the room, bringing everyone together, that now looks ter-rifying in its friendliness. Chelsea rests her head on Edison's shoulder, and Edison struggles to keep his eyes open. Sepp and I play cards.

The Duvals aren't staying at Cross Cove this week; they have business out of town and friends to visit in the Hamptons, they say.

Since Edison leaves in the morning, I take a guess that he will be at the half-built house tonight to see me alone one more time before he goes. But when I arrive, the house is empty, the platform is dark.

Chapter 44

With the Duvals gone for a week, Chelsea and I spend the next few days on our own beach. Phoebe has developed a cough that has Trisha and George keeping her inside, steaming up the bathrooms to help her sleep, so Chelsea and I are mostly left alone.

It's just us in the water, in the sun, sometimes laughing, sometimes lost in our own thoughts. We can be quiet together, and I like that. Sometimes we float listlessly on our inflatables, sometimes we ride together on the same paddleboard, trying to go faster but always giving up before we get to the other side of the cove.

No matter how close I get to Chelsea, it can never be as close as I wish. I can still feel the wall between us, put there by me, built strong by the betrayal of knowing that Edison is pretending with her and I am, too.

We're lying in the sand under the shade of the giant red beach umbrella we dragged out of the garage, eating apricots and salt-and-vinegar chips and drinking sparkling water, laughing about the sand that comes out of our hair every time we move. Somehow, over these past days with Chelsea, I feel comfortable with a perfectly predictable day.

"What do you want to do next year?" she asks, something she's inquired about before.

"I don't know," I tell her, a particular kind of sadness creeping over me, knowing I have no plans and no idea even how to start thinking about the future or how I fit into it. "It'll come to you," she says. She sucks the last juice off her apricot and tosses the pit, aiming for the center of our tube. When she misses, she gets up and retrieves it.

"You know what scares me the most?" Chelsea says later that night. The two of us are sitting on lawn chairs eating popcorn, waiting for the fireworks we never miss.

"Spiders? Snakes? Sharks?" I tease her. She throws popcorn at me.

"Bats!" she screams. I'm not sure if that's what she was going to say originally, but then she launches into a story about camping with George and her mom, before Phoebe was born, how they found the perfect spot in the forest to set up their camping gear, and then when the sun started going down, they looked to the sky and saw a cluster of bats above them, dipping and diving, and she spent the rest of the night in the tent, even when George tried to get her to come out for s'mores.

George never took me camping. But we have old sleeping bags

and a red tent collecting dust in our garage. And we have photos of when he and my mom would go, when they first started dating. They look delighted and fresh-faced, so much hope in their eyes and smiles that didn't know any better. I saw those photos, and I felt bad for them. I wonder what Chelsea would say if I told her this; if I were allowed to let her see the dark parts of me that I hide; if I were allowed to be as open with her as she is with me.

Some nights, watching George be gentle and sweet and loving with the New Brown girls, I feel overcome with confusion. Who is he, really? What else is in his past that no one in his life knows about? What's his role in the threats that Senator Stevens had to be protected from? Is he really safe from it now? Are the rest of us? Who is this man who has so many sides to him that he can conceal so easily?

"Chels?" I say. She turns to look at me. "What really scares you?"

"Loneliness."

"Me, too."

The next morning, Chelsea and I visit North Point Beach and later, when I'm flipping through the photos we took of ourselves in the matching sunglasses we bought on Main Street, I stumble upon the pictures from the masquerade party. And I remember what we should really be scared of.

Chapter 45

I leave for a run as soon as the sun goes down, fueled by adrena-line and fear and excruciating curiosity, stubborn determination. I'm scared I'll miss them, afraid even more that there'll be no trace of them. I sprint to the same bend in the road where I saw the men from the island the last time, telling myself if I see the SUV parked under the trees tonight, it was meant to be.

It's there, as I'd wished, and I walk right up and rap on the win-dow. At first I think maybe they aren't here yet. But soon I hear movement on the other side and the murmuring of voices. I keep knocking until I hear the click of the handle and the door slowly draws open.

The taller one, who was in the red hat on the island, opens the door and steps out of the SUV. He is not wearing the red hat and he isn't dressed like the wait-staff downtown. He is in khakis and boots, with a plain shirt under his black canvas jacket. There's a gun strapped against him. He appears exactly how I'd expect an officer to look.

Face-to-face with him like this, I freeze. Up this close, I can see the sharpness of his features and the seriousness of his eyes. His hair is parted and combed. He stands tall with rigid posture and his arms crossed in front of him. He takes a deep breath like he is collecting himself. This was a bad plan. I don't really know who these men are, even if I think I've figured them out. I close my eyes for a moment and try to steady my breathing, still going rapid from the run over here. I remember what I decided scrolling through photos on my phone of the Hanover Estate, thinking of Edison's secrets, and of George's, how they're intertwined. How they're dangerous, but I don't know the extent of it, or how badly it can come back to bite him, or the rest of us. Unless I ask. Edison won't tell me. But these men might. This is taking a risk, and there's a chance I could be getting myself in even more trouble. But it is better than waiting for whatever inevitability is about to come.

"I have something you might be interested in," I say.

He keeps his expression neutral, so I can't tell if this has surprised him or not. I like that he's at least not pretending he doesn't know who I am.

I add, "Information," and he still doesn't give away whether or not this interests him. He scratches his chin, checks the road, then nods. He opens the back seat door and says, "Get in."

When I hesitate, he clears his throat. This is what I've decided to do, and there's no going back now. I climb inside.

As soon as I'm seated, the door shuts. I hear someone stir behind me and turn to see the third row of seating is missing, and the shorter one is sitting on the floor wearing headphones and watching a few small monitors stacked in the corner.

"What the hell?" he says, when he notices me. He throws a dark cover over the monitors before I can make out what was on them.

The taller guy joins me in the back seat.

"She has information," he explains quickly to the shorter guy, who has his arms up in protest.

The shorter one leans forward. "Well, this is an interesting turn of events."

The taller one starts to speak, "We're going to need—" but the shorter one goes off, "How did you know we were here?" he says. His voice is noticeably friendlier, with an accent that tells me he grew up somewhere around New York City, something I hadn't picked up on at the island.

They both watch me closely as they wait for my answer.

"I saw you when I was going for a run the other night."

They are quiet again and I wait for their cue. A chuckle comes from the back. "That's unlucky." I don't know if he's talking about them, for being seen by me, or me, for having spotted them. "Don't leave us in suspense. What are you doing here? You discovered us, fine. But why approach us?"

"First, give me your phone," the taller one says, presenting his hand.

"My phone?"

"Protocol. So we know you aren't recording this," he explains.

I hold it out to them and bring the screen to life so they can see I am not using it as a recording device. Still, they have me take off the light pullover I'm wearing and empty the shallow pockets, revealing lip balm and an extra hair tie.

"Can I ask—" My voice catches and I realize I maybe should have done this before I agreed to get in the car. "Do you mind telling me who you are?"

The shorter one looks at the taller one, but the taller one keeps his eyes on me. In that moment I wonder if they'll pretend to be associates of Archaletta or if they'll confess they're exactly who I thought they were when I came here offering information.

The taller one reaches into his jacket. He pulls out a wallet-looking object. He shows me his ID and his badge. Agent Brent Ryan. The shorter guy gets out his, too. Agent Aiden Hall.

"Guess you've officially blown our cover," Hall says. But neither of them seem particularly concerned—probably because I came promising information, they think I am on their side regardless. Also, I likely don't have a choice.

Knowing they are federal agents is at first a relief, but dread immediately follows. These are still the two men who witnessed Edison and me on the island with Archaletta. They were paid off at the Duval offices under the guise of these men. They are the ones who could confirm that I lied to the police. They could provide a motive as to why Edison might have wanted to get rid of Archaletta.

I remind myself that what I can offer will be valuable to them, since what I overheard at the private meeting at the Hanover Estate could prove that the Duvals are involved in Archaletta's disappearance, because the agents were undercover with Archaletta and are well aware Archaletta was in the process of blackmailing Senator Stevens.

Their next question is, "Does Edison Finn know you're here?" and I am not surprised they bring him up.

I shake my head.

"Is this the part where you tell us the truth about what happened to Luke Archaletta?" Hall asks from the back.

"I want to know if my father is in danger," I say.

"What makes you think he's in danger?" Ryan asks.

Since they know about the blackmail and they know its source, they must be aware of how George is involved. They are cautious about revealing this to me, probably because they don't want to let me in on what they know, until they are sure that I know it, too.

"I witnessed a private meeting with Senator Stevens and the Duvals."

"You were in a private meeting at the Hanover Estate?" Hall does nothing to hide his disbelief.

"They weren't aware I was in the room. I can show proof of the meeting."

"And you're here to give us your account of this meeting, and the proof?" Ryan says.

"And what do you want for it?" Hall knows that nothing is free. "Protection for your father?" he guesses. "Protection for your family?"

I hadn't considered that they could provide protection. But before I can ask for this, I still need the most basic information. "I want to see the recording that Archaletta was using to blackmail Senator Stevens. I know you supposedly turned it over to Sepp and Edison, but since you're not who they think you are, I'm guessing you still have a copy. If you show me the recording, I'll show you the proof of the private meeting at the Hanover Estate. I'll tell you everything that was said."

They glance at each other, a wordless exchange that reveals nothing to me about what they are going to say next.

"I know George—my father," I correct myself, "is on that recording. I need to see it."

"Edison never told you about it?" Ryan asks, keeping his expression as even as his tone.

Edison said he didn't know. But I'm not going to reveal anything to them that will encourage them to draw conclusions about Edison's involvement, or my own. "Why do you think that's something Edison would tell me?"

"If you didn't know about the blackmail, then what did Edison say to you to get you to hide out and help him that day on the island, if it wasn't for your father's benefit?" Hall says. "Why would you lie to the police when they questioned you about Archaletta?"

I foolishly think of the affectionate way Edison looked at me in the cottage, how it felt like he at least broke the surface of truth with what he told me.

Ryan and Hall won't believe wrong place, wrong time—or as it seemed at the moment, right place, right time. They think I was a plant, put there in case Edison was seen. They think I was Plan B, to help him get away.

Hall smiles, but in such a way that it's clear that whatever he's about to say next is not meant to be friendly. "I guess it's his charm and charisma and the way he kisses that won you over, then?"

They want me to know that they've seen all the ways I'm involved with this, and with him. Maybe they want to discourage me, or embarrass me. I ignore this comment.

Ryan sighs, like he might recognize all of this and can see that it's fueled me instead of deterred me.

"If you show me the recording of my father that was being used to blackmail Senator Stevens, I'll tell you whatever you want about the private meeting between the Duvals and the senator at the masquerade party at the Hanover Estate, and show you proof of the meeting," I repeat.

Hall readjusts and leans in closer. "If we do this, we need to know you understand how important it is that you do not tell Edison, or anyone, that we met, or that we exchanged information. Or, that you know who we are at all. Do you understand how that could get you into trouble? Do you understand that this is the kind of thing Edison Finn cannot protect you from? And if it gets out, it will ruin our case and then we won't be able to protect you either."

"I understand."

Hall looks to Ryan and Ryan's forehead wrinkles with uncertainty.

"The thing about the recording of your father," Ryan starts.

Hall interrupts. "I've got it right here." He holds up a thin, black laptop. "First show us proof of the meeting."

I do as he says. They both lean in, examining the photos on my phone. Ryan sighs. "That's them, all right."

Instead of handing the laptop to Ryan, Hall gets out of the car through the doors in the back and walks around to the side door, to take Ryan's place. Ryan moves to the front seat.

Hall pulls up the video, and turns the screen so it's facing me. Ryan keeps his back turned.

"I feel obligated to warn you that you definitely do not want to see this," Hall says. But he doesn't hesitate before pressing Play.

Chapter 46

The recording starts with a close-up of a girl's face. She has dark makeup outlining her blue eyes, and her blond hair is pushed back with a thin pink headband. She looks like she might only be a few years older than I am. The girl smokes a cigarette as she adjusts her camera, or whatever she's using as a recording device, glancing behind her like she's checking to make sure the side of the room with the bed is in full view. From where she's positioned it, we can see the bed, the bedside table, a chair in the corner, and the door to the bathroom.

There's a knock in the distance.

"Coming!" she calls, checking the angle of the device one more time before she stands up.

Voices are low and muffled in the distance. Followed by the sound of a door opening and closing. More inaudible speaking; faraway laughter. Two figures come into view: the girl, still smoking, dressed in black fishnets and a pink tube dress, and a much older man, dressed in a suit but wearing a black baseball hat. He has a six-pack of beer that he sets on the nightstand. He lets his briefcase fall next to the bed. The girl helps him take off his jacket and tosses it on the chair in the corner. When she sits on the bed and puts out her cigarette, he sits next to her. He removes his hat. It's Senator Stevens. He doesn't look much different from when I saw him last weekend.

"Hello, sweetheart," he says, tilting forward to give her a kiss.

She leans away from him, laughing. "What did you bring me?"

"What are you talking about, baby? I'm right here."

She laughs again but shakes her head. "You know the rules."

"You want the cash so you can freeze your ass off waiting outside of some dirtbag's apartment to score mediocre shit, or do you want the special stuff I've got coming here? It'll be any minute, I swear."

"You have a dealer coming *here*?"

"First-class delivery, just for you."

"Your special stuff better be fucking *special*."

"Only the best for you." He leans in and kisses her, and she lets him. She wraps her arms around him and falls back on the bed. I can't hear it on the recording, but the way she springs back up quickly makes it clear there was a knock on the door. The girl rushes up to answer it but Stevens catches her arm.

"You mind giving us some privacy to handle this, baby?" Stevens says. The girl groans but marches into the bathroom and closes the door.

Stevens leaves the picture to answer the door and comes back with a man. He has dark hair that's longer than it is now that he has started to lose it. The weight in his stomach is leaner. He has the goatee he wore when I was around twelve, shaved off by the time I was fourteen. George.

"What do you have for me?" Stevens asks George.

George takes a yellow pill bottle from his messenger bag and hands it to Stevens.

"And you've been paid?" Stevens says.

George nods.

"Thanks, man." Stevens shakes George's hand, and then George leaves.

Stevens cracks open two of the beers. He takes a long sip of one and sets it on the nightstand. From the pill bottle George gave him, he takes out a small vial. He dumps the contents into the other open beer. He replaces the empty vial in the pill bottle and puts it in his pants pocket.

"Can I come out?" the girl calls.

Stevens reaches in his briefcase and pulls out small baggies full of white power and a square mirror.

"Come on out, baby."

They sit on the bed drinking as Stevens arranges the cocaine on the mirror. They do what I saw Trevor do a thousand times, except Trevor wasn't so concerned with what kind of surface he used.

When they are done, Stevens and girl finish their beers. Stevens leans in close to her.

I look away from the screen. Hall moves to close the laptop.

"She needs to see how it ends," Ryan says.

Hall skips the recording ahead by a few minutes. When he turns the screen back to face me, Stevens is sitting up, opening another beer. The girl is next to him in bed wiping her eyes like the room is too bright for her to look at. She tries speaking to Stevens, her words stringing together in slurs. She grabs her throat. Her arms flail. She leans forward on her hands and knees and vomits all over the comforter. Stevens jumps up. He puts on his pants. Grabs his jacket and his briefcase. The girl is still clutching her throat, still vomiting. She falls forward. She convulses twice, and then she is perfectly still.

Stevens takes out his phone and moves so close to the recording device that he blocks half of it. "Hey," we can hear him saying. And then: "Yeah, it's done."

He hangs up the phone and takes another long sip of his beer. He sets it directly in front of the recording device, so all we can see is a blurry beer label. We hear when he leaves because the door slams so hard the beer presses forward, knocking the recording device on its back. The screen goes dark, then cuts out.

"Do you understand now how serious this is?" Hall says.

Ryan turns around and looks at me. "Start talking."

My throat is dry and eyes are wet. I feel like I'm in a daze, my thoughts like wisps that disappear before I can accept them. I don't know what I was expecting. Not that. I can't decide if it's so horrific it warrants Edison keeping it from me, or if because it's so sickening, he should have told me, if he knew. George. My father. The man I know to be hateful and greedy and selfish. Someone who kept a lot of secrets.

The agents start asking me questions. They ask if I heard the Duvals or the Senator threaten George. I nod. I tell them Stevens suggested taking care of him at the party. *Where the walls don't talk*. They ask what else was mentioned and I close my eyes, my head still reeling as I tell them what I overheard: the upcoming infrastructure meetings with the Smiths, and the obvious trade in secrets and the mention of Ellis Exports.

"Did they say anything else about Ellis Exports, or anyone who works for them?" asks Ryan. He's got the laptop in the front seat and he types furiously.

"No—I . . . No." I see the girl again, the look on her face when she realized she was about to die. My father, that girl; his fault.

"I think I'm going to be sick," I say, fumbling with the locked door until I finally manage to get it open.

"Stay here," Ryan is saying as I fall out of the car. I lean against the side, bending forward, resting my hands on my knees. I let the fresh air fill my lungs and I close my eyes.

"Maris." I blink and stare at my shoes pressing into the cool dirt, when I hear Hall's voice. "I'm sorry, but you can't be out here like this."

I straighten up slowly before getting in the car. Hall produces a warm water bottle.

"This is all we have," he says.

They let me take a few sips before they start questioning me.

"Did they say anything else about Ellis Exports in this meeting?" Hall asks.

"No." I pinch my eyes shut, waiting to feel better. "What happened to her?" My voice comes out hoarse. My heart is heavy with dread and I am very much afraid of the answer, even though I'm sure I already know it.

Ryan sighs. "She died."

"Tamoxide poisoning," Hall adds after a while. "An awful poison. Inhaled, injected, or ingested, it's a terrible way to go."

Ryan closes the laptop and rests it on the center console. "We won't let anything happen to your dad," Ryan says.

I'm dying to get out of this stuffy car; I want to run home, try to erase what I've seen from my thoughts, try to think over what it means and what I should do next. But I can tell that this is something I can't walk away from so easily.

"Does anyone know you overheard the meeting?" Ryan asks.

I shake my head. The agents already suspect I am allied with Edison; there is no need for them to know he's been the source of most of my information, when I can point to the Duvals as a whole.

"Does anyone know you met with us?" Ryan's voice is low, serious, not calm at all.

"I told you, no one knows," I say.

"It's very important," Hall says, "that you understand why you can't tell anyone about this, not our meeting, not who we are. Do you understand?"

"Yes," I manage. My throat is still tight, but I am out of water.

"Tell us why," Ryan says. Hall nods, encouraging.

"Because—" I close my eyes again, try to focus. It seems clear now. "The Duvals don't know about you, that you're undercover. They think they've paid off the guys working with Archaletta to make the blackmail go away."

Someone pats my knee. I open my eyes and see that it's Hall. "Very good."

I see the image again—the girl convulsing and then dying, the scared look on her face as she held her throat. I could run and run and run and never get her out of my mind. I'm hit with another wave of nausea, wondering if George knew what he was giving to Stevens and how it would be used.

The Duvals seemed to think George was clueless enough that

they didn't need to worry about him as a liability. But I don't like that Hall and Ryan knew about George on the recording, even though when they approached me, they spoke only of Edison and Archaletta. Is the coincidence that I was on the island with Edison when he was meeting Archaletta or that I am George's daughter? What are they really after?

Ryan gets out and walks around the front of the SUV, coming to open the door for me, and Hall gets out to reenter through the back doors, to assume his position in front of the monitors. The black tarp draped over the monitors falls loose as Hall slams the door. A view of a nice restaurant. A blank table. No telling who they are really monitoring or why, but it explains their outfits the first night I noticed them. They were planting a camera. Maybe a bug, too.

My pullover is off and dangling over my legs. The laptop is resting on the center console. Black plastic on dark leather, it nearly blends in. For the moment, I am the only one in the car. I carefully slide my long-sleeved shirt over the laptop, moving it closer to me. Casually, I press it against my chest, burying it in the shirt.

Ryan opens the door and I climb out.

"Do you know who the girl was?" I ask not wanting to appear in a hurry to get away, but also craving more information about her.

Ryan is silent, but Hall comes clean. "Archaletta's sister."

They give me one final wave, and I leave quickly, running immediately down the hill. I am clutching my pullover tight against me. I listen to the noise of their engine coming to life. And when they don't turn around after heading up the hill, I know I've gotten away with it.

Chapter 47

The second I get home, I rush up to my room, ignoring Chelsea's commentary of, "You missed a great fireworks show." I turn on the shower so she won't disturb me and sit on the tile floor, quickly unwrapping the agent's laptop from my pullover.

When I open the screen, I'm relieved to see it hasn't powered itself off; the sleep function must not be turned on, or it hasn't kicked in yet. This is the best stroke of luck, since I'm sure this computer has a login password that's impossible to crack. I run my finger over the touch pad. I look at the file names. They are all coded with letters and numbers. I click on a random folder, but it's password protected. I try to open five more and get the same result. Password required.

All I can access is the document that was already open—what Ryan was typing on as I told them what I saw at the Hanover party.

It's a simple text file. *Ellis Exports* is at the top, in bold. And then: *Notes: Hanover Estate Private Party—June.* And: *Confirmed shipment.* Below that is a list.

Case File 78651. Victims—"Dr. Alic":

2015—Missing—Proof of Death [Video A3479]—
Distribution: Ellis Exports—Goodman Pharmaceuticals
Rep: George Brown—Order from "Dr. Alic"

2000—Missing Person [Evidence file 674Y]—Distribution:
Unconfirmed—Goodman Pharmaceuticals Rep:
Unknown—Order from "Dr. Alic"

1995—Missing Person [Evidence file 4949F]—Distribution:
Unconfirmed—Goodman Pharmaceuticals Rep: Ken
Coleman [Deceased]—Order from "Dr. Alic"

1992—Missing Person—Proof of Death [Medical Records,
Evidence file 89786P]—Distribution: Unconfirmed—
Goodman Pharmaceuticals Rep: Landry Myers
[Deceased]—Order from "Dr. Alic"

1989—Missing Person [Evidence file Q9147]—Distribution:
Unconfirmed—Goodman Pharmaceuticals Rep:
Unknown—Order from "Dr. Alic"

1984—Missing Person—Proof of Death [Photographs, Evidence
file G1987]—Distribution: Unconfirmed—Goodman Pharmaceuticals Rep: Lyle Harris [Deceased]—Order from "Dr. Alic"

2015. That year makes sense based on George's appearance in the recording and for the summer he took me across the country with him to that ratty motel. This case has been active for decades it seems. And these dates are spread out. I bet that makes leads hard to follow, victims hard to track. And if evidence comes in late, the way the 2015 recording from Archaletta only surfaced recently, then who knows how many other victims there are that they haven't discovered yet? This almost seems like a lost cause. No wonder the agents were so anxious about any new information I might've had to offer.

But this case file isn't on the Duvals or Stevens—the label was "victims" and "Dr. Alic." What does any of this have to do with the Duvals and Edison? According to this list, George should be an important part of the evidence, since all the other Goodman Pharmaceuticals reps involved are either unknown or dead—so why haven't they reached out to him? What does Ellis Exports have to do with this case?

I go to bed with more questions than answers.

The next day I keep the laptop with me, hidden in my beach bag as Chelsea and I spend another day basking in the sun. I don't know if the agents will show up at any time demanding I return it to them. They could even bring me in for lying to the police, have Edison taken in for questioning; or George. But as the day wears on, I think of the case notes and the recording, and I think I understand what's happened, what the agents are truly after. This may have nothing to do with the Duvals or Senator Stevens at all. But a decades-old murder case that accidentally uncovered extortion.

Chapter 48

They find me on the road that night. I'm in running attire but walking since I've got their laptop with me, wrapped in my pullover.

"Get in." Ryan's face is tense. His voice matches.

I climb in the car. Hall is already in the back seat. I hand him the laptop.

"You understand this was a major violation?" Hall says.

"Major!" roars Ryan. "A violation of our trust, that's for sure. Not to mention it's completely illegal to steal the property of the federal government, so we'll add that to the list of *completely illegal* things you've done that you're lucky—so damn lucky—we're not charging you for. Yet. As long as you continue to cooperate."

When I'm sure he's finally done, I say, "I'm sorry."

Ryan lets out a long exasperated sigh. His knuckles are white on the steering wheel.

"What did you hope to gain from taking this?" Hall asks.

"I only wanted to know what kind of trouble George—I mean, my dad—was in. After . . . after what I saw on the recording."

"Oh, really? You were concerned about George, were you?" he says, showing me it's not lost on him that my relationship with George is so strained it's not natural for me to refer to him as *my dad*. But he's wrong; I do want to know about George, how he's connected, and what he knew about the vial he delivered.

Ryan is still seething. "If you showed anything on that laptop to anyone—"

"Everything on your computer is password protected," I say, jumping in before he can get too riled up.

Hall says, "But were you able to see anything on the laptop at all?"

"Out with it, Maris," Ryan says. "What did you see?"

They're going to know what I saw the moment they power on the laptop and see the open notes.

"Who is Dr. Alic?"

Ryan slams his hand down on the steering wheel. He goes off again, scolding me about breaking trust, telling me I don't get to ask questions.

"If we knew who Dr. Alic was, we wouldn't be here," Hall says.

So it's true, what I suspected. Ryan and Hall don't care about Archaletta or his disappearance. They don't care about the Duvals trading in secrets to get what they want from Senator Stevens or that the Duvals tried to protect him from blackmail. They don't care about the extortion or bribery. And they definitely don't care about Edison or that I lied to the police. They only wanted me to think they cared about these things in case they needed something to leverage against me since I know the truth about them. All they really care about is finding Dr. Alic.

"But you have his name," I say, turning to Hall.

"We have *a* name pulled off the blurry photo of the label of a pill bottle from the scene at one of the deaths we believe him to be responsible for."

"You think George knows who he is?" I say.

They exchange a look and they're quiet; my heart beats fast as my mind races through the possibilities of what this could mean. What if George does know and he's been helping him all along? "Is George in trouble?" Not with the Duvals or Stevens, but because of Dr. Alic.

To my surprise, Ryan answers. "George has been questioned. Everyone has. And now we're taking a different approach." Ryan shifts in his seat; he chews on his lip. "But, just in case." Ryan reaches into the black canvas bag at his feet and pulls out a small dark object. It's a rectangle, about two inches long and one inch wide. It's thin, not even a centimeter in thickness.

He hands the device to me; it's very light. "If you think your father is in danger, or that you are, you'll need to flick the on-switch, on the side. Feel it?"

I run my finger along the edge of the object and I nod.

"What is it?"

"It's a tracker," Hall says. "There's a GPS inside. We'll be able to find you, wherever you are."

The tracker is practically weightless in my hand, the corners sharp against the skin on my palm as I close my fist around it. It's not lost on me, what it means that they think I might need it.

"Why did George do this?" My throat tightens. I'm so mad at George for being involved in this, but so sad at the same time. There was a night when he didn't come back until late, past midnight, when we were staying in that motel with the green pool. Maybe he was with Trisha. Maybe this is what he was doing. "For money? Is that it?"

George did get a promotion that summer after I turned twelve. George started traveling more, spending more time on the East Coast, more time with the girls who would become the New Browns.

Ryan and Hall are quiet. It's clear I'm not going to get an answer on this. And they don't owe me one.

I can't help but say, "You have enough on that recording to arrest Senator Stevens."

"Believe it or not, we don't," Hall says.

"What about George?"

"Not yet."

According to the victims list on the laptop, Ellis Exports was in charge of delivery—connecting Dr. Alic to some of the Goodman Pharmaceuticals associates. Ellis Exports was mentioned in the private meeting, and the agents asked me to elaborate on this.

"Are the Duvals involved?"

"Don't try to piece this together yourself," Ryan says. "There is a lot you don't know."

They round the corner, where they'll be dropping me off.

Even if they don't care about Archaletta's disappearance because it has nothing to do with their investigation into Dr. Alic, they still have something real they could threaten me with. And they could threaten Edison, too.

"Hey," Hall says as I'm about to open the door and get out. "I don't know what's really going on between you and Edison; but I wouldn't make the mistake of trusting him."

Chapter 49

It's been a week, but the Duvals are still away, and Phoebe's cough is completely gone, so the New Browns and I go to North Point Beach. We eat lunch on the patio of Redfin Grill and stuff our faces with the seafood platter, enjoying a view of the boats docking and the trail of families biking to the lighthouse. We're close enough to hear both the sounds of the ocean and the laughter and chatter of the people on the beach.

It's been a while since Trisha and George have had a day to enjoy Cross Cove, so we leave them on the patio sipping sparkling wine and take Phoebe with us down Main Street. They're sitting next to each other facing the beach, with their legs outstretched under the table as we're walking out of the restaurant. George looks so peaceful I hardly recognize him.

"We have to keep Phoebe awake," Chelsea says, "so she'll sleep when we're back at the house."

And this becomes our mission. First, we take her to the Ella Jack's Toy Shop, where we build tracks out of a wooden train set and take turns seeing how far we can get the train to go before Phoebe inevitably reaches in and breaks it apart. The farthest my train makes it is to the drawbridge. Chelsea's train makes it all the way under the cave.

She doesn't talk about Edison, but I know she's thinking about him whenever I catch her with a faraway look in her eyes or smiling to herself. Every time she checks her phone. And when we pass a 3-D puzzle of Big Ben, she lets her finger run over the lettering on the box.

"It doesn't bother you," I say, "that he's so far away?"

She shrugs. "It's where he goes to school. And besides, next year I'm going to visit him." She's beaming as she goes on about all the castles she wants to visit.

I can't imagine Edison would take it so far as to let her visit him. But then he's never told me his plans for letting her go—only the obligatory reasons he started dating her in the first place.

Phoebe does fall asleep on us. But it's for the best because Chelsea is craving ice cream and Phoebe isn't old enough yet to have any.

We cross to the side of the street nestled in shade and walk back toward the beach until we reach the Big Scoop Ice Cream Parlor. I glance past that familiar alley as Chelsea opens the door and a chime rings, welcoming us inside. Chelsea samples all the flavors before she finally chooses the lavender, rose, and vanilla combo, and I decide on the maple-bacon flavor.

Phoebe starts to wake up now that her stroller isn't moving and we're inside where the air-conditioning is turned all the way up. Chelsea takes her outside while I pay.

"The maple bacon is my favorite," the boy behind the counter tells me.

He's got a youthful face, and he's skinny, with floppy blond hair and a dark golden tan that tells me he's been spending a good amount of time in the sun. He looks younger than I am by a couple of years. He watched me closely when we were picking out our ice cream, but now that I'm standing in front of him, he can hardly meet my eyes.

I look around and notice that from where he's standing at the register, he can see directly out the window behind the counter next to the door that leads to the alleyway. A clear view of anyone who might've been walking past the Dumpster.

It's a chance, but what've I got to lose?

"Hey, have I seen you before?" I say.

"Probably," he says, still not looking up as he taps his fingers on the counter, waiting for me to pass him the cash in my hand. "Like, probably, I've seen you around, and you've seen me around."

"Probably." I give him the twenty. "Were you working the day of the clambake?"

"Yeah," he says, counting out the change. "That was a wild day."

"Did the police ask you about that missing guy?" I worry this is too forward, in case he was the eyewitness that pointed me out, but he starts nodding, so I press on. "Me, too. He actually talked to me. He was so wasted."

"Tell me about it," he says. "He barfed all over the side of the building. Regurgitated seafood is not a good smell. It was so rank."

"He threw up?" I know it might be a jump to link whatever happened to Archaletta to the girl on the recording when I saw how drunk he was—drunk enough that throwing up doesn't seem far-fetched at all.

"It was an insane amount of throw-up." He leans toward me as he gives me my change. He's not shy anymore now that we're on a topic he seems to like. "I saw it." He motions to the window. "I hauled ass out there to hose it down before the heat made it smell even worse. I even tried to bring the dude a cup of water. But he wasn't there when I went outside."

"Like he really just vanished." I act overtly fascinated, and this makes the boy's smile get bigger, the way I'd intended.

"That's what I thought at first," he says. "But his buddies probably scooped him up, took him home."

"His buddies?"

He shrugs his right shoulder. "That's what my crew would've done if I was crashing around a back alley blitzed out of my mind."

"Did you see anyone pick him up?"

"No, but the car could've picked him up on another street; no one would've noticed."

"But there were so many people here for the clambake. Someone would've seen that, don't you think?"

"Probably not. I mean, you know what they say about downtown Cross Cove?" He pauses for effect. "If it's not Main Street, it's minor." He looks like he expects me to laugh at this, so I do.

"But he's still missing."

He does the half shrug again. "So I guess it wasn't his buddies that picked him up after all."

I smile at the boy, and he smiles back. He asks me if I'll be at the party on the Fourth, tells me the shop will have a stand and he'll be working it. I lie and tell him I'll look for him.

I step out into the sun and walk with Chelsea back to meet Trisha and George so we can return to the beach house.

"Edison will be there," she says, her voice full of delight. "He's back, and he's coming for dinner."

I remember what Archaletta said to me the last time I saw him—the last time anyone saw him: *All that money. Who could stay away? I couldn't. I couldn't.*

He'd laughed and coughed, and his eyes were lost and faraway like they were fading.

He'd said, *It's a curse, though; I hope you know that.*

And now I really do.

As we travel back to the beach house, my nerves are jumping and the pit in my stomach is growing deeper the closer we get.

Edison's waiting for us outside, waving at us as we pull into the driveway. He's smiling and his hair is windblown and his tan is setting in and his eyes are bright with an excitement that I know is mostly because of me, and for a moment, I forget that he's as much of a liar as I am, except his lies are shielding millions of dollars; his lies are holding people in power and covering up death.

I am not the dangerous one, Archaletta had said.

No one will ever find him, was what Edison said.

I follow behind Chelsea as she runs up to greet him and watch as she gives him a giant hug. I thought I was being clever and that between the agents and Edison, I'd gotten all the secrets I needed to uncover the truth, but I was very wrong.

Chapter 50

I expect to be angry when I see him at the half-built house that night. He is standing by the stairs, waiting in the lantern light, and the moment I'm through the door, he's surrounding me, a hand behind my neck, the other pressed into my back. I see a flash of his face before he kisses me—a fixed expression of desperate relief. I can feel in the firm press of his lips, the way his fingers grip my shirt, how much he has hated the days we spent apart, how glad he is to have me with him now.

"I can't stand being away from you," he says, his voice muffled against my neck. All I can do is nod. I'm holding on to him so tightly my hands are throbbing.

By the time we are upstairs, lying side by side on the blanket

272 • Alexis Bass

and the tarp's been pulled away, letting in the summer breeze and the moonlight, I wish he was Finn again, full of mystery, the kind that kept me guessing. Not like this quiet deception from both of us, where being with him and ignoring everything else is the most delicious form of denial.

But I can't forget what the boy working at the ice cream shop told me about Archaletta, his last moments. Maybe the agents are closer to discovering the truth behind Dr. Alic than they think, now that they have uncovered the business of the Duvals and Stevens. I brought the tracker with me tonight, but I didn't turn it on. If I did, would that summon them? Or would they only start watching me, monitoring my whereabouts? Maybe they would know to come here tonight or any other night when I might meet him like this. I don't want them to know I'm here. I like that the rest of the world is out there, and Edison and I are alone in here.

"If you could go anywhere, where would you go?" I say, thinking of that evening when I wanted him so badly it felt like I was vanishing. "I guess, you can go wherever you want, can't you?"

"I can't go anywhere whenever I want." He readjusts next to me and I take it as a sign he's said something he wishes he could take back. "But I liked Europe. I liked being far away. Sepp wants to go to South America next. It's his favorite."

"Is there any world where I get to come with you?" I ask. I've never been outside of the country, but I can imagine being somewhere far away with Edison, somewhere unreachable, that would be so unrecognizable and unfamiliar to us, that we really could let go of the secrets we're holding, leave behind the danger we could be in. We wouldn't have to pretend to run away; we'd really do it.

I can tell by the way he breathes out that he's smiling. "I think there is. One day. You and me."

"When it's safe?"

"Hey." He rolls on his side and looks down at me. "Not 'when it's safe.' It's already safe for you and your family. You understand?" He waits for me to nod. "One day when this is all behind us, is what I meant."

I think of what he said in the cottage when I asked him about what he knew and his answer was, "too much . . . enough that I'll never get away."

"Are you safe?" I sit up on my elbows and he lets his arm drape over my stomach.

"I'm always safe."

The money protects him, as long as he does what's required from Oswald and Warren and Karen and Stevens. And Sepp. He was in danger on the island because of what he was doing for all of them.

"Are you afraid of them?" I ask.

He's surprised. But he's careful. He lets the shock pass over his face for only a second. His mouth turns down. His eyebrows lower. He looks away. I reach up and grab his chin, force him to look at me.

"Are you?"

"No," he says with no hesitation. "The Duvals saved me." He focuses his attention on the string of my sweatshirt, twisting it between his fingers. "After what I saw they didn't have to take me in, but they did. They made me one of them. They took care of everything after my mother died. They've always been there for me."

"What did you see?"

He pulls tighter and tighter on the string, until the fabric bunches around my neck. "Hey," I say. He's smiling. He lets go. "I saw them at the quarry," he says. "Making the cement."

It mimics the story Oswald told me about how they discovered Edison when he was young. But now there are obvious pieces missing. "I don't get it," I say.

He leans down and kisses me. "Because there's nothing to get." I roll onto my side, so we are lying with our knees touching, staring into each other's eyes instead of at the sky.

"I don't want to let them down," he tells me.

"Why do they trust you with so much?" They put him alone on the island; they're using him to keep George close—this kid they found at their quarry. It doesn't make sense.

"The same reason I trust you. I just know I can." He moves forward and kisses my neck, right below my jawline. "Can't I?"

I nod into him. I shrug down so we're nose to nose and he has nowhere to look but right in my eyes. "You're the one with the secrets."

You have them all, I expect him to say, a syrup-sweet lie, but that's not what he says. "One day I'll tell you everything."

"Tell me now." But I know he won't. I know he'll kiss me instead. He'll take my hands and circle his arms around me, repositioning us so we're looking at the sky. That's exactly what he does and all the while I'm wondering if it's equal between us now, since I am keeping so much from him, too.

I take a chance and ask about the one secret that's going to keep me awake at night, leave me restless with agitation during the day. "How did Archaletta die?"

He gets very still beside me. "No one told me," he says. It must be a gamble for him, to know how much to trust me, what he can reveal to me without going too far. And maybe it's because he can feel how much I care for him that he said, "No one told me," instead of denying that Archaletta is dead altogether. He's trusting me not only to keep his secret, but also to understand that if no one told him, he truly doesn't know.

In this moment, I hate not being able to come clean and tell him what I've been through with the agents, what I saw on the recording. But he's still with the Duvals; he still did what they wanted to protect Senator Stevens; there is still more he's covering up.

"It's late," he says. "Do you have to go?"

"No," I say, wondering if this is a test to see if he's gone too far now that he's told me something that should scare me. "No, I don't have to go."

He kisses my temple, the place easiest for him to reach, and his arms squeeze tighter around me. We're quiet as we stare through the skylight. And when we see the shooting star, I wonder if we've both made the same wish.

Chapter 51

When I wake up the next morning, it is just another day at Cross Cove. Chelsea humming to herself as she curls her hair. George watching the news while he drinks his coffee. Trisha playing peek-aboo with Phoebe to make her laugh.

We all have lunch together on the screened porch. Phoebe chooses me to hold her after she's done eating, leaning in my direction with her arms stretched out. I stand in the sunlight with her as she pulls on my hair and pinches the sides of my arms, giggling and shouting the whole time. She is strong and excited, and this makes me glad.

A little after noon, we cross the cove. Chelsea is eager, not at all trying to hide how much she missed spending time at the Duvals' beach as she runs off the dock and jumps into Edison's arms. Oswald, Warren, Karen, and Sepp are there waiting for us. I think we all missed it, the beach games, the lounge chairs, the fluffy towels, the ease of being here.

It doesn't look any less luxurious than it did when I didn't know how the Duvals made their money. But I do wonder if what they've done haunts them, if they have to run away to Europe or South America the way Edison does. If they can see the blood on their hands or if the money and comfort is truly enough and they believe in their souls that whatever they had to do was worth it.

Edison is quieter than usual. He didn't sleep, not a wink; the wind blew the tree branches right against his window, and the tapping kept him up all night, he claims.

I couldn't sleep either.

This makes Chelsea extra chipper, like her good mood will douse us all in her sunshine until we glow as brightly as she does.

We play badminton, we swim, we lie in the sand with our feet in the surf.

Katherine Ellis and her brother Michael come by, and Sepp is on his best behavior, slapping his knee while he laughs at Michael's mediocre jokes, paying Kath compliments left and right, and doting on her: dipping her sandals in the water before she puts them on after they've been lying out on the dock, getting hot with the sun, holding her iced tea as she takes a turn flying the drone. Warren asks how their father is doing and Michael launches into some story about his father spending the week in Atlantic City and drunkenly tossing his chips in the air after winning a high-stakes game of blackjack.

"What does your father's company do?" I ask.

Sepp laughs. "Ellis Exports, take a wild guess, Maris."

George speaks up. "They handle distribution and equipment transportation for Goodman Pharmaceuticals." He nods at Kath. "Isn't that right?"

"Goodman Pharmaceuticals has their own distribution center," Kath says. "We take care of their special shipments. But we're a primary distributor for many other wholesalers."

"And you work with the Duval Cement and Gravel Company?" I say.

"They are not one of our clients currently," Kath says.

"Maybe one day." Sepp nudges her with his elbow. "Now that Kath is the head of their logistics department."

"We're all very excited for her," Michael says. His voice is so deadpan I can't tell if he means it, though I don't detect any animosity from him either, if he is jealous of her position at the company.

"I've still got a lot to learn," she says, downplaying it in a way that makes me think he might be.

"Don't be modest," Sepp says to her. "You're doing great."

"I have appreciated your help," she tells Sepp, lowering her voice. "Your advice."

He leans in toward her, as close as he can get without touching her, and her smile is as bright as the sun.

Michael and Kath don't stay for long. The moment they leave, Sepp downs a vodka tonic and falls groggily onto a lounge chair.

Sepp comes off careless and flippant, but I'm curious if it's ever too much for Sepp to bury what they've done and put on a smile, to carry on with whatever agenda will lead to the biggest paycheck or keep Senator Stevens from losing his power. If that's why he drinks so much; if that's why he's so good at distracting himself with jokes.

When he peels himself off the lounge chair to get a refill, I ask him if he wants to take the boat for a spin. He seems glad for a reason to leave the beach. I am, too, to be honest.

Sepp lets me drive so he can lie back and close his eyes and sip on his drink. I steer us far enough so we are away from the beach, but not out so far that we're in the middle of the boat traffic in the bay.

Chelsea and Edison are miniature people walking along the surf.

"Stop torturing yourself," Sepp says, nodding in their direction, noticing I've been watching them.

"I'm not."

He laughs like he doesn't believe me.

"It's a beautiful day." I change the subject.

"It's paradise, Maris. Every day is fucking beautiful." He finishes his drink and roots around in the cooler for a beer. He drinks it too fast, and it drips down his chin. He lets out a belch.

"It's a good thing Kath's not here to see you in all your glory."

He smiles, wiggles his eyebrows up and down. "Are you jealous?"

"At least with me, you don't hide who you are."

He laughs, loud and deep. I look back to the shore as goose bumps creep up my arms, thinking of all the things Sepp does hide. "If you have something to say, why don't you go ahead and say it?"

"Are you with her for any reason other than because your family approves?" Like the reason Edison is with Chelsea. My heart races, but I keep my voice steady.

He shakes his head, muttering, "Unbelievable." He finishes his beer and says, "You know what? Fuck off, Maris. I've had enough of your holier-than-thou commentary about me and Kath, your insistence that I'm somehow putting on a show for her and lying to her. And this is all very rich, by the way, coming from you—the one going behind Chelsea's back all summer." He tosses the empty beer can in the corner of the boat. "Are you with Kath and me every second we're together? Do you understand what we're saying when we're talking in French?"

"Fair enough."

"Damn right, fair enough. This is something you have no idea about; you couldn't even begin to understand. You don't know what it's like when it's just her and me." He bends forward and fumbles with the lid on the cooler. I nudge it open all the way for him. He nods at me, and though he doesn't say thank you, I can see he's already softening toward me, maybe even feeling sorry he got so worked up.

"So what's it like, then? Between you and Kath?"

"I'll have you know she could drink me under the table if she was in the mood to do so and that she does nothing but curse when we speak French." Sepp looks straight ahead at a group of boats trying to anchor next to each other, the people in each boat motioning for the opposite boat to stop, stretching out their arms like they can reach one another, then giving up and jumping into the open space between the boats and laughing when they hit the water.

"It's great," he finally says. He rubs his eyes and looks at me. "It's perfect."

"Then why do you seem sad?"

I think he's going to deny this, throw a joke my way. He turns his head so I can't see his face.

"Maybe this is just how I am."

I join him on the bench seat, and he scoots over to make room for me. We watch the boats and the people; we don't say anything else. He slings his arm around me, and when I turn to look at him, he doesn't look at me, but he does let a small smile spread across his lips. He knows I am watching. This is what he wants me to see.

I think I do believe him when he says he likes Kath and likes the way they are together. I think it's the Duvals who want him to be a certain way, who think Sepp needs to hold himself back in order to keep her impressed. And I think he knows that whatever is between them isn't real, even if he'd like it to be.

Before we go back, Sepp kisses me on the forehead. "I can't stay mad at you," he says, his voice as light and carefree as his expression, his disposition as sunny and perfect as the day.

Chapter 52

We have dinner in the grotto that night. All the adults are a little overserved; Oswald's laughter a little freer, Karen's eyes a little heavier, Warren's stories a little more exaggerated. George hoots at everything and repeats things he said ten minutes ago, though no one else seems to mind. Sepp turns clumsy, and when he knocks over his full drink, spilling dark liquid down the center of the table, I volunteer to help him to bed. I know the line that's going to come out of Edison's mouth before he says it.

"Let me help you."

Chelsea asks if there's anything she can do. Sepp laughs heartily. He has one arm over my shoulder, the other over Edison's, and as we attempt to steady him while he walks, he starts singing, "It takes two, baby."

Oswald, Warren, and George all find this hilarious.

Edison and I shuffle Sepp into the house. We move past the tall windows letting in the light from the outside and up a flight of stairs.

"You got him?" Edison says. Sepp is leaning on us to make it up the stairs. His head is bobbing like it's too heavy for him.

"Yeah," I say.

"*Yeah*," Sepp mimics.

We move in zigzags, laughing, down the dark hallway, a few narrow skylights making the darkness more gray than black, so it's possible to see the outline of the hall. We lead Sepp through the third door on the left. We attempt to ease him onto his mattress, but he falls forward, flopping down on the bed. He kicks off his shoes and mumbles as he scoots forward and buries his face in the pillows.

"Is he okay?" I say.

We hear the sound of snoring.

Edison smiles. "He's fine."

Edison shuts the door lightly behind him as we return to the hallway. We walk a few feet down the hall, drawing closer to each other with each step, and I know we won't be able to ignore the electricity in the air between us any longer. Our eyes meet. Sometimes it's very simple, the way I want him.

He presses me against the wall, kissing me like he is thirsty. I let my hands sneak up his shirt, over his bare stomach. His kisses travel down my neck, and his hands travel past my hips and up my dress.

"Hello?" We hear a voice coming from the staircase. Chelsea. She grumbles as she trips up the last step, her eyes still adjusting to the dim lighting. I duck into the closest room and gently close the door. I listen as Edison says, "Over here." A glow comes through the bottom of the door like he's turned on the hall light. He tells her that I'm in the bathroom and will meet them outside. The sound of their footsteps slowly descends until I can't hear them at all.

I glance around at the room, faintly lit because of the large open window. It takes only a quick scan for me to realize this must be Edison's room. That's his navy sweatshirt slung over the back of the chair. And his shoes kicked off in the center of the room. I turn on the lamp next to the bed. His room has abstract paintings hanging on the gray walls. A perfectly made bed, with a red duvet covering a down comforter and dark blue sheets. There is a quilt folded at the end of his bed. I run my fingers over its fabric. It's an assortment of colors, random and haphazard, a little worn. But beautiful. The way it doesn't fit in this room, I think it must be something his mother made. I examine the bookshelf and see more evidence of her, photos of the two of them together. She was a woman with a big smile and dark curly hair, and he was a child who looked at her with luminous eyes, like she was the whole world. I can see what came before all this, what he had before the Duvals took him in. Before he lost her. A life that money could never replace.

Now he lives in a castle, but there are gates and a moat and rules he has to follow, conditions he has to meet. Some secrets are traps, he said, and this is his cage.

Chapter 53

The windows of the half-built house are dark when I arrive, but Edison is standing on the platform next to his car.

We drive past Main Street and North Point Beach, even past the lighthouse. It's quiet as we turn down a gravel road that leads to a peninsula and park. I walk to the end, getting as close as I can to the water before it touches my toes. The night air turns warmer as we edge into July. He comes up behind me and wraps his arms around me. We have a view of the ocean and the sky and nothing else. We can't hear anything except for the distant sound of waves. It's us, invisible to the rest of the cove, pocketed away like we're the only ones who exist. I love him for bringing me here.

"I might have to leave before the summer is over." He dips his head into the curve of my shoulder. "But maybe, later, after all the dust has settled, if you're up for it, and it's something you want, you can spend some time in London." I spin around to face him. We've never made plans before, outside of this place.

I don't know what to say, but I can't stop myself from smiling. "I can't promise no rain." He glances to the ground, like he's even a little nervous. "But I promise I'll do whatever it takes to see you again." He can't really promise me anything, the way he could never really promise Chelsea. He's not free, not really. And this hope Edison has for us is false. I try to remember the girl at the beginning of the summer, who only wanted this cute boy who made her heart race, who didn't care about sneaking around and didn't care about Chelsea.

I smile at him, and he takes this as my answer. When he kisses me, it is slow and soft.

He is going to want me to say that I can't wait, that I believe we'll see each other again after this vacation is over. I won't lie to him. Not about this.

"Do you want to go swimming?" I am already pulling off my sweatshirt, my T-shirt, letting my shorts drop, and walking toward the shore, and in a flash he is out of his shirt, out of his shorts, coming up from behind me and grabbing my hand, pulling me faster into the water.

I don't know what's coming for us next. If this careful construct of what we have together, a whole summer of nights staying awake and stolen kisses, can sustain time apart, as well as all our secrets.

Probably, this is it, and when he disappears from Chelsea's life, he'll disappear from mine, too, and we have to enjoy these moments when it's the two of us and a calm ocean and a cloudless night sky. We have to make the most of it.

There's still a chill in the air every time the wind blows, and the water is not as warm as we'd prefer, but he is here, and so am I.

We soak each other with splashes, and Edison lifts me into the air, tossing me in the water. I dunk him. We try kissing underwater, but it's too dark to find each other and I poke him in the eye with my nose and he knocks his head against my chin, and we always break the surface swallowing water from cracking up. Like this, we cancel out all the worst parts of each other. We are not the terrible things we have done. We are Edison and Maris, full of light and laughter. We don't have any secrets. We've never disappointed anyone. We've never lied. We've never cheated. We've never hurt anyone.

We swim out far enough that the water reaches our necks. I pick my feet up off the ocean floor and let myself float, resting my arms around Edison's shoulders. We get very quiet. I don't know what he's thinking. I don't even have a guess.

I lean in and kiss him. I hold him close. I stare at him, wishing it didn't feel like what we have is bound by a rapidly ticking clock.

After we get out of the water, pat ourselves dry, and put our clothes and shoes back on, Edison pulls me close, so I'm slanted against him. Maybe the agents will come for the Duvals, maybe they won't. Maybe I have to tell myself I've done the right thing by taking a risk that could bury the only family that he has left. I twist so I can watch him as his head tips back and he stares at the sky. He is wearing the same expression of abandonment as that night we made the boat go as fast as it could and jumped into the ocean. And I know like I know the feel of my own skin that on Edison's eighteenth birthday, when he let the horse out, it was not a drunken mistake. He was setting the horse free.

288 • Alexis Bass

He drops me off at the half-built house, like he always does, since it's safer that we won't be seen. But this time I forget my sweatshirt, and as I'm walking up the New Browns' driveway, I hear a car pull up behind me. I hear a door open. It's him, waving the sweatshirt I left behind, and I run up to him, taking back the sweatshirt and stealing a kiss.

I am smiling as I walk away. But as I'm about to go around the side of the house to climb up the terrace, I notice the front door is cracked open a few inches.

I walk slowly to the door, panic flooding me. A surge of all the dangerous secrets I carry with me. I am someone who knows too much about the Duvals. I know that Dr. Alic and the senator are somehow linked. And George—if so many of the other Goodman Pharmaceuticals associates were deceased, what makes me think George isn't in danger of more than just going to prison?

I grip my phone in my hand, ready to call 911, depending on what's inside. I am ready to scream. I am ready for someone to jump out at me. I pull my arm back ready to hit them in the face.

I am ready for everything, except for what I find.

Chapter 54

George is holding a bottle, and Phoebe is asleep in his arms. He paces in front of the large window that would've given him a full view of the driveway, a full view of Edison and me.

I close the door softly behind me. He turns his back to me. This probably simply confirms all the horrible things he already thought about me. I decide to walk away from him, since I know how he prefers avoidance when it comes to me, even when he knows I've been getting into trouble.

My foot is on the first step when I hear him say in a low voice, "I'll kill him."

I spin around to look at him, and his face is red and stiff; he's frowning. This is the face of the father I'm used to. The father who is unhappy and disappointed. The father who didn't want me to come on this trip finally being given validation for everything he had tried to forget about me.

I'll kill *him*, he said—but he doesn't get off that easy, talking around the issue, focusing his frustration on Edison. He's never once said to my face how he really feels about me. Actions speak louder than words, but that's been the coward's way for him. He probably still tells himself he's done nothing to me that warrants how I've acted because he never yelled at me, never scolded me, never told me I'd done something wrong, only treated me as though I had, and that began long before I ever started acting out. He keeps himself in the dark on purpose. With me, and with what he did for Dr. Alic, the delivery he made. I see the girl again, the fear in her eyes, the way she'd been excited at the start of the recording and facedown in her own vomit by the end of it.

"What about me?" I say to him, my blood boiling. "I did it, too. It wasn't just Edison."

"I'll deal with you later," he says in a hushed tone, cradling Phoebe closer and moving toward the stairs, using her as an excuse to get out of this conversation. I know how he'll deal with me. He won't.

"What are you going to do, call my mom?" I say. "She'll know exactly where I learned this kind of behavior."

Now he looks hurt, and that—for some reason—is much worse. Because I've never confronted him either. And this is why— because I didn't want to see the pain I could cause. I covered my ears and left the room when he yelled at my mother. I played the part of the withdrawn, troubled daughter who kept to herself when I'd visited him. All along I knew if I confronted him, he would get to claim me as the cause of his pain and all the things I said would only be stacked against me..

I step aside so he doesn't have to walk around me to go upstairs. The boat keys are sitting on the long, slender table backing the sofa, resting neatly in a sea-green glass bowl.

When I hear the sound of Phoebe's bedroom door clicking shut, I grab the boat keys. I charge outside, through the screened porch and down the stairs. I'm not even to the bottom when the first pangs of helplessness hit, and I know that if I keep going down these steps and into that boat, I will have nowhere to go. What am I going to do, drive out into the ocean like Edison does? Scream into the wind? I sit on the steps and press my forehead to my knees. I take deep breaths until I feel steady, until I feel calmer; until I can feel in my bones how it's closer to sunrise than sunset and I am achingly tired.

When I come back inside, George is standing at the counter sipping water. Like he was waiting for me. His eyes travel from my hand, clenching the boat keys, to my face. He gives me a slight smile. I do not smile back.

"I'm glad you didn't leave," he says, keeping his voice quiet. "Destruction can be tempting, I know. Sometimes it's the only thing that makes sense . . . but I'm glad you decided not to take off in the boat tonight."

My eyes sting from holding in tears. *Destruction can be tempting, I know.* How does he have the nerve to say that to me? As if we're somehow alike, and the things I did in Phoenix are the same as the horrible things he's done, the way he went behind our backs and would have been content lying for who knows how long if Trisha hadn't gotten pregnant. And what he did to get a promotion at Goodman Pharmaceuticals; he couldn't have assumed what he was doing was harmless when it was a lie. It was cheating. It was the kind of destruction that left someone dead. And if what I did was dangerous, at least I knew the full weight of the risks I was taking; at least I owned them. George thinks he can see through me, but I'm the one who can see through him.

"I know all about you," I say. "And we're nothing alike." I grab my beach bag from the hooks on the wall and let the screen door slam on my way out.

Chapter 55

I don't drive into the middle of the ocean. I go across the cove. I pull in behind Edison's black speedboat at the Duval's dock. I call his phone as I walk through the sand, and when he doesn't answer, I call again as I'm charging up the stairs etched in the cliff, taking them two at a time.

When I reach the top, I'm out of breath, but I keep going, calling again and again as I move past the garden, past the grotto. There are lights on in the main room, and through the windows I can see figures moving. Warren strolls from the drink cart to the sofa, where Karen is sitting. They are both wearing silk robes over their pajamas, and they have slippers on. They are deep in conversation. There are papers laid out over the coffee table. Warren points to his wrist as he speaks, as if referring to the time, though I don't think he has a watch on right now. Karen nods, sips her martini. Whatever she says to him has him leaning forward and writing something down. I didn't think anyone would be awake at this hour. I duck behind the retaining wall and ease myself to the left so I'm hidden by the tightly trimmed shrubs heading off the garden.

I call Edison one more time. "What are you doing here?" he'll say; there'll be excitement in his voice, and when I've finally made it past Karen and Warren and into his room, there'll be relief in his expression. I'll tell him everything: what happened tonight with George, about the agents and their interest in the Duvals because they are searching for Dr. Alic. I'll give up all my secrets and he'll give up his. And then I'll do everything with him that I've always wanted to do; I won't hold back anymore and neither will he. But his phone rings and rings, until it cuts to voicemail again. Instead of leaving a voice message, I send a text: *I'm here. Coming to your room now. I'll be careful not to be seen.*

The living room is vacant now. From the mirror hanging over the fireplace, I can see Karen and Warren walking down the hall. They open a door at the far end; they both go through it.

I slip in through the side door, closest to the kitchen. Through the mirror, I can monitor the hallway to make sure they do not come out of the room they've ducked into. They don't close the door. I walk slowly so there's no way they'll see a sudden movement out of the corners of their eyes.

Papers containing whatever Karen and Warren are discussing so intently in the middle of the night are spread out over the coffee table. Perfectly readable, if I alter my route slightly. I step cautiously into the living room, moving around the large leather chair. I bend forward and examine the papers. They are blueprints of what looks to be a shipyard or storage units. The label reads: *Ellis Exports—East Port.* There are arrows drawn roughly around the containers, but they seem too random for me to make sense of. Another sheet of paper has lists of times: a schedule of arrivals and departures. Goodman Pharmaceuticals is named as Shipment Arrivals on July 4th. Tomorrow. This sheet is labeled: *Logistics Department.* Underneath reads: *Katherine Ellis, Head of Domestic Logistics.* A loose purple Post-it note lies amidst the papers, reading, "Thanks for taking a look. Let me know if you have any suggestions. Je vous dois."

A tablet is lying there also. I press my finger to the screen and watch it light up to reveal an accounting ledger. At the top it reads, *Liability Transfer. First installment: $300,000. Second installment: $200,000.* The number listed as the third installment of $500,000 is recorded as pending. The date listed is July 4th.

My heart beats quickly as I move toward the stairs. I see in the mirror that Warren and Karen are leaving the room down the hall; they are taking their time, talking among themselves. But I pick up my pace, and I crouch to the floor, listening to their voices get louder as they return to the main room. I can't make it to the staircase without them noticing, so I turn into the first open room. Luckily, with their backs to me and their focus on mixing drinks at the bar, I can carefully open and close the door without them noticing. There is one light on in the room coming from a short green lamp atop a large oak desk. Surrounding me are file cabinets and bookshelves; a circular red-and-gold rug rests in the middle of the room and behind the desk is a large black armchair. On the wall next to me hangs a Renaissance painting of a young prince with a crooked crown.

The problem now will be knowing when it's safe to exit this room. I press my ear up against the door and listen.

"Sepp has done well," Warren says.

"He's really surprised me," Karen says.

Their voices are getting louder—so are their footsteps. I scramble away from the door. There isn't anywhere good to hide in this room. There is no closet, no space behind the shelving, and my only choice is the least ideal. Under the desk. I secure myself in position right as they open the door. I hold my breath. If either of them decides to sit at the desk, they will see me. If either of them steps too far to the left or too far to the right, or gets too close, they will see me. Thankfully, they don't turn on the overhead light as they enter.

"What do you want to do about this?" Karen says. My view is of their lower halves, cut off at their knees.

"Shred it," Warren says. "It's been destroyed in the hospital records and Sepp swears Edison didn't know what to make of it. Edison doesn't lie to Sepp."

"Are you sure?"

They are quiet.

"We'll have Sepp ask him about it again," Karen says. "Tomorrow. After."

"It's been seven years and we still can't really trust him. He either needs more to lose, or he needs out."

"I know." Karen sighs. "The problem is he doesn't seem to love anything. She died and he turned heartless."

They are moving closer to the desk—I can see the ties of their robes; Warren's hands dangling at his side. Karen is holding a large envelope. If they take even another step forward they are going to see me. It's a gamble, but I slide farther under the desk. Now, if they happen to turn around and look back after they leave the room, they will definitely see me. But in the meantime, as they walk behind the desk and Karen lets the package she was holding drop into the wastebasket, where it lands with a thud, I am out of their sight. Sweat forms on my hairline and my heart is pounding in my chest. I pinch my eyes shut and listen as their footsteps recede. I hear the door fall shut behind them. Letting all my breath out at once and scooting frantically behind the desk, I am almost noisy. But they don't seem to be coming back.

I reach into the garbage can and pull out the package. Immediately, I notice the return address scribbled in the corner. Francesca Finn. I remember the way Edison' reacted when he got the package. How he shook his head, like he didn't understand.

I take the package and move closer to the light. Inside is a stack of papers about thirty pages thick. Medical records, it looks like. Rows of vitals and bloodwork. How did Edison say his mother died again? A sudden blood disease. I don't know much of what I'm looking at, but many of the pages seem repetitive, like they are an accumulation of the tests they gave her when she checked into the hospital. The last few pages have red ink. They are marked as "Alert." I don't know what any of the abbreviations stand for, but I can see clearly the element abbreviation that killed her. And then on the next page, there is a summary. In red ink, the words: *Alert: lethal levels of tamoxide detected.* I drop the papers, feeling a surge of panic rising in my chest. I gather them quickly, flipping to the next sheet—nearly identical except "Alert" is listed farther down the page, next to a different abbreviation. Then on the next page, for the summary, it states: "Alert: subject tested positive for blood poisoning."

I wonder if Edison looked at this. If he thought it was normal. Karen said: Sepp swears Edison didn't know what to make of it.

Quickly, I turn back to the page with the tamoxide detection;

I scan over the sheet. It pops out at me clear as day. The doctor who issued the report.

Dr. Alice.

It's too much of a coincidence. Dr. Alic. Dr. Alice. If the agents were basing the name they had off a blurry image of a pill bottle, maybe they couldn't see the whole name, the last letter cut off.

The realization compounds heavy in the pit of my stomach. It turns my throat to ashes. If Dr. Alic is really Dr. Alice, then either the Duvals know Dr. Alice and they use him to get rid of people—or they are Dr. Alice. I look back through the whole stack of reports. Dr. Alice is listed only on the results with tamoxide.

And Edison's mother knew, I think.

Before she died she arranged to have these sent to Edison. She must've known that she didn't end up in the hospital for no reason; that it wasn't a sudden illness. She told Edison, "You're going to have a beautiful life, my boy." If she knew the truth about what the Duvals were, she must've known they wouldn't hesitate to kill her. It must've scared her enough that she didn't want Edison to know until after she was gone. My hands shake as I fumble with the papers, putting them back in the envelope. I stuff the package in my bag and get ready to exit.

There's nothing but silence on the other side of the door. I inch it open slowly. The coast seems clear. The second I step out of the office I hear them, coming down the hall, from the room they were in when I first arrived. I can see them getting closer through the mirror. I don't have time to be stealthy and careful. I only have time to hurry as fast as I can toward the stairs.

When I reach the dark hallway at the top of the stairs, I'm faced with rows of doors, three on one side, four on the other. I thought I would remember which door led to Edison's room from the last

time I was here. The memory comes hurling through my mind—
Edison pressing me against the wall, his lips hard on mine, his
hands reaching up my dress. It was on the left side—I'm almost
sure. Maybe the third door—or was that Sepp's room? My head
spins; my heart is still racing. Taking a guess, I quickly walk
through the third door on the left. The room is full of gray light,
the darkness subdued from the glow coming in from the open
window.

Someone registers my presence and I hear a low moan. Not Edison. A lamp flicks on. Sepp is on his stomach, half under the
covers, resting on his elbows on the edge of the mattress by his
bedside table and the lamp. He squints as his eyes adjust to the
light.

"Oh, you've got to be fucking kidding me," is what he says when
he realizes it's me.

"I'm lost—I meant to sneak into Edison's room."

"I'm sure you did," he says. He pushes away the covers and gets
out of bed. When he looks down and realizes he's only in black
boxer briefs, he turns off the lamp.

I'm about to get out of there, but his hand covers mine over the
doorknob.

"You can't let anyone else see you," he says in a low voice. "Does
Edison know you're here?"

I shake my head. It's important that Sepp know Edison would
never be so careless as to invite me here and risk the Duvals discovering that he's gotten himself involved in something that could
effectively ruin what he's built with Chelsea and cut off their access to George. Sepp needs to know I came here on my own, no
matter how pathetic or desperate or weak this makes me look
to him.

"I'll be really careful," I say.

"Famous last words," he says. "Do you have any idea what time it is? And—wait—weren't you who he was out meeting tonight?"

I nod. He's looking down at me and I can see the astonishment in his face, his eyebrows lowered like he's trying to read me, like he can't tell if it's believable, from everything he knows about me, that I'd sneak in here to see Edison after just having spent hours with him. I stare back at him, seeing him for who he really is for the first time. He knew what was done to Edison's mother and he must've been responsible for killing Archaletta, probably the one who slipped the tamoxide in his drink at the clambake. We are muted versions of ourselves in this foggy light, but he is still striking as his lips curve up into a slight smile.

"Maris," he says, sighing. "Are you familiar with the expression 'get a grip'?"

"Pretend you never saw me. Or better yet help me, cover for us—"

"Oh, no, no, no—no way," he says, moving between me and the door. "I already cover plenty for Edison—and for you. You're not going back out there. Not with my parents still up working. You can see him when they finally go to bed."

"Sepp. It's not that big of a deal. It's only one door over!" I get as loud as I can while still whispering.

He holds up his fingers. "Two! Two doors over, Maris. Wow, I thought you were supposed to be good at this whole sneaking around thing."

"I usually am." I step back from the door and sit on the edge of the bed. I'm still really shaken up. I should get out of here as fast as I can. Sepp knows about everything, all the secrets too risky for Edison to know. But Sepp doesn't know about the agents. And he doesn't know about me. To him, I still look like a reckless girl, blinded by love. "I wasn't trying to get Edison in trouble."

"They're big on loyalty, our family. Big on respect, too. They wouldn't like Edison sneaking around with anyone behind their backs. But now they've got this friendship with George based on his relationship with Chelsea, so you can see how that makes it worse." He shakes his head. "Also, I retain the role of the family fuckup. No need to go passing the torch to Edison just yet."

I know he wants me to smile at this, so I do it. It doesn't relax him the way I'd hoped it would. He walks over and sits down next to me on the bed.

"You can stay here until it's safe to go to his room. But . . . why are you really here, Maris?"

Right now, I should lie to him. But even for all the secrets Sepp keeps, he has always let me see the truth about who he is and what he feels.

"George caught me tonight. With Edison. Edison doesn't know— he was gone when George approached me." While I talk, Sepp is covering his mouth, shaking his head. "George is mad, but what he said to me . . ." Remembering makes my voice catch in my throat, raw tears form in my eyes.

"What did he say?" Sepp's hand comes down on mine; his voice is soft.

"He said—" I can't get it out. It wasn't anything new, George's disappointment in me, the way he wanted to ignore how I am or pretend to understand it—but for some reason I think about Chelsea's diamond necklace, an identical one purchased for me. I think of George's arms around me when he hoisted me up when we played badminton. I think of the relaxed smile on his face, the way he beamed at Trisha, when Chelsea and I entertained Phoebe downtown for the afternoon. I thought I'd already let George go, written him off. But it's like losing him every day, all over again, the same pain as when I was young and wished for a father who loved me and wanted to be with me.

Tears glide down my face. I wipe at my cheeks and Sepp puts his arm around me.

"I thought I'd gotten over it, stopped expecting anything from him. I thought I was used to him not caring about me."

"Maris." He pulls me in closer. What he says next surprises me. "I know how you feel."

But maybe it shouldn't. The things I've done pale in comparison to the horrible things he's done. Maybe we were both led astray somehow, products of whatever came before us, whatever happened to us when we weren't old enough to know better or how to protect ourselves, how to save ourselves.

"You do?" I turn toward him. I'm distracted for a moment by his nearness. His arm gets tighter around me in a way that doesn't make me feel afraid. It makes me feel safe. Comforted. I let myself lean into his warm skin.

"Of course I do," he whispers. "So that's why you wanted to see Edison tonight? You were sad and he'd make you feel better?"

I shake my head, then change my mind and nod. I came here to feel better, to forget, to distract myself—I came here to be reckless, let all the secrets drop not caring what would become of the wreckage. Because for me, that is what feels best.

There's a burst of noise and the door swings open. The overhead light is turned on.

"Sepp?" Karen's voice.

"What's going on here?" It's Warren.

I blink against the light and they come into view. Warren's gaze shifts between Sepp—disheveled hair, wearing only his boxers—and me, looking equally as unruly, but at least fully clothed.

Sepp lets his arm drop from around me and stands up. I follow his lead and do the same.

He reaches for a robe hanging off the chair at his desk.

"Oh." Karen shakes her head. "Sepp?"

"I was just walking Maris out," he says.

My heart is racing. I try to think of what to say, how to play this—but I am utterly terrified. I don't look at either of them.

"How is she getting home?" Karen says.

"My boat is at the dock." I speak up right away.

Sepp nods once; he puts his hand on the small of my back, nudging me out of the room. He stays close to me as we walk down the hall.

Karen and Warren are on our heels.

"Maris can show herself out." Karen has her arm extended; she touches Sepp's shoulder, stopping him. "Can't you, Maris?"

Sepp's hand is still on my back, but I nod. My legs feel like they're going to give out at any moment as I move swiftly down the stairs. Sepp doesn't follow me. My heart is still racing and my breath is coming out in large gulps. I round the corner at the bottom of the stairs where I am out of their view, and I lean against the wall, trying to pull it together. A painting of the Duvals stares back at me on the opposite wall. Oswald, Karen, Warren, and Sepp, looking like he couldn't be any older than ten. None of them are smiling, and this makes them appear both sad and regal.

When I'm about to run toward the back door, the sound of yelling from upstairs stops me.

"You couldn't help yourself, could you?" Warren shouts. "What the hell is the matter with you?" I hear the hollow slap of a fist hitting skin and listen as Sepp lets out a sharp gasp.

"How long has this been going on?" Warren demands, but he continues on, not waiting for an answer. "You better hope she doesn't say anything that jeopardizes what you've built with Katherine Ellis."

"She won't," Sepp says, his voice weak.

"She's unpredictable," Warren says.

"What if she's jealous? What if she . . ." Karen says. "She's just a girl, Sepp."

"This is the most idiotic thing you've done in a long time," yells Warren.

"You don't have to worry about her," Sepp says.

Warren says, "You better pray that's true." His voice is gruff.

"We still need information from Katherine," Karen says. "She has to trust you."

"I know that," Sepp mutters quickly.

Warren's voice booms again. "If you knew that, why would you take such a risk with a damn teenager? Especially one who is with us all the time. She could cause a scene over this whenever she wants!" There's a loud thud. Sepp cries out again. Sepp gasps for air; and then he starts coughing.

I hear the sound of a door opening.

"Go back to bed, Edison," Karen says.

"What's going on?" Edison says.

"Go back to your room," Sepp says in a raspy voice.

"What's happened?" Edison says.

"Good night, Edison," Sepp says again, his voice still strained, but more forceful this time.

"You don't want to know what I'll do to you if you fuck this up," Warren says.

There's the sound of a door slamming. Another door clicking shut.

I peer around the corner and climb the steps just enough that I can see down the hallway. Sepp is leaning against the wall, his nose dripping blood. Karen is standing with her back to me. She holds out an old phone, like the one I found that first day I met him—Edison's phone.

"You gave her this number?" Karen asks.

Sepp lets his head hang for a minute, eyes closed, before he finally nods. "I guess I did."

"You're too quick to like people," she says to him. "Even when I've told you your whole life that no one is good."

"Maybe she's not good and that's why I like her. It takes one to know one, isn't that what Oswald is always saying?"

Karen's hand flies across his cheek.

"I'm sorry," Sepp croaks. "I promise it will not be a problem."

Karen turns her head slowly in my direction.

I whirl around and run. I don't stop. As I create distance between me and the Duvals I am aware of every rustle of leaves, the sudden offbeat whoosh whenever a wave crashes the shore faster than the waves that came before it. I imagine a hand reaching out to grab me. Someone already waiting for me on the dock.

Can I leave Edison here, with these people who murdered his mother? What other choice do I have? If the Duvals suspect something's off with Edison, with whatever they have planned tomorrow, they won't hesitate to fix the problem, or make it go away entirely. I can take the medical records and show them to the agents—they'll have to look into it as another Proof of Death to add to their case. I'll turn the tracker on the second I get home; that should be a red flag to them that something is wrong, and they'll come looking for me.

I get in *Vienna* and speed across the cove. Everyone is still asleep when I get home, but I know that with the thin walls of this house, there are sure to be questions.

Chapter 56

Chelsea startles me awake, waving a steaming maple scone under my nose when it's almost noon. I scream so loudly that Chelsea drops the plate and Trisha rushes in from her bedroom down the hall.

"I'm sorry!" Chelsea says. Trisha breathes out in relief with her hand over her heart.

They both look at me like they are very concerned.

I fell asleep over my comforter, still in the clothes I'd worn to meet Edison, with my bag containing Franny's medical records and the tracking device from the agents around my arm. I turned it on last night and sat on my bed, staring out the window to see if their black SUV would pull up outside. That's the last thing I remember.

I dig out my phone and bring the screen to life. No missed calls from my mother, which means George hasn't resorted to looping her in yet. Maybe he won't, and when I am safe and sound in Arizona, he'll go back to pretending that none of this happened. And until then, he'll bide his time, keep the peace between me and his new family until I leave. Chelsea will never have to know what I did to her; George will never have to have another conversation about how similar it is to what he did.

Edison is in the living room with Chelsea when I come downstairs. He stays through the afternoon. George is not ever in the same vicinity as Edison and me and busies himself wiping down *Vienna*, collecting all the beach towels and shaking them free of sand, going to the market to get eggs for the pancakes he insists he's going to make us tomorrow morning. He packs up the boat two hours before we planned to leave for North Point Beach and the Fourth of July party.

Chelsea and Trisha question his behavior; they say, "You've been going nonstop, take a minute and relax; sit with us," but he gets out of that conversation, too.

"I've been running around all day," he tells them, "getting things ready for us to go to the Fourth of July party, and now I have to shower."

I suspect they don't notice that he's only greeted Edison in passing, or that he's not said one word to me or even looked in my direction.

But I am more anxious than George, and his behavior is the least of my worries. I keep Franny's package with me at all times, stuffed in my purse that's always strapped around my shoulder. I stash the tracker under my left arm, held tightly to my body by my bathing suit. It's a comfort to know all I have to do is squeeze my arm to my side and I can feel it's with me. I've decided the agents probably won't approach me while I'm at home or at the beach behind our house. They're going to wait for the party, where it's easier for them to blend in with the crowd.

We go to the party later in the afternoon.

It's like the clambake, except the beach is even more crowded, dotted with lawn chairs and towels, as everyone has claimed a spot for watching the fireworks. Instead of paddleboard rentals, the booths sell sparklers. Instead of steamed seafood, it's hot dogs and burgers and ice cream and pie. We've been there for about an hour when Edison announces the Duvals are arriving. George goes with him to greet them at the dock.

Chelsea, Trisha, and I are sitting with our lawn chairs in a circle around Phoebe, all of us ready to catch her if she tries to crawl away, which she's been wanting to do ever since we got here and she saw the red, white, blue, and silver balloons lining the dock posts and the entrance to Main Street.

Chelsea leans close to me. "Are you mad at Dad?"

There's no point in lying to her now that she's noticed the tension between George and me. "Yeah, I am."

"What happened?"

"I don't want to talk about it."

"Well, okay, but have you at least talked to him about it? If he did something wrong, I'm sure he'll apologize for it. But he can be pretty clueless sometimes." She shakes her head and laughs, but it's a nervous laughter.

"He doesn't want to talk to me, Chelsea."

She shakes her head again like she's sure this isn't true.

"I know things are great between you and George," I say, not caring that Trisha can hear me, that Phoebe is pushing against my arms trying to get to a stray beach ball that's rolling past us, "but that's . . . that's not how it is with George and me. It's more complicated."

"But you guys have been getting along so well this summer."

"That was fake, Chelsea. I wanted a decent vacation, and he didn't want you and Trisha to know that he wished I wasn't here."

"He wanted you here," she says. "He was glad to spend the summer with you. We all were."

"Why? So you could feel better about breaking up my family?" Chelsea lets out a gasp. "The truth is he's lucky you and Trisha were so welcoming to him, even though he was lying and cheating. He's lucky the two of you could look past that and forgive him. But he's always hated being tied to my mother and always felt like he was stuck with me. I've never been anything more than a burden to him and I'm never going to forgive him for not doing a better job at hiding it."

Her eyes well with tears, and her mouth drops open, ready to protest. But I don't want to hear it, her sweet interpretation of George, or what she'll say to defend him. I know she doesn't want to confront the truth, that while he was being her hero, he deserted me.

"You don't understand—" I'm shouting before she can speak and it's loud enough that Phoebe turns away and crawls into Trisha's lap. "Everything that's wrong with me is his fault." All that I kept from her that day on the Duvals' dock is spilling out, no one around to stop me. "He brought me with him once, some week he had to work conveniently where you and Trisha lived. He left me all alone in a motel. I didn't have anyone to talk to except an alcoholic fortune-teller who told me the best thing to do was to prepare myself to leave him. She was right." I'm omitting the truly horrible things I know about him and what he's done to get ahead. Maybe they'll never have to know about the girl who was poisoned and the suspicious timing of him getting a promotion; but they at least need to know what he did to me. I don't think it was my fault anymore, just like it wasn't the girl's fault on the recording. "He was never there for me, Chelsea! And I never understood why—I still don't."

"I'm sorry, I'm sorry," she's saying, tears streaking down her cheeks. "I didn't know—I . . . I wish he'd been there for both of us. I wish he'd figured out how."

I get up, ready to storm off, right as George and Edison come back with the Duvals. Edison has his arms crossed. He's careful not to look at me. Maybe George said something to him when it was only the two of them walking to the dock to get the Duvals; maybe it was obvious George was mad because of how closed off he's been toward Edison.

Sepp has a faint bruise on the right side of his cheek, near his nose, that I might not have noticed if I didn't know what happened last night. He is also careful not to look at me.

But Karen and Warren and George don't take their eyes off me as we make our way to the Duvals' beach setup, under a canopy, with their own lounge chairs and drink cart. Karen and Warren are watching to make sure I stay away from Sepp. George is watching to make sure I stay away from Edison.

I make it easy on all of them and leave.

"Where are you going?" Trisha calls.

I walk faster, hoping to get lost in the crowd.

Chapter 57

I stroll up Main Street, ducking into the back streets, hoping to see the agents' SUV. The streets are all empty, as I knew they would be. I walk toward the path to the lighthouse but don't follow the trail, thinking that will lead me too far away from the beach. I circle back to the party, watching a cluster of boats pull up to the docks to let people off and anchor near the shore.

Kath and Michael Ellis drive up to the dock. Sepp is there, waving to greet them.

I don't trust any of them.

I don't trust the Duvals in this crowd where it's so easy for them to hide right out in the open. I don't trust the way Sepp is holding

Kath's hand so carefully, the way he always is around her. I don't trust the way she smiles at him.

I don't trust the way Oswald has his arm around George. I watch from across the beach as Warren offers him a cigar and Karen lights it for him. Edison holds Phoebe while Trisha and Chelsea make air-hearts with their sparklers.

The party is filling up and getting louder. I walk farther away from the Duvals, to the edge of the beach, by the rocks. Why haven't the agents approached me? Why haven't I seen them disguised as waiters or dressed as partygoers, their faces hidden under caps? Haven't they wondered why the tracker was activated? Maybe they are watching and this time I can't see them.

My phone buzzes. I have two texts from Chelsea and Trisha, asking where I've gone. The sun is going down; it will be time for fireworks shortly.

The latest text is from Edison: *Where are you?*

And then: *Meet me.*

Where? I ask as I feel a wash of relief that maybe for now the right thing to do is get him away from the Duvals.

Now, he says. *Behind the Dragonfly Inn, in the parking lot.*

The Dragonfly Inn is nestled between two restaurants, both starting to clear as people make their way to the beach. I walk against the flow of people around the building to a small but full parking lot, tall slender trees lining the back. When I arrive, his car is there, idling with its brake lights on in the rear entrance of the lot. He's ready to get out of here? Good. We'll get in his car and drive and drive and I really will tell him everything so he'll know just what to say when the agents find us. The fireworks will start right as we leave, distracting everyone so no one will know we're gone until we are miles away and too far to reach. I am almost there, my arm outstretched reaching for the door handle, when someone yanks on my dress. I fall back, hitting my head hard against the ground. My vision blurs in and out. A hand comes down over my mouth. It's holding a cloth and it covers my whole face, white static obscuring the gray air, though the pressure is over my nose and mouth. I smell something sweet—but wrong. The hand tightens around my mouth as I try to cough. I kick my legs, which is no use, because there is weight over me like someone is sitting on top of me. I try to scream and I try to move my arms, but those are being pinned back, too. My head grinds against the cement as I try to shake off whoever has hold of me. Everything turns dark.

Chapter 58

I wake up to a headache, a dry throat, and a slow mounting panic as I realize I don't know where I am. I'm on the floor, lying on cold, damp, hard carpet. The floor bobs up and down, jostles side to side. I let my eyes adjust. I'm on a boat. But when I look up, I do not see the sky. I see a roof, high above, like we are in a warehouse.

There are voices from the other end of the boat. This boat is bigger than the Duvals' speedboats but smaller than their yacht. It's older and beat-up, with faded and torn leather bench seats, rust traveling up the entrance to a covered room with the steering wheel and navigation panel. It smells like mildew and fish. It is long, with a large front deck that stretches past the steering enclosure, according to my view from the floor, where I am lying on the back deck, a much smaller area.

When I try to sit up, there's a sharp pain in the base of my head. I feel a surge of nausea and have to lie back down. The world goes dark and slowly comes into focus. My skin feels clammy and cold. I can't see who's with me on this boat, but I can hear them.

"And look," Karen says. "Look what I found in her bag." I hear the rustling of paper.

"How did she get these?" Oswald mutters.

"Why would she have these if she didn't intend to do something with them?" Karen says. "If she didn't understand what they were?"

Someone sighs.

"Sepp wouldn't have let it get this out of hand," Oswald says. "I understand that the two of you have no faith in him, but he's done well. He knows what's at stake. He'd never tell her anything. And he'd know if she was using him for information."

"I don't think it's Sepp we have to worry about," Karen says. "Did you see Edison's face tonight when it'd been hours and no one had heard from Maris? He looked the same way when we took Franny to the hospital. Sick with worry."

"If Sepp was covering for him, it must be bad," Oswald says.

"I knew it," Warren says. "I knew one day it would catch up with us and he'd be a liability. Just like his mother."

It's quiet for a while and then Oswald speaks. "Have you checked on the girl? She's here?"

"I looked in on her ten minutes ago. Still out. She inhaled enough that she won't be regaining consciousness. And if she does wake up, she won't be awake for long."

Hearing this makes me take a deep breath, just to make sure I can. I start to wheeze and bury my mouth in the crook of my elbow to muffle the sound. I blink and blink and blink. I am awake—sore and pulsing with pain and dizzy and disoriented, but awake.

"Tonight, after we're done, we'll take her to the quarry. We'll get rid of her," Warren says.

My mouth drops open. The realization takes the wind out of me, makes me cough again. The day Oswald discovered Edison hanging around the quarry. Not because he liked destruction. Because he saw destruction. And there was a choice. They could kill a thirteen-year-old boy, throw his body in the rock crusher, make him disappear forever—doing exactly what he saw them doing when he wandered into the quarry that day. Or they could make him a part of it. They spared him, and Edison knows it; that's what he was talking about that night at the half-built house.

"And what about Edison?" Karen asks. "He's lied to us. Sepp even went as far as to lie for him. And now the girl shows up with the bloodwork from the contaminated IV with Dr. Alice down on record."

After a moment, Warren says, "Father?"

Karen speaks up instead. "They'll say the two of them ran off together. It won't be hard to believe. They'll be searching credit card statements and airline and hotel reservations before they start looking for bodies. And of course, that's never really been a problem for us."

My stomach convulses and I don't know if it's from the tamoxide she must've had me inhale to knock me out and bring me here, or from the reminder of what the Duvals do—what Karen wants to do to Edison and me.

"Okay," Oswald says, his voice rough. "Tonight?"

"We have what we need here to get it done," Warren says.

Oswald says, "You be the one to tell Sepp. After it's finished."

"Sepp will understand," Karen says. "He knows we do anything to protect family."

Oswald clears his throat; when he speaks, he sounds aggravated. "I hope you're right."

I roll back and close my eyes, waiting for the nausea to pass. The tracker digs into my side. It is still there. The agents could still find me; maybe now that it's late, and they'll see I'm no longer at Cross Cove, and they'll be on their way. They could be here to save me anytime. They'll arrest the Duvals before the Duvals have a chance to get to Edison. And if they take care of me first? Then the agents will be able to follow my body, from where it was seen at Cross Cove to the Duvals' quarry, where it disappears forever. And then they'll know the truth about all those missing people.

The voices of the Duvals are far away now. With every breath my chest has started to burn. But in the distance, getting closer, I hear the familiar sound of the speedboat.

Chapter 59

I listen to the speedboat slow down and then stop. I hear the sound of footsteps on the dock, moving away from me. I attempt to call out, but my voice is weak and they are gone too fast. Edison is apologizing to Oswald and Warren; Sepp is firm when he says, "It'll be okay. It's okay. It's fine."

But Oswald and Warren don't say anything.

"Where are they?" Sepp says. "It's five minutes past the time they said they'd be here."

My mind races. There's no way out of this. If I try to get Edison's attention and warn him, and succeed, the rest of them are sure to notice and it might make things worse for us—might make things happen faster. I need more time to think, to figure something out.

Karen said that it's too late for me, but it doesn't have to be for Edison.

Their voices get farther away, though I can still hear them.

"Here they come," Warren says.

"I'll get the money?" Edison says.

"Not yet," Oswald says.

I hear a mechanical sound, like a giant garage door lifting then shutting. The sound of a car driving up. Car doors opening and closing.

I hold my breath. I wait to hear Stevens, or maybe someone from Ellis Exports, like Kath or Michael, or someone whose voice I wouldn't recognize, who I'd guess would be their father.

"Sorry we're late." This voice is familiar, but I still can't place it.

The next voice I hear is unmistakable.

"Do you have it?" *Hall.*

There's a small stretch of silence. I can hear the rasping of my own breath, growing rapid now that I know the agents are here.

"Not so fast," Oswald says. "Is it done?"

"The search warrant has been issued to Ellis's East Port. Officers are on-site," Hall says. "They'll find what they're looking for, I presume?"

"Yes," Oswald says. "That's been taken care of."

"What about Katherine Ellis?" Sepp asks.

It's quiet again and Warren says, "Well?"

"She's in holding," Hall says, clearing his throat. "We have one more matter to settle first."

"What are you talking about?" Sepp says. "We've done our part entirely. You've got your money, we got the shipment information and led you right to the tamoxide, delivered Katherine Ellis on a silver fucking platter—all you have to do is take the damn money and destroy the recording."

"If there's someone else here, you need to have them come out. The deal was everything out in the open, right?" Ryan says loudly.

"Actually," Sepp says, "the deal was we'd give you Ellis, you'd take the money and stay out of our affairs." His voice is angry. "There's no one else fucking here except for the five of us and you two. Look around—this is it."

"Okay, okay, take it easy," Hall says.

"Maris Brown," Ryan says. "Where is she?"

"Maris Brown?" Oswald says.

"She's been missing since this evening," Edison says.

Ryan says, "We're going to need to take her back with us."

"What do you mean *back*?" Sepp says.

Oswald laughs, a loud, bold sound that echoes. "I'm afraid there has been quite the misunderstanding. We won't be returning Maris Brown, certainly not."

This is the time to make my presence known, I think. The agents want to help me—even if they were here to get paid off. Even if they are overlooking the Duvals' involvement, ready to blame it all on Ellis Exports, and take the Duvals' money and the credit they'll get for finally capturing Dr. Alice.

I yell as loudly as I can, my insides tightening and head aching in the attempt to get any sound out. I writhe and push against the side of the boat until I bring myself to my knees, then to my feet. I am still so weak from the poison Karen made me inhale, but I manage to stay standing. I look around. On one side, a place for shipments to be dropped off or collected by land; the other side has an inlet to the ocean. Edison's mouth hangs open in surprise when he sees me—his hair is disheveled and his eyes are wild. Sepp rushes toward me, jumping in the boat, his face colored in surprise. I don't know if I can trust Sepp, but there's nowhere for me to go except in the water, and right now I can't rely on my body to be able to swim. Edison starts to run after Sepp, but Warren takes him by the arm, yanks him back. Edison calls out as he hits the ground.

Hall and Ryan are alarmed by this commotion. Ryan has a hand over the gun in his waistband. Hall is frowning.

I meet their eyes. I don't know if I can trust them either. It seems like they were trying to bring me back with them, but maybe they just don't like that I'm a loose end, someone with incriminating information, and they want to know for themselves what becomes of me. Edison struggles to get up, and Warren kicks him each time he tries, until finally, Warren pulls a small black gun from behind his back and points it at Edison. Edison turns to look at me in the boat, but he stays on the floor, his shaking hands held up in surrender. Ryan's hand tightens over his own gun, but he doesn't take it out.

I only know how to risk chaos instead of doing nothing. There's something I could say now to the agents, a blatant lie, but one they're sure to believe now that they see how I've been beaten and stashed, a lie that will unearth all the fears they should have about making a deal with a corrupt family like the Duvals. Sepp is coming toward me and my legs are too weak to move. I scream, "Run! It's a trap!"

Hall and Ryan immediately reach back and pull out their weapons. Warren's eyes are on them, and Edison takes the opportunity to knock Warren's gun to the ground. Warren fumbles to retrieve it.

"You know the beautiful thing about Dr. Alice?" Oswald says. "Her victims never saw it coming."

Karen comes up from behind Hall and rams a syringe into his neck. He falls to his knees, grabbing at the protruding object, his mouth open in a soundless scream. Ryan watches in terror and turns his gun on Karen.

I don't know who takes the first shot, or the next, only that bullets are being fired. I fall against the bench seat, as I hear them clang off the sides of the boat and ricochet off the walls of the warehouse. Sepp rushes to the steering wheel and starts the engine. I try to find Edison as we back away from the dock, the boat's engine grinding. But we are moving too fast and my head is thick with fog and my eyes are watering as my vision blurs, and I can't make out what's happening back at the dock. Our boat travels past the other docks, the engine growing louder with speed. Sepp groans at it and yells, "Come on, come on!"

I'm screaming, "What about Edison? We can't leave him!" But I'm too far away from Sepp, and he can't hear me over all the noise. Soon the engine is roaring, and we're headed farther and farther from the shore until we can't see it anymore.

Chapter 60

We've been driving for a while in the open water when the engine lets out a gurgle. We slow to a sputter before the boat jerks forward and stops. Sepp curses and hits the steering wheel; he pounds on the navigation panel.

I haven't moved from the bench seat. I haven't been able to. The cold wind helped with my nausea, but there is a pain in my chest that won't let up. Every breath feels like it takes a great effort. Karen said I inhaled enough tamoxide to never wake up again and I wonder if it's only a matter of time before the poison spreads. If I die out here, I won't know if Edison got away or what happened to the agents. I won't know if the risks I took were for nothing. I close my eyes for a moment and when I open them tears rush out.

"How could you leave Edison like that?" I scream, confident Sepp can hear me now that the boat is no longer running and I don't have to compete with the noise of the engine. "You just left him!" Sepp doesn't turn around. I hoist myself up and use the side of the boat to keep steady as I move toward the navigation panel. I feel weak, like I'm going to collapse any second, but I need answers from him. When I'm close enough, I tug on the back of Sepp's shirt. "I tried to get you to stop. How could you leave him there with *them*? Do you know what they were going to do to him?" I cry.

"I know what they were going to do to you," Sepp says, still facing forward, not turning to face me, even as I pull harder on his shirt. "The most important thing was getting you out of there; Edison would agree. He still had a chance, but he wouldn't have been able to handle it if anything happened to you."

"But—I heard them—your family was done trusting him. We have to go back for him."

"We're out of gas." Sepp turns around slowly; it's the first time he's looked at me since we left the warehouse on the water. His face is stricken with grief. The front of his shirt is covered in blood.

"What happened—?"

He lets out a laugh as he looks down at his entire front, dark and sticky. He walks past me, a certain grace about him for someone with a bullet wound, and stumbles as he makes his way to the back of the boat where he slides into the bench seat. He shifts in the direction of the wind and closes his eyes against the breeze.

"We have to try to stop the bleeding." I gather the blanket bunched next to a box of canned bait and drag it over to him. The wound is on his stomach. When I try to put pressure there, he coughs, he cries out, he jerks away. His mouth is bright red, blood starting to drip from the corners of his lips.

"You have to let me," I say, being gentle this time as I find the place that's letting out the most blood and apply pressure. The blanket soaks through in seconds. I notice his arms are limp by his sides.

I stand up and walk back to the steering enclosure, grabbing on to whatever I can to balance myself to keep from slipping back and forth with the rocking of the boat. I flip all the switches on the navigation panel. I pick up the radio. "Hello?" I scream into the microphone over and over again. There's no answer. I can't even hear static. I'm sobbing as I try the engine again and again. I search for Sepp's phone and find it in his pocket. There's no service. No matter where I am on the boat, the front, the back, the left side, the right side, I can't get a signal.

"It's no use," he says. He motions for me to come over to him and I do it. I fall next to him on the bench seat. "I always thought I'd be in Brazil on the beach sipping a caipirinha when the FBI surrounded me. That's the ending I was hoping for." He takes one long ragged breath. His lips are a shade closer to blue.

"I thought it'd be exactly like this," I say. We are both clammy, coated in droplets from the mist in the air. We both take big breaths and choke on the exhale. "I always knew it would happen too soon."

"Maris," he says. He smiles. "You're not dying."

"I inhaled tamoxide. Karen held it to my mouth until I was unconscious." I've worked out what happened, how I was taken to the dock at the warehouse. The night Karen and Warren found me in Sepp's room, she had Edison's phone, but I hadn't remembered that and assumed it was Edison when I got those texts at the Fourth of July party. It was a ploy to get rid of me because she thought I was with Sepp, before she realized the truth of what I knew, and it turned out to be the perfect trap. "I heard her say I wouldn't be awake for long, if I woke up at all."

"And yet here you are, wide awake."

I shake my head. More tears spill down my cheeks. "Sepp—I'm not." It's all I can get out. There is a price for everything, and maybe this is the cost of living fast, taking risks, and playing the odds for love.

"Hey," he says, leaning into me. "It's going to be okay."

"Don't start lying to me now." This makes him vibrate with silent laughter.

"Not a lie," he says and I watch his face relax. "Bribing federal officers can only go one of two ways. When Edison and I met them at the office and made the deal, it seemed like we were really going to pull it off. But I knew what I was getting into." A small smile forms on his lips, but his eyes turn glassy. "We've been ruining ourselves, all along. I don't know how it was for them—my parents, my grandfather—if it got easier every time, and they stopped feeling guilty. It never got easier for me. I hated myself, knowing how we were setting up Kath."

"The agents had already linked Ellis Exports to the Dr. Alice murders."

"Ellis Exports had nothing to do with any of that. They were easy to frame once we got the shipping schedule from Kath, and could make sure that when Ellis' East Port was searched, there would be incriminating evidence. They were the perfect target because of the shipping they did for Goodman Pharmaceuticals."

"That's why I spoke to the agents," I admit. "I found out George was involved and I was scared. I couldn't trust Edison to tell me if I had any real reason to be."

"You definitely should have been afraid. My family is ruthless about keeping power." His expression flattens and the sadness behind his eyes turns to anger.

I feel the same fury, thinking of my own father. "It's George's fault. He could've refused to do the delivery, he could've—"

"It's not that simple," Sepp says. "Who would turn down the promotion that a sizable order from Dr. Alice would earn them?"

Archaletta really had spelled it all out for me that day, that greed was at the root of every sinister thing that I would go on to discover; his parting message. *All that money. Who could stay away? I couldn't. I couldn't.*

"Who is Dr. Alice?"

Sepp smiles again. "He's whoever we needed him to be. An alias that sends untraceable messages to desperate Goodman Pharmaceuticals reps about to be let go, and gives instructions for a hand delivery, with the promise of a bulk order, the kind that always resulted in a promotion due to some dated company policy. It's genius, when you think about it, and I have to admire that, at the very least. It was our way of keeping our distance. Creating a trail that didn't lead to us. If there was a trail at all."

"But you were still the ones who used the tamoxide, who went through with the killings then made the bodies disappear at the quarry."

His expression darkens. "That's my biggest regret," he says. "Edison. I was the one who saw him in the quarry, caught him watching us. I was only seventeen, but I knew what we did; I knew that if anyone found out, we'd lose everything. I was afraid. I was so relieved when Oswald wanted to bring Edison closer instead of getting rid of him. And I liked having a brother. It was lonely before he came around. But if I could go back, I would've pretended I hadn't seen him. I would have, for once, kept my mouth shut."

I see flashes of them together—their embrace on the roof of the Duval office building, the two of them warring as they balanced on paddleboards in the cove. "What about Edison's mother? How could you do that to him?"

He closes his eyes for a moment; he doesn't seem surprised that I know, or maybe he is too weak to show it. "She wanted a payoff, too. She was making threats, getting difficult. We didn't tell Edison what she was asking of us. There was only one way we knew to end her, but we wanted her to die in the hospital, where he might be able to prepare or better accept it."

"Sepp, come on." I put my hand over his. His skin is cold. "She was killed like that because it would be harder to trace back to your family. Nothing suspicious about a hospital death unless you see the bloodwork on the original medical records."

"Nothing ever gets past you." He smiles weakly at me. "I like that about you."

"She sent the medical records to Edison. But he didn't understand what to look for like I did."

He nods. "She was getting too suspicious of us. She knew whatever we had to hide was big, the way we treated Edison so well and inexplicably gave in to her demands. She wanted the world from us, but we couldn't give her the world and keep it for ourselves also."

He smiles at me again his lips are turning pale, and his mouth is red with blood. "We didn't want him to know that she was blackmailing us. She was his mother, and he loved her. So I thought, better to let her die a saint." He's wheezing as he talks, his voice getting weaker. "I'd do anything for him, you know?"

More blood is gathering around his mouth. His head is damp with sweat. He shivers, and I pull up the blanket, tuck it around his shoulders.

"Maris," he whispers. "I'm sorry. Please don't hate me."

I shake my head, trying to stop the tears from falling. "I can't stay mad at you," I tell him.

The realization settles in slowly, what's happening to Sepp, and how quickly, and how he must feel it, too, if he's trying to make amends.

"I told Edison to stay close to you," he says, his voice getting lower.

"I understand." I was a liability and Sepp didn't want me to end up like Archaletta.

"Because he needed you—someone like you. Someone he could trust."

I cry harder. "But I went behind his back and spoke to the agents."

"For your family, I know. But also for him, right? When I heard you saved his life on the island, I wondered if you would save him in other ways, too. You didn't disappoint."

Since it's impossible for me to speak through the tears and the sobs stuck in my throat, I can only shake my head. I was reckless, and now we don't know what happened to Edison, or the Duvals, or Ryan or Hall. We might never know. I remember the very first thing I really noticed about Edison and let it fill me with hope: on the island, when he was bleeding and injured and trembling and terrified, he didn't give up; even when he was scared he was going to die, he kept going.

"Maris," Sepp says. He shivers as he struggles to lift his hand and clutch the front of my dress, so I'll look right at him. "You took all the right risks."

He trembles harder and I scoot closer to him. I fold my arms around him as best I can without hurting him, and rest my head next to his. I am glad to be with him now, if this is the end. I only wish he wasn't fading faster than me, and I feel intensely how it really is impossible to let people go, even if they're in your arms when they slip away.

"It's beautiful, isn't it?" he says.

I follow his gaze out at the night sky, the dark water, the stars all around us. A few tears fall from his wide, unblinking eyes. I lie back, wondering why I don't feel weaker.

"Listen," he says. "Can you hear it?"

I can only hear the sound of the waves, the water hitting the boat. And now his breathing, getting shallower.

His eyes are lit up as he stares out ahead. He laughs one more time, then coughs. And after that, he is completely silent.

Chapter 61

The sun is rising when the coast guard finds us. Edison is on the boat with them. His arm is in a sling. There's a gash across his forehead, freshly stitched. Ryan is there, too.

Edison doesn't believe them that Sepp is gone. He keeps trying to wake him up. He won't listen to Ryan, or to me. The EMTs onboard check my vitals. I can't stop shaking, no matter how many blankets they wrap me in. I tell them about the tamoxide. This makes their eyes get wide, and suddenly everything is urgent. They strap a mask over my nose and mouth and hook me up to an oxygen tank, as we speed back to shore. I can hear Edison crying next to me, but I don't have enough energy to move, not even to open my eyes and tell him goodbye.

When we reach the hospital, I am almost completely numb. I can feel myself slipping away, slowly moving in and out of consciousness. My mind can't land on a single memory for long, so I get flashes of them. A collection of moments that made up my life; too many to count, to keep track of. But I feel grateful for every single one of them. They fade from my mind all at once. Except for one lingering voice.

Maris, you're not dying.

Except, I *am*, I think. This is why the fortune-teller wanted me to know about letting go. This is why she said I probably wouldn't make it to my eighteenth birthday. It wasn't all bullshit, she said. *Every person we come into contact with plays a role in our future, if we let them*—and I try to visualize the collection of people who made up my life, who got me here, like she said.

And yet here you are, wide awake.

My eyes pop open. My shoulders are being shaken by a man, saying, "She's awake, she's awake." He introduces himself as Dr. Landon.

There is a lot wrong with me, he says. Dehydration and a head injury, but the tamoxide, well, good news, I have arrived in time for the antidote to work. He straps a mask over my mouth and the medication is administered in the form of a mist, inhaled into my lungs.

It wasn't too late for me, he keeps saying. It wasn't too late. I missed my own death, is all I can think. I wait to feel relief, but I just feel sad, and then so, so tired.

After it's done, Edison finds me. Before we give our official statements to the federal agents and local police, Ryan comes to talk to us.

"The Duvals and Agent Hall didn't make it," Ryan says, new

334 • *Alexis Bass*

information to me, but something Edison already knows because he was there. Ryan's hair is greasy, and his eyes are red and tired. There's gauze visible under his collar, but he assures me that like Edison, he wasn't hit, only grazed. "We're closing the investigation on Dr. Alice and making arrests. The Duvals are dead, the case is unfolding as we speak."

"What about us—Edison and me?"

"You both were victims who didn't know anything. You'll both be declared innocent of all this."

"And Sepp," I say. "He didn't know anything either."

Ryan stares at me, considering this. I wonder if he can see in my eyes that there's only one acceptable answer, if there's a hint of determination left in them or if it's only sadness, and he suspects that he should do whatever I ask, so I won't open my mouth about the bribe they'd agreed to before I'd convinced him it was a trap and everything fell apart.

He nods. "Okay."

"I'm sorry about Hall."

Ryan stays stoic. "He knew what he'd signed up for," he says. "It was always a risk. But this case is closed for good now. And Hall's part in solving the investigation will not be forgotten."

It's later, after we've been interviewed by Ryan's associates and the detectives, when I'm gathering my things at the hospital and Edison and I are finally alone, and he tells me he offered Ryan the money after all to keep our names out of the investigation, and that Ryan accepted it, that I actually believe Ryan will do whatever it takes to close this case for good and won't let the investigation steer toward Edison and me.

After I'm discharged, we sit on the curb outside the hospital with nowhere to go. If George has been arrested and is in custody, as Ryan said he would be, and the Duvals are all dead, I wonder if there is anyone left who could be coming for us. It's late in the afternoon, and the air is hot and still.

Nothing feels real, and I expect us to dissolve.

Edison leans forward. He cradles his head in his hands. "Why did I survive?"

And I know he's not thinking of Ryan's explanation of the events, that Edison being unarmed, and not fleeing the scene in a boat like Sepp, but flailing in the water, having tried to jump on the boat as it left the dock, he was not a target of the gunfire and was also very lucky. He's thinking back to that day in the quarry when he was thirteen.

I don't know what to say, but I take both his hands, squeeze them tightly in mine. *You're free now*, I want to tell him. But I can see on his face that the price of his freedom is intense grief.

It's Trisha who comes for me eventually. Edison has nowhere to go, so when she opens the car door, she motions to both of us to get in the back seat. She gasps and reaches out when she sees us, Edison with the cut on his face, his arm in a sling, and me, eyes red and tired, bruises blooming all over my body. But she doesn't hug us. She puts her hand on our backs as we climb into the car.

The New Brown beach house is quiet when we enter and there are suitcases lined up by the front door. My navy duffel is packed and stacked on top of the pile. Trisha says they'll drop me off at the airport this evening on their way out of town. I initially think they want to get rid of me, but then I get a call from my mother and discover she was the one who bought the plane ticket, intent that I return as soon as possible.

Edison stands in the living room, hands in his pockets, shift-

ing his weight from heel to heel, like he can sense he doesn't belong here. But has nowhere else to go. His phone still works, so
he calls the Duvals' lawyer. I tell him he can go in my room to have
some privacy and he seems relieved to have somewhere to hide.

From the living room, I can faintly hear his voice talking on
the phone. He sounds practiced in the way he speaks and I can't
make out his exact words, but I imagine him saying things like,
"I really appreciate the information" and "thanks for your time."

A second later, his phone rings, and this time he doesn't say
much to whoever is on the other end. But when he does speak, he
sounds relieved and grateful.

Then it's quiet for a while and I wonder if I should go check on
him. I'm at the bottom of the stairs when I hear him again. His
tone is different now; it's softer. I hear her voice next and imagine
she's standing there in the doorway of the adjoining bathroom. She
sounds completely deflated and she sniffles as she speaks; I can
hear each time her voice catches. But all I can think about is how
much courage it must've taken for her to face him after learning
that we deceived her. Even if she has not yet pieced together that
their relationship existed only to aid the Duvals in their cover-up,
and that whatever Edison knew about George and however he
felt about me were things he kept from her. I wonder if she knows
how strong she is. Every cell in my body is curious about what they
are saying to each other. But whatever was between the two of
them isn't my business. I walk outside, so I'm not in earshot of
their voices.

For a moment, I wish I were brave enough to approach Chelsea, to look in her eyes and tell her I'm sorry, or that I felt like it
would be okay for me to join Trisha in her bedroom, where she's
napping with Phoebe, and put my arms around her, and tell her

how sorry I am that George disappointed her, too. But it feels like I do not have the right to do the things that would make me feel better, and I should wait for their cue, to see what they need from me next.

Edison joins me on the steps of the porch twenty minutes later.

"All the Duvals' money and assets are frozen," he tells me. "The Smiths called to see how I was doing. I was surprised to hear from them. They're going to meet me at the Duvals' after I collect my things, so I'll have somewhere to stay while this is all sorted out." He rubs his hands over his thighs, like he is nervous. "They didn't know about our arrangement with Senator Stevens."

I nod. The Smiths were just another part of the trail distancing the Duvals from their crimes and had no idea the Duvals abused their power to ensure they both were successful.

Edison was going to take a cab to the Duvals' When I tell Trisha I want to go with him, she lets me take her car.

Everything at the Duvals' is being seized as evidence. The foyer is missing the round table with the fresh roses. The offices are bare. All the curtains are gone and the windows are open. The grotto is void of its usual wrought iron furniture. We walk down to the Duval beach. There are no boats parked at the dock. The beach looks abandoned.

"I can't believe this place ever existed," I say as we stand side by side a few feet from the surf.

We look around as though we'll find any answers on this deserted beach, the ocean still lively with activity. What we went through felt strong enough to shake the world, but the world didn't even notice.

"It was my home," he says. *But it had to be destroyed*, I want to tell him, in case he still doesn't believe it. But then he adds, "I'm glad it's gone," and I know he's starting to accept the truth about the Duvals and the role they played in Franny's death.

Ryan took the money and the Duvals are gone and my father and Senator Stevens will probably go to jail, but Katherine and Ellis Exports will be cleared and Edison will never have to lie again if he doesn't want to. After one last reckless act, one last pay-off, one last lie, it's over now and we are both free.

"Was *this* real?" he asks and I know because of the way his voice has turned scared, and his eyes determined, that he's talking about him and me. We both had reasons to keep the other close that had to do with protecting secrets and uncovering them, and nothing to do with being in love. I don't know why, but I immediately think of him on the boat at the island the day we met, the day I saved him, his whole body relaxing as I pressed my hand against his shoulder when the cold pack touched his face. There is a cavalcade of memories I am not ready to give up, even if they will always be tied to the ominous events of the summer.

"I think it could be," I say.

I watch his eyes fall shut for a moment, but when he opens them again, he seems content.

"Okay," he says.

We don't say anything else. We stare at the beach, waiting for answers to questions we don't know to ask, and a while later, when the Smiths arrive for him, and he hugs me goodbye, and I can't seem to stop crying, he whispers in my ear.

"I promise I'll do whatever it takes to see you again."

And then he is gone.

Chapter 62

The desert floods this time of year. Epic, end-of-the-world down-pours that wash away cars and leave the sidewalks dirty with gritty sand. Fences and mailboxes are stained with white spots and splashes. And sometimes the air smells like sulfur.

I return home to a mother who wraps me in her arms and a room that's been redecorated and scrubbed free of any traces of my old life, but it hardly feels like a homecoming. Not the sort that's celebrated or even a relief. It's the kind that makes you think of that quote, "You can't go home again," said by some man, putting words in our mouths, whose words have grown beyond whatever he meant by them when he first wrote them down.

My birthday comes and goes, with no ceremony or surprises; no new beginings and no diamond necklace.

Trevor hears about George, and he texts me to tell me he always knew my father was a "piece of shit"—the kind of thing we used to say all the time when we talked about unfair adults. I know he means well, but I don't respond. The next text he sends asks if I'll come over. I delete his number and it feels like nothing, and I wish letting go of someone was always this simple, this easy, this painless.

I knew Sepp for only a few weeks, but his voice still echoes in my mind and I'm tricked into listening. He was the only one who never lied to me. And I can see him clear as day if I want. He is easy to conjure and I think some people are like that by design. Impossible to forget, burned into memory.

There's a clear day, the air still heavy, a sign of the rain coming back soon. I drive to Camelback Mountain. I start running but have to walk when it's too steep. I like the ache in my muscles from the climb, I like the view of the top, no ocean in sight. And I like the pain in my lungs running down, letting my legs lose themselves for a moment, sometimes falling because of it. The hurt reminds me I am tough, I can take it.

When I get to my car, heavy droplets have started to fall from the sky. I have a missed call from Trisha, the first time I've heard from her since I left Cross Cove. There is a voice message letting me know George is taking a deal, pleading guilty. His sentence will be minimal. If I'd like to visit for his sentencing, before his incarceration, I am more than welcome to stay with them.

I tell my mother about it that night after dinner. She asks what I want to do, and I tell her I don't want to see him.

"So that settles it," she says, wiping her hands off on her apron.

She returns to the lasagna pan she was scrubbing. "You'll stay here, let his other family deal with it."

His other family.

Trisha, who has a natural way of starting a conversation, and knows when it's kindest to say nothing at all; who would sometimes flash me a subtle smile when her eyes met mine across the room, almost like a wink. Phoebe, with a strong grip and a loud giggle. Hands reaching out for the world. Legs charging forward even before she could stand. Chelsea, who is earnest and genuine—traits that can be perceived as weak and naïve, but to me they were her greatest gift.

I think of the three of them, together—will they ever be that happy and whole again? Will they ever forgive him? Does he deserve their forgiveness?

That night, I lie awake, with Sepp's words haunting my thoughts.

All of life is a test.

Fake it till you make it; works every single time.

You took all the right risks.

The New Browns were living in bliss and then I went for a walk on the island and thought I saved Edison's life. If I wouldn't have fixated on Edison and the men on the island, I wouldn't have seen Archaletta, wouldn't have witnessed that secret meeting at the Hanover Estate, wouldn't have noticed Ryan and Hall. Without Trevor I never would've known they were undercover. If I weren't so scared of regrets and so reliant on doing things that made my heart race in order to feel alive, I never would have been banished to Cross Cove. Sometimes it feels like I can so clearly see the trail that brought me here. So why don't I know what to do next? Why don't I know what happens now?

I dial Edison's number, the first time I've tried calling him since we last saw each other. But his number is disconnected and I knew there was a chance it would be, since the Duvals had paid for his phone.

I'm invincible—I fall asleep thinking of Sepp screaming from the roof of the Duvals' offices and I see Chelsea's face, full of worry as I stepped toward the edge with him. I think of the night at the boutique when she chose the perfect dress for me to wear to the masquerade party. And the way she danced in the surf during the fireworks shows, even though there was never any music, and was always so concerned whenever I missed them, because: *When else in your whole life are you going to be treated to a private fireworks show every night?* I remember the boat ride back from Honeycomb Island after I'd been gone for too long, when she sat beside me.

When I wake up the next morning, I know I have to go back to see her.

Chapter 63

We sit behind George in the courtroom and listen to him enter his plea.

From what I've heard of the rest of the case, it's wrapping up nicely, with no loose ends. The way life never does. Senator Stevens throws the Duvals under the bus in an attempt to get a shorter sentence, but with the recording as evidence against him, he doesn't have a lot of negotiating power. It's revealed in the news that Luke Archaletta's real name is Patrick Lowe, and that he's been seeking vengeance since his sister died, but had been hiding from the police for a stack of charges out against him, including attempted murder, assault, and armed robbery, so he never showed them the recording he found when he'd retraced her steps looking for her. He'd been aware that she was recording her conquests in order to blackmail a powerful, rich man she'd been sleeping with in exchange for drugs, but it was only last year, after he saw Senator Stevens on the news, that he recognized him from the recording and decided to go through with the blackmail after all, knowing he could get more money for a recording that looked like murder than he ever could for proof of adultery.

We wave goodbye to George as he's escorted away in handcuffs. And all I can think about is when he said, *Destruction can be tempting*, and thought I would understand.

In the courthouse parking lot, Chelsea finally speaks to me. She hadn't returned any of my text messages and voice messages, telling her how sorry I was, letting her know that I'm here if she ever wants to talk, even if she can't forgive me and only wants to vent about what's going on with George. And she didn't say a word to me when I first arrived, not in the car from the airport to the house, not across from me at the dinner table last night, and not this morning, before the hearing.

"I feel helpless," she says, her voice shaking but determined. "How can people say they're one thing and be something else? How can they just lie? How can they do horrible things and think it doesn't matter?"

She breaks down. She sobs loudly, her hands in fists pressed against her eyes. Trisha is holding Phoebe, but she manages to free her left hand and she reaches out to rub Chelsea's back. Chelsea cries so hard she starts coughing, she turns red.

"I'm sorry about George," I say. I know there is nothing I can say to comfort her, but I try to at least clear the air. "I'm sorry I went behind your back with Edison."

"You are not," she cries. "You knew the truth about him, about all of them—and you didn't care. I don't even know Edison; I couldn't have loved him because everything he said to me, everything he did, was a lie. But I thought I knew you."

"You did." I can't stop how fast the tears are coming, and I wish they would quit, because here with her, I don't feel like I have the right to them. "I didn't mean to fall in love with him." She brings her hands to her ears for a moment, shaking her head.

"He lied to me, too," I say, in case she doesn't understand that part of his deception was self-preservation. "He lied to everyone."

"I know he lied to everyone!" Her face crumples and another sob ricochets through her. "Just like you did."

I move closer to her. "I know. And I'm sorry. I'll never lie to you again. I wish you could believe me." I reach out with both arms and hug her. It's a risk. There's a chance she'll push me off, tell me to leave her alone. But the moment my arms are around her, she falls against me. She grips the fabric at the back of my dress and cries on my shoulder.

She doesn't speak to me during the drive back to her house, or during dinner, but Chelsea and I are afraid of the same things, we are part of the same family, and Chelsea was always honest; she meant it when she said that love makes the unforgivable things forgivable. And that's why, one day, I hope she'll forgive me.

That night I get a call from a number I've never seen before.

"I thought you might be in town," he says when I answer.

It's a relief to hear from Edison and I tell him so. We make a plan to meet tomorrow, but around midnight, I get a text.

Come outside.

The house is dark and silent and I don't make a sound when I slip out the front door. He's on the path to the house and I like that he's not hiding.

He shrugs. "I couldn't wait."

I can still feel the ache that comes with having him in front of me and not knowing where I stand with him. The mixture of being relieved and desperate and happy and furious. But my legs keep moving toward him until there is nothing to do but hug him.

We end up in his car, something on loan from the Smiths. He tells me he's not going back to school in England; since we're well into September, he's missed the deadline to attend this year. He thinks he might work for the Smiths, or attend a local college or one in a whole new state. His future is blank and unknown and I realize this is all I wanted for him, even though it's scary in a different way.

He nods toward the back seat. It's dark, but in the shadows I make out a tall clear bottle sitting upright against the seat.

"What is that?" I say.

"It's Sepp," he says.

"What?"

"His ashes."

"You keep his ashes in an empty bottle of . . ."

"Tequila."

I burst out laughing at this, but my chuckles slowly morph into sobs. Edison cries a little, too. It's the kind of thing Sepp would've liked, and I tell Edison this. He wipes his cheeks and he nods.

"I don't want to keep them there forever though," he says. "I want to spread them over his favorite places."

I picture us in the black speedboat, going as fast as we can, with nothing to run from, soaring under a sky that changes colors—pink, and orange, and yellow—as I steer and he leans over the edge of the boat, spreading Sepp's ashes along the coast of Brazil. My hand finds his across the console and I hold on to it gently. He feels the side of my wrist, but that wound has completely healed and it didn't leave a scar.

"I thought we'd have to start all over," he says. "That I shouldn't see you right after your dad was getting sentenced and so soon after Sepp—" He shakes his head instead of saying what happened to Sepp and I understand what he means when he says that maybe it's too soon. "I thought I should wait, maybe find you in Phoenix next year. It would be sunny and warm and when I took you out to dinner, it would be like a first date. And we'd get to do things the normal way." I try to imagine this, the proper date, him, holding the door open for me, me, all dressed up to see him. I can't. He shakes his head again. "But it won't ever be normal with us, will it?"

He's right. We'll always have a first meeting of him just having stabbed someone and me on the hunt for adventure. Me, thinking I was going to die too soon that summer, and him, thinking he could deceive me.

"I hope not," I say and I watch his smile appear and fade. He observes my face, too, the flux of joy, the grief we both share, the confusion over how to move forward. What to do next. We'll have to keep the wrongness of our first kisses, all our kisses that summer; the lying and the secrets; losing Sepp. But we'll get to keep the night on the boat, the relief of not feeling alone; the joy we felt that night under the stars, swimming at the peninsula.

The last person to see the fortune-teller before I was busted for being in the bathroom was a middle-aged woman with short brown hair and kind eyes. When she saw me crouched on the floor when she opened the bathroom door, she said, "Oh, my goodness." But before that, she was asking the fortune-teller if there was a secret to life. "There are many secrets to life," the fortune-teller said. "But here is the most important one: nothing will be how you thought. This is a very good thing. It means there will be lots of surprises." The woman wanted to know if all surprises were good, and the fortune-teller said, "No, of course not, but that is life, and we have to take it all—all of the good with all of the bad."

Edison and I talk until the sun comes up. We get out of the car to say goodbye. We listen to the birds and let the morning sunlight warm our faces. We haven't made any plans for what's next. But I think of the very first promise he made to me, when we were leaving the half-built house, the first time I kissed him. *You'll see me again, Maris.*

We still don't know what's coming for us, tomorrow, next year, ten years from now. But he takes my hand and draws me close to him. I tilt my head up and he looks down at me, and we exchange giant smiles before our lips meet.

Right then, I wish for a fortune-teller. I understand the need to hear about the future, just to have something to defy.

Acknowledgments

Thank you:

Amy Stapp, my editor, for guidance in writing suspense, enthusiasm for this book, and for seeing its potential from the start. Melissa Frain, Lucille Rettino, Zohra Ashpari, Daniela Medina, and everyone at Tor Teen.

Suzie Townsend, my agent, for always having great insight, and for reading so many drafts of this book. Joanna Volpe, Pouya Shahbazian, Cassandra Baim, Mia Roman, Veronica Grijalva, and the entire team at New Leaf Literary.

Writer friends who read the very first draft and gave me impeccable notes (always!): Jeanmarie Anaya, Tanya Spencer, and Shelley Batt.

Virginia Boecker, Kim Liggett, and Kara Thomas for always *getting it* and never being more than a text message away. The Northern California writers; I feel so grateful to be close to such an amazing group. My favorite hags for their support and friendship and laughter.

And to my family and friends: my parents, Karisa, Rowdy, Tom and Sheri, Sarah and Lucas. Lea, for visiting when I was in the revision dungeon and making me dinner, and for obsessing with me about WWII and the Winnie the Pooh movies (that somehow were about WWII also). Brittany, for the perfect advice. Kelsey, for the hours you spent reading and painting next to me while I worked on this book in Pittsburgh and Versailles. Shaun, for being a bright light in our lives; we'll always miss you. Justin, for brainstorming with me, for never-ending encouragement, and for our version of what it means to be happily and madly.